MY ANYWHERE

My Anywhere

Isabelle Van Buren

Copyright © 2017 Isabelle Van Buren

All rights reserved. No part of this publication may be reproduced, distributed, or transmitted in any form or by any means, including photocopying, recording, or other electronic or mechanical methods, without the prior written permission of the publisher except for the use of brief quotations in a book review.

Printed in the United States of America

ISBN-13: 978-1974170005
ISBN-10: 1974170004

A note to the reader:

There's some French content sprinkled throughout the book but have no fear if you don't know how to read or understand French because neither does Mandy. It doesn't take away from the story in any way.

A note to my northern Maine readers:

This is where I'm supposed to tell you that the content is merely fictional and none of the places or people are real, but if I said that, I'd be lying. With that said, the story is fictional, but it's also mostly set in northern Maine—specifically, The County. And if you're from that area, you'll recognize many of the places, businesses, and even some individuals in the community that are mentioned. Most of the names have been changed, not to "protect the innocent," so to say, but for various reasons. And not all the details about the places and businesses included in the story may be how you recall them since some particulars have been embellished and changed to fit the story. Also, much of the book is set in a particular time period, but don't expect the places, businesses, and happenings to have all existed during that time—some happened prior, during, or after, and some never existed and likely never will. Remember, this is a made-up story, told for sheer enjoyment. It is not intended to be picked apart to separate the facts from fiction or to find the inaccuracies. This was by far my favorite story I've written. And even if I pen another hundred books, I believe this will always remain my favorite. My hope is that it's your favorite to read as well.

This book is dedicated to the girls in my Badass Book Project group. Thank you for helping to mold this story into what it is.

Chapter One

— Virgin in a Coffee-Stained Dress —

"We're going streaking!"

Caps, gowns, and so much more litter the air.

My eyes frantically dart between my mom and the countless bare asses passing us by.

"Goodness! Timothy! Don't you dare look at that. How could they?" My mom yanks my little brother toward her and, in one swift motion, smothers his face against her chest.

"Mmoooomm," my brother mumbles, through gasps for air.

Sure, Mom, poking an eye out with his mother's nipple is better than allowing him to see a stranger naked. She seems to have forgotten that he is thirteen years old, has access to the internet, and was caught watching *Naughty College Girls on Spring Break* or *Pop Stars Gone Bad* just about daily. *Great* judgment call.

"Mandy, will you marry me?"

I turn to my right to find Walter, my boyfriend of two years, shakily trying to hold his balance while down on one knee and holding up a Tiffany box—the exact same Tiffany box he's held up at least three times before.

"Walter, first, get up off the ground. And second, you'd have to open that box so I can at least see what's inside. But don't bother. Do we really need to go over this again?"

"I...I know, Mandy," he stutters, reaching out for my hand to steady him as he stands. "I just thought maybe this time would be the right time."

"Oh, Walter, don't be silly. You know Mandy has a lot she wants to do before she gets married," my mom interrupts with pursed lips. "She can't run the world with distractions of a husband and kids, can she?"

She loosens her grip on my brother's head, and the poor kid gasps for air as if he was drowning.

"Can we leave now?" My dad appears out of nowhere. "I have to get to the office," he states, waving his phone in the air. "Sorry, baby girl, but I just got a break on a case, and it can't wait much longer."

My dad's a private investigator, and while he takes his work seriously, his family always comes first. So, during moments like this when he's distracted, I know it has to be something really important, so I don't take it personally in the least.

"Mandy!" a rugged voice calls out among the mass of mostly drunk and naked graduates.

Scanning the crowd, I quickly spot Tom, my bestie. He's not difficult to pick out of any crowd, especially when he doesn't have a shirt on. He towers over everyone, and the boy's got so much hair all over his body that he's most certainly the easiest person to spot.

He trots over to us, and I quickly squeeze my eyes shut, turning away when I see so much more of my good friend Tom than I've ever wanted to.

"Let's get a selfie," he proclaims.

My mom shields her eyes. "I cannot be caught here like this," she whispers, leaning into me. "All it takes is one photographer to get a picture of me with all *this*," she warns, waving her hand wildly in the air.

"Fish face," Tom sings, raising his cellphone in front of us.

"I have to leave now," my dad states, leaning down, kissing the top of my head.

"Photobomb," Tom proclaims, the click of the camera going off.

He tugs on my arm. "You have to join us."

"Don't you dare, Amanda Marie O'Reilly," my mom scoffs. "It's one thing for a photographer to snap a picture of the mayor of New York City on the sidelines of this circus show, but another for them to get a distasteful nude picture of her daughter."

A sly grin creeps up, and I scan from my agitated mom to my distracted boyfriend, who I now realize I've seriously got to dump. And then over to my brother—my mom's midlife crisis—whose eyes are glued to the female species in all their glory. I let out a giggle before I glance over to my dad who's tapping his foot in annoyance of having to wait for my mom. And my twin sister who's been sitting on the curb, talking on her cellphone the entire time she's been here.

"Sorry, Mom," I announce, reaching up, grabbing my cap and tossing it in Walter's direction. I make quick work of shedding my gown, shoes, shirt, skirt, and bra. It was a good judgment call this morning when I decided to go without underwear, a timesaver in this moment.

Grabbing hold of Tom's hand, my mom grumbles.

"And, Walter, we're done," I proclaim.

"What? What do you—"

"You're gay!" I exclaim above the noise.

"What are you—"

"Walter, I'm standing here completely in the flesh, and you haven't batted an eye my way. You haven't been able to peel your eyes off Tom since he appeared. You owe it to yourself to throw that closet door open and show the world who you really are."

"Walter?" my mom manages, mouth agape.

I shrug.

"You're as gay as I am, baby!" Tom bellows. He blows Walter a kiss. "Even my mama pointed that out."

I lace my arm in Tom's, and we trot away, joining the growing mass headed toward the common.

"Excuse me, are you—"

"Yes. I'm her daughter," I respond, not looking up, pressing *Send* on my cellphone.

"Whose daughter?" the voice asks. I turn his way to see a bald, freckled man staring back at me. "I was just alerting you that your drink was ready because you're holding up the line."

"Last call for Wonder Woman," a voice calls out from behind the counter.

I roll my eyes at the bald, freckled, and annoying man.

Ding. I look down at my phone to see if it's a response from Jayde. *Where the hell is she?*

"For goodness sake, lady. Get your drink and get out of the way," an annoyed voice hollers from behind.

I huff. They obviously wouldn't treat me like this if they knew who my mom was.

I step forward and reach for my latte.

"She's clearly an impersonator because Wonder Woman would never be this slow," another voice states.

I roll my eyes and straighten up, making sure to stand a bit taller. No one is going to ruin my day. Especially now with my skinny vanilla latte in hand.

Spinning on my heels, I turn toward the crowd and offer them an exaggerated smile before taking a long sip and then licking my lips. "Have a good day, folks."

Trying to balance my phone and plane ticket in one hand, the latte in another, and my carry-on bag—that's currently sliding off my shoulder—I confidently saunter away.

While glancing down at my ticket to see what terminal I need to get to, my phone chimes again so I quickly swipe the screen to see the message when... *suddenly*, I'm tossed face down to the floor. My phone goes flying and lands with a crash, scattering pieces in all directions. But that's not the worst part because I'm now covered in scolding hot skinny vanilla latte.

"Shit! I'm sorry," a husky voice coated in a thick accent calls out in a panic. I feel a hand grabbing at my arm. "I'm so sorry. I tried moving out of your way, but I guess you didn't see me. Are you all right?"

Too astounded to reply, I jerk my arm out of his grasp. Does this idiot really think that I'm all right? Doesn't he see that I'm face down on the floor, lying in a pool of steaming coffee?

I prop myself onto my knees and look down at my dress.

"Oh no. Was that hot coffee? Are you burned? Do you need medical attention?"

Glaring up and over my shoulder, I freeze the moment my eyes lock with the guy standing over me. My mouth forces open to offer a snide response, but not a single word comes out.

I close and reopen it, hoping this time I can at least offer a sound—any sound. But nothing.

Swallowing, I look away, trying to compose myself.

"Let me help you up," he offers, reaching for my arm again. Feeling too weak to shrug him off this time, I let him.

Now onto my feet, my voice has returned. "Are you fucking blind?" I blurt out without looking at him.

"Mandy?" a familiar voice is heard. Tom and Jayde scurry in my direction. "Are you all right?" Jayde asks, examining me.

"Do I look okay?" I quip, annoyed. "This idiot rammed into me." I point a thumb over my shoulder.

"I'm sorry. But, in all honesty, you were the one not looking where you were going. And I tried to walk around you, but you didn't see me."

Did he really just say that to me? I turn and glare at him. And... *again*, I'm left unable to speak. *What in the world is happening to me? Do I have a concussion or something?* I swallow hard, and without speaking a single word to him, turn back around.

"Just get me out of here," I direct my friends.

"I'm sorry," he repeats, bending down to collect the pieces of my phone.

"Just go. You've clearly done enough here," Tom advises, grabbing the phone out of the stranger's grasp.

The boy reaches into his pocket and then extends his hand to me, holding out what looks to be a few twenty-dollar bills. "At least take this so you can buy yourself another dress."

"Evidently, he's not only blind, but he's deaf too," Jayde announces.

Shaking my head, I raise both hands in his direction. I may not be able to speak, but at least I can still gesture.

I scoff and turn away.

"Mandy! Hey, Mandy! Wake up."

I lazily open my eyes.

"Do you have your seat belt on?" Tom asks in a panic.

"Yes." Did he just wake me from a really good sleep to ask that? I haven't slept in days since we've been busy celebrating being done with four grueling years of college. "Are we already in Bermuda?"

"Um, yeah…but they just announced that they're having a bit of a problem."

"What?"

"Ladies and Gentlemen, remain calm and in your seats. We're having a small issue with our landing gear, but not to worry, we'll continue to work on getting it properly down for our landing while we circle the airport."

"What?" I repeat, sitting up straight in my seat.

Jayde grabs my arm, digging her nails in. "Oh, hell no, I didn't prepare to die today," she claims in a panic.

"How does…landing gear not work?" Tom questions, in between deep breaths. He's clearly hyperventilating. *Aren't those little oxygen masks supposed to pop out of the ceiling at a time like this?*

I reach into the pocket of the seat in front of me and fish around for a barf bag. *I'm evidently the only person in this row who can still think clearly.* But there's only a lone magazine and a couple of candy wrappers inside.

A hand holding a paper bag appears between the seats in front of us. I pause, but hastily, Tom yanks it.

"Marc! Why'd you give them our only yack bag?" the guy sitting directly in front of Jayde asks.

"Thanks," I offer, sheepishly.

"No problem," the guy says. His voice is familiar—that unforgettable accent. He's the one that I rammed into at the airport.

"We need to document this." Jayde swipes at the screen on her phone. "What is that new thing called where you can do live videos?"

"Facebook Live?" I shrug.

"No. There's another one. It's like Telescope, or something."

"Periscope," the boy, who I now know is Marc, calls back.

"That's it," she confirms, tapping at her screen.

"Jayde, we tried getting internet earlier, don't you remember? You obviously can't do a live video if there's no internet." I'm apparently *still* the only voice of reason in this aisle.

She huffs. "Then let's do a regular video that I can show my dad. He needs to see this because we should not be treated this way. My dad will be able to get us compensated for our distress."

"Can't your dad do something about this too?" I overhear one of the guys sitting with Marc ask him. "Doesn't he have connections as the town manager?"

"*Folks, remain calm. We seem to be experiencing a mechanical malfunction that is preventing us from extending the landing gear. Our pilot is confident that he has full control of the aircraft and can successfully perform a belly landing. Remain in your seats with your seat belts fastened. You'll experience what feels like turbulence and then hear a loud noise as soon as the underside of the aircraft touches the ground. This may result in being tossed around if you do not have your seat belt properly secured. Once we touch ground, we'll wait until the aircraft comes to a full and complete stop. From there, you'll be escorted out safely. It is of utmost importance that no one panics and that everyone remains in their seats during this process. Thank you.*"

"Uh, ma'am." The guy sitting next to Marc throws a hand up, trying to get the stewardess' attention. "Can't they turn this plane around and…uh, get us back to Van Buren…Maine?" He fumbles, anxiety filling his tone. *He may need that barf bag next.*

"I don't want to die. I should have kissed Jackson when I had the chance," Tom whines, gripping the arms of the seat.

"And I'm still a virgin in a coffee-stained dress," I add, now panicked.

Chapter Two
— A Dream, Nightmare, or Reality —

Beep...Beep...Beep...Beep...Beep...
I take in some air.
Whish. Woo. Whish. Woo. Whish. Woo.
I try to open my eyes, but my eyelids feel like they have a bungee cord attached, pulling down toward my chin.

"Pensez-vous que le docteur va venir aujourd'hui?"

"Oui. Her vitals are good today and she's breathing more on her own. I'm sure he'll want to take her off the ventilator."

My toes burn. They feel like they're frostbitten. I hear a constant hum, a buzzing within earshot, to my right.

Beep...Beep...Beep...

My body feels like it's sinking into a waterbed. And my tongue feels inflated like the throat of a frog.

Beep...Beep...Beep...

I wiggle a finger, hoping the rest of my hand will follow. I need to turn off my alarm, but I can barely move. The constant beeping continues on like it's leading a choir.

"Paging Dr. LaBrec to the nurse's station. Paging Dr.—"

Tick. Tick. Tick. Tick...

I flutter my eyes open just enough to see partial sunlight. The room around me is all a blur, like everything's encapsulated in a cloud.

"Her eyes are open! Get the nurse."

The sound of shoes clatter against the floor, and then the noise disappears in an instant.

I feel something touch my arm, but I can't move my head to see.

My eyes blink sluggishly, and my throat is dry, thirsty.

"She just opened her eyes. See?"

"That's a great sign. Now, let's see if we can get her to respond to us."

"Sara?"

I remain silent. I blink rapidly, trying to clear my vision, but all I see are ghost-like images floating in front of my face.

I shut my eyes.

"Elle a ouvert les yeux hier."

"That's good. She's doing good."

"Oui, mais—"

"Non. Non. Don't go there. Don't talk like that. She'll come out of it."

"Mom?" I croak out.

"Oh! Get the nurse."

I force my eyes open again.

A short, round-bodied woman with milky white skin stands over me, staring down wide-eyed, looking like she's waiting for me to do a trick.

I swallow and close my eyes, wincing. My throat feels like it's been scraped by a thousand razor blades.

"Je peux lui donner un peu d'eau?" the round-bodied woman calls out. "Can I give her some water?" she repeats.

"Juste des ice chip, the nurse said."

I hear a bit of clatter. And then a cold sensation hits my lips. My tongue instinctively responds, stretching out to meet it.

"She's responding?" another voice questions.

"Oui. All of a sudden, she said 'Mom,'" my new friend—the round-bodied, but attentive woman—answers.

"Open your eyes for me, dear."

I do as the voice requests.

"Hi. Can you see me?"

I can only slowly blink my eyes shut in response. My head feels too heavy to nod a reply.

"Good job," she answers. "Do you know where you are?"

I blink my eyes closed again. I know I'm in a hospital.

When I reopen my eyes, I see that she's a nurse; she's wearing scrubs decorated in little puppies dressed in hospital gowns.

"Good. Now can you try to say something? Can you tell me your name?"

I extend my tongue, pushing the ice cube back into my new friend's hand. I suck in my thick saliva and swallow, quickly reminded of the pain that radiates up and down my throat.

Feeling exhausted, I force open my mouth, but no sound comes out.

"It's okay. Take your time," the nurse advises.

My eyes wander to the right, and I'm met with another face. When she sees me looking at her, she smiles. "I'm right here, sis."

Sis?

"Can you try to tell us your name again?"

I drop my mouth open and fill my lungs up with an excessive amount of air, hoping that it will help to push the words out of my mouth. "Mandy," I breathe out in a low growl.

"No. You mean—" the lady to the right, who claims to be my "sis," quickly interjects.

The nurse looks from side to side to each of the women, and she mouths, "It's okay."

"Jump out," I say. *Why did I just say that?*

"What was that you said?"

All three ladies lean in, their faces so close that I'm afraid to speak again because I know my breath must smell like a donkey's behind.

"The beach," I croak. I wanted to tell them that my name is Amanda O'Reilly. I wanted to ask them where my mom was.

"We all wish we were at the beach," the nurse quips before offering a hearty chuckle with the other two. "Let's give you a bit of rest. The doctor should be by shortly." She tugs and tucks the sheets, covering my toes.

The instant warmth of the blankets makes me close my eyes.

I awake to the sound of sobbing. Not the kind of sobbing from a small child whose ice cream just fell on the ground, but the kind that signals anguish.

I clear my throat and the crying pauses.

The room goes silent.

"Sara?" This is the second time I've heard that name being called. *Can someone please just respond?* "Sara," the voice repeats. I feel a warm hand touch my arm.

I blink my eyes open. Standing beside me is a gentleman sporting a crisp, long white medical jacket with a crimson red tie around his neck.

"Hi, Sara, I'm Dr. Gagnon. It's good to see you awake. How are you feeling?"

I shake my head with creased brow. "No. I'm not—"

I feel the need to sit up, so I push my hands deep into the mattress.

The doctor notices my attempt so he extends his hand, and in an instant, the head of the bed begins to mechanically rise.

My head is loopy, but my lungs suddenly feel less restricted. "I'm not Sara," I finally blurt out, directing my attention to the doorway where the lady from yesterday enters.

"Sara, you're up and talking," she proclaims, strutting to my bedside.

"I'm not Sara," I push out again with greater force.

"It's all right," the doctor says. "Do you know where you are?"

"The same place...I was yesterday...when the nurse asked me," I bark out, between long breaths. *Why are they asking these same stupid questions?* "Where's my mom? I *want* my mom."

The lady looks at the doctor with a fearful expression.

"Okay. We'll get to that. I just want to ask you a few more questions. Do you know what happened to you?"

"I was in an accident," I tell him, my breath jagged.

The doctor leans over, reaching behind the bed, and strings an oxygen tube around my head. The air fills my nose, and I immediately feel my lungs respond.

"Good," he states. "Do you know what kind of accident it was?"

I close my eyes for an instant, allowing the oxygen to calm my spinning head.

"The airplane," I answer, not opening my eyes.

"No. Not quite. Do you recall anything at all to do with the accident?"

He clearly mustn't have heard me, so I repeat myself. "The plane. I was in an airplane accident."

"Sara, you were in a car accident," he clarifies.

Rage fills me. I widen my eyes and sit up straighter. "My name is *not* Sara. My name is *not* Sara," I declare again and again with greater force.

The doctor puts a hand on my shoulder, but I shrug it away.

"Get me the puppy nurse. Call my mom. Where is Tom?"

"Tom is in the cafeteria," the woman answers warily.

"Tom is here?" I question.

She nods, looking terrified.

"Is my mom here too?"

She shakes her head, looking sad.

"My cell phone," I state. "I want my cell phone."

The lady looks at the doctor for guidance.

"I think you've had enough questions for now," the doctor announces, scribbling something onto a paper attached to a clipboard.

"No!" I squawk. "I need...I want my mom. Where's my dad? Where are my sister and brother? Where are they? Tell me now!"

The woman approaches the bed. "I'm your sister. I'm here, Sara. I've been here the whole time," she answers, tears forming in her eyes.

I shake my head, feeling defeated. *Why do they insist that I'm Sara? And why does this woman think she's my sister?* She looks old enough to be my mother.

"I'm Amanda Marie O'Reilly. My mom is—"

"No!" the woman interrupts angrily.

I ignore her and continue. "My mom is Theresa O'Reilly. My dad is Robert O'Reilly." I pause to take in some air. The woman continues to look me square in the eye, shaking her head. "My twin sister is Rebecca O'Reilly. My brother is Timothy O'Reilly." My lungs feel restricted. I feel like I just ran a marathon, but I have so much more I need to confess. "I was in a plane accident with my friends Tom and Jayde. I just graduated from Columbia University yesterday. My mom is the mayor of New York City—"

"Stop! Just stop!" the woman shouts. "Make her stop," she demands, glaring at the doctor.

"It's okay, Megan. It's common for patients to be confused after being in a coma for such a long time."

"No, I'm not confused. Ask me anything," I demand, confident that I know who I am and what happened to me. He offers me a pitiful smile. "Ask me!" I repeat just as a familiar face enters the room.

"You," I exclaim. The woman smiles and scoots across the floor to the end of my bed.

"You're awake. You're up," she announces, excited.

"Elle est très perdue aujourd'hui," the woman claiming to be my sister whispers to her.

What did she just say? What language is that? German? French? It's clearly not Spanish. What language do they speak in Bermuda?

"What did you say to her?" I point a finger toward both women.

They remain silent.

The doctor pulls a chair close to the bed and lowers himself in it.

"It's clear that you don't remember much of anything," he states, leaning back in the chair, folding his hands in his lap. "Your name is Sara. You're in Caribou, Maine. You've been in a car accident. You hit a moose. You've been in a coma for thirteen days. This is your sister, Megan. This is your mother-in-law, Claudette."

I'm so shaken. These people are obviously the ones who are confused. "Where is Tom?"

"Va chercher Tom," the lady who claims to be my sister says to the other lady.

She scuttles out the door, shuffling her feet.

Once the woman has left the room, the doctor begins to speak again. "You should know that the baby didn't make it," he announces, scanning my face.

I narrow my eyes. *Baby?* I'm unmistakably the wrong person. I'm a virgin. I clearly couldn't have had a baby.

"I'm a virgin." I roll my eyes.

The doctor and the woman shake their heads in sync. "Sara, you have four kids. And you were pregnant when you had the accident. The baby didn't make it."

I let out a chuckle. "That's not possible. I'm only twenty-two years old. I can't have four kids."

"You're thirty-four years old, Sara. Your memory has been affected by the accident," the doctor explains.

I swallow hard, feeling like I was gut-punched. I hesitantly grab hold of the blankets and raise them in the air. Peering under, tears trickle to the corners of my eyes when I see the silhouette of my figure through the robe. This isn't my body. This can't be.

"Sara," a deep voice calls out from the doorway.

Lowering the blankets, I see the woman from earlier enter the room, along with a priest. *What is he doing here? Are they preparing to do an exorcism?*

"I'm so happy to see you awake and responding. Our prayers were answered," the priest exclaims.

He hurries to my bedside and bends down, wrapping his arms around my shoulders. I stiffen and clench my jaw, feeling uncomfortable with this strange priest hugging me.

He pulls away but places a hand on both of my shoulders and looks into my eyes before he leans in and kisses my cheek.

"Sara woke up a bit confused today, but she did ask for you," the doctor utters.

I look over to the doctor, narrowing my eyes. "I didn't ask for *him*. I asked for my friend Tom."

"Yes. I know. This is Tom. Your good friend, Father Tom."

Without moving my head, I look to my left at the priest. *That's Tom?* That's not possible. He's at least four inches shorter than Tom, and he has much lighter hair and a smaller build.

"It's all right, Sara," the priest says, returning a hand to my shoulder. "I think it's a good time for all of us to pray. God will hear our words, and he'll restore your memory."

The four of them stand around my bed, holding hands and lowering their heads.

"Sara?" a concerned voice calls out from the end of the bed.

Everyone opens their eyes and looks to the doorway. Another gentleman stands there.

"I'm sorry, I thought you were still in ICU. I ran all the way here when they told me that they transferred you to a regular room. I'm sorry I wasn't here earlier," he breaths out.

"Thank goodness you're here, Marc," the round-bodied woman proclaims, walking toward him. She pronounces his name in a molasses-thick accent. "Elle se réveilla confuse," she utters in a low tone.

He takes a cautious step in my direction.

When he gets close enough for me to see into his eyes, I feel a sense of familiarity. I know him. I've seen him somewhere. And then it hits me, he's the guy from the airport, but he looks older. His hair, while still a light blonde, is sprinkled with glistening greys. And he has frown lines surrounding his mouth when he smiles. But there's no mistaking those eyes. He has crystal blue eyes, as blue as the summer sky. And when he looks at me, it feels like no one else is in the room.

"Daddy," a tiny voice whispers from the doorway. "Do we really need to wait out here?"

The man turns and a little girl peeks around the corner into the room. She sees me looking at her. Her eyes widen and a huge smile forms on her face. "Mama!" she exclaims. "You're awake." She barely gets the last word out before three other faces peek through the doorway next to her.

"Mom," a little boy exclaims before he bolts in my direction.

This can't be real. It must be a dream—a nightmare. I squeeze my eyes shut and hope that when I reopen them, I'm sitting on a beach in Bermuda.

Chapter Three
— Anywhere, But Here —

"Mommy, are you sleeping again?"

I squint one eye open and swallow the golf ball-size lump in my throat.

"Why are you crying?" another tiny voice questions.

With a shaky hand, I swipe a runaway tear as it rolls down my cheek. I look to the doctor in horror, pleading with him to make it all go away.

"Come on kids, let's go get a snack," the round-bodied woman announces, extending a hand to help them down from the bed.

"I don't want to go," a little boy with strawberry-blonde hair shrieks, clutching to my arm.

"Can she come with us?"

"No, she's tired. I'll go with you guys too," the priest interjects, tugging lightly on the little boy's arm.

Three tiny humans climb down from the bed. But the moment their feet touch the floor, they race out without looking back. "I want chocolate ice cream," one of them calls out.

While watching them all leave, I see another boy, maybe eight years old or so, standing in the doorway with his arms crossed and looking down, an expression of anger plastered on his face. I can't help but think that I must be wearing a matching expression on my own face.

"Those are not my kids. They can't be. I never wanted kids," I blurt out the moment the tiny humans disappear from sight. "I want my cell phone," I bark, tears bursting from my eyes. "I want to call my mom. Give me my cell phone."

The guy from the airport shakes his head slowly and his brow creases. "We don't have cell phones, Sara," he whispers barely audibly.

I yank the IV tube out of my arm, causing a sharp pain to radiate all the way up to my shoulder and blood to spurt everywhere.

"Hold on...don't—" The doctor jumps from the chair and tries to shield the stream of blood.

"I don't care. I want to go home. Give me my things," I demand, scooting myself to the side of the bed and lowering my feet to the floor.

"Looks like your kids were happy to see—" the nurse enters the room and stops abruptly when she sees that the doctor's white medical jacket now matches his crimson red tie.

"I've got this. Get Dr. Bouchard down here," the doctor advises.

"Where are my clothes? I want to go home. I'm an adult. You cannot keep me here."

"Okay. You will go home, but you should at least eat something first. You haven't eaten any food in nearly two weeks. Just eat something and then we'll let you go home," the doctor advises while applying pressure to my arm to stop the bleeding.

The lady who claims to be my sister rolls the hospital table close to me and uncovers a plate. The platter is covered in brown gravy, with what looks to be mashed potatoes and sliced turkey peeking out from under it. The smell makes my stomach do somersaults.

"Get that away from me. I'm a vegetarian," I protest, rolling my eyes in disgust.

The guy from the airport chuckles and the lady smiles in response.

"Sorry," the lady says. "It's just that you haven't been a vegetarian since you were twenty."

Why do they keep claiming to know me? How could I possibly look like the person they think they know?

"I don't know who you guys think I am, but I'm not that person. Just get me my things. You guys don't need to stay. I will find my own way home."

The doctor finishes bandaging my arm.

"I'll get the discharge paperwork ready," he announces before walking out of the room.

The lady walks to my bedside and sits next to me. I don't care to look at her; I look down and fold my hands in my lap.

"When you were sixteen, you snuck out of the house to go to a party in the city. I refused to go; I was too scared to get caught. You thought the back door was unlocked, but when you got back home around three o'clock in the morning, you were locked out of the house. You threw a rock at my bedroom window..." she pauses and quietly laughs. "You threw the rock too hard, and it broke the window. I was so mad at you. I was scared to tell Dad that it was broken so I didn't say anything until after school the next day. When I got home, I found that it had rained into my bedroom, soaking everything that was on my desk. I lied to him, telling him it wasn't broken when I left for school that morning. Luckily, he didn't press for the truth because I think I would have caved."

I raise my head, looking at her from the corner of my eye. *How could she know that story? Who is she?*

"I had you do my homework for an entire month in return for keeping quiet." She offers me a soft smile. "A few months later we got matching tattoos," she adds, leaving me speechless.

Tears tickle down my cheeks.

She reaches a hand across her shoulder and lowers the top of her shirt to reveal a tattoo that reads "If the door is closed, open a window."

A sob escapes me. I have that exact same tattoo on my shoulder. It was our inside joke, but also our reminder that we'll always have each other's back.

She leans in and envelops me in a hug.

"How?" I cry out into her shirt. "How can this be?"

"It's okay, Sara. You'll be all right. You're alive, so you'll be okay."

When I raise my head from her shoulder, I notice another man in a long white medical jacket standing beside the guy from the airport. "I hear someone's ready to leave," he declares when we make eye contact. "I'd prefer it if you stayed a little while longer, though."

I shake my head, feeling too overwhelmed to speak.

He extends his hand for me to shake. "I'm Dr. Bouchard. I'm a psychiatrist. Do you mind if we talk a bit?"

I steady myself on the rail of the bed and stand.

"Where are you going?" he asks.

"Anywhere, but here."

My legs aren't as stable as I thought they'd be, but it doesn't stop me. I wobble to the bathroom.

"Can I get some clothes?"

The lady follows behind me, and holds onto my elbow, steadying me.

"I brought you some clothes a few days ago," the guy from the airport answers.

Flicking on the light in the bathroom, I see my image in the mirror before me. I look like myself, but about ten pounds heavier and with shorter hair than I remember.

I glance at the woman standing alongside me, and she looks *exactly* like me. And I realize that we both look like my dad. *How can this be?*

"I don't know," she mutters as if she can read my thoughts.

"You're really her?" I question, shaking my head in disbelief.

"I am."

Feeling like I'm going to collapse, I bend down, grasping the edge of the sink for support.

The guy from the airport pulls a chair into the bathroom, positioning it behind me. I lower myself into it and bury my face in my hands. A sob forms that quickly escalates into a body-wracking cry.

My sister crouches down and wraps me in a bear hug. We stay like this until there are no more tears to shed.

"Why aren't Mom and Dad here?" I question, pulling away.

She swipes a runaway tear from my cheek. "They died seventeen years ago."

My chest tightens and I replay her words in my head.

"How old am I?"

"We're thirty-four," she answers.

"That's not possible," I say to her, doing the math in my head. "They were at my college graduation when I was twenty-two. I can't be thirty-four if they died seventeen years ago. That's not possible."

She shakes her head. "No, Sara, they were never at your college graduation. They died two months before we graduated from high school."

"No!" I growl angrily. "No, they were there. Timmy was there too. I remember it."

"It's common to confuse the dream you had while in a coma with reality," the doctor advises from the doorway.

I glance over my shoulder, not knowing he was there the entire time.

"It's likely you had a dream that your parents were at your graduation. While in a coma, your mind was creating a world to contently live in. It's possible that it chose to include your parents since I'm assuming you miss them, and the accident was a traumatic experience for you."

The guy from the airport hands me a cup of water.

I take a sip and let out a quivering breath.

"I don't know why this is happening to me. Did Timmy die too?"

My sister shakes her head and furrows her brow. "Who is Timmy?" she questions after a long moment.

"Our brother. You know, our baby brother."

"We don't have a brother, Sara."

This is all so confusing. "I could really use a Starbucks right now," I murmur to myself.

"You're most definitely still the Sara I know," the guy from the airport jests, smiling.

"I'd like to get dressed now. I want to go." I'm feeling overwhelmed with all these people who I don't know looking down on me.

The guy from the airport hands me a bag. I unzip it and begin to pull out its contents.

"While I'd prefer that you stay a few days longer, I know I can't keep you here. It's evident that you suffered from traumatic amnesia, but your brain scans yesterday didn't show any significant neurological damage. Possibly if you get back to your life, you'll start to remember the pieces you've forgotten," the doctor says. "I can tell that you have a very loving family that will help you. I'd like to schedule a follow-up with you in a week or so. And be sure to call your doctor if you should feel sick or have problems holding down any food. But, otherwise, I agree that going home is probably the best thing for you right now. I'll let the nurse know," he states before walking away.

I unfold a T-shirt and raise it in the air in front of me. It has a large red cracked heart and the words *Achy Breaky Heart* are scrolled across it. I scoff. "What is this?"

"It's your favorite T-shirt," the guy mutters. "I thought you'd like to wear it since you say it's the most comfortable one you have."

"And you have a crush on Billy Ray," my sister adds.

"Who the hell is Billy Ray?"

"One of your favorite singers," she states, and I'm somewhat reminded of who this guy is.

"Why would I have a crush on a guy that's twice my age?"

"He's younger than we are. He's in his early thirties."

I start to do the math in my head again. "What year is it?"

"Nineteen ninety-three," the guy answers.

"No, I wasn't asking what year I was born. I'm asking what year it is right now."

"It's nineteen ninety-three right now. We weren't born in ninety-three, we were born in nineteen fifty-nine."

My jaw drops open, feeling like it'll slam to the floor in one big thud.

"Can I have some privacy so I can get dressed, please?" I demand, angry with myself for remembering my life different than I'm being told.

After dressing into my broken-hearted T-shirt and a pair of grey sweatpants—not the more stylish leggings that I recall owning a closet full of, but the elastic at the bottom, drawstring on the top, jogger-type that I wouldn't want to be caught on my deathbed in—I sign some release papers, and I'm wheeled out in a wheelchair to a van parked outside of the hospital entrance.

"Ta-da! Your chariot awaits," the guy from the airport sings, opening the passenger side door. "I knew how much you loved your old van that now sits in pieces in Roland's junk yard, so I made sure to buy you a new one before you came out of the hospital." *A van? I loved a van?*

"Do I not own a Mercedes?"

Both the guy and my sister laugh. "This is your Mercedes."

"Great."

"I found some vegetable broth in the pantry. Are you sure that you wouldn't prefer some chicken broth that my mom made instead?" the guy questions.

I shake my head, still unable to look him in the eye without feeling weak in the knees.

The guy—my husband—hands me a cup, along with a plate of buttered toast.

Megan and I are sitting on the porch of a massive, modern-style, white farmhouse. It has a wraparound covered porch, held up by pillars, and lined with multiple wooden rocking chairs. Large, bright orange tiger lily plants outline the porch and stairs. And beyond that, the home is surrounded by endless fields of grass.

I still can't get myself to enter the house that I'm told I live in with a husband and four kids. I've only made it as far as the porch. The kids from earlier, and a few others, play Mother May I in the front yard.

"I'm sorry. I don't mean to be rude, but what is your name again?" I ask the guy I last remember seeing in the airport, feeling shameful.

"I'm Marc," he answers, but like the round-bodied woman in the hospital, he pronounces his name in a molasses-thick accent. "Like Mark, but pronounced in French," he clarifies. "But you always call me 'handsome,'" he adds, smiling a beautiful genuine grin, making me feel embarrassed.

"I need to get going," Megan states, standing.

"Where are you going?" I ask, feeling alone and scared.

"I need to get my kids to take a shower and off to bed. They have school in the morning. But don't worry, I'm not that far away from you. I'm your neighbor," she announces, pointing off to the side.

I squint my eyes and can barely see anything but fields of grass. "Where?"

"Just around the corner."

I look at her, pleading with my eyes for her to stay.

"I'll stop by in the morning before I head to school." She leans down and hugs me. "You'll be okay, Sara. Marc is a great guy. He and the kids love you so much," she whispers before turning away and walking to the stairs.

She spins back around before ascending and blows me a kiss. "I'm so happy you're alive and awake," she declares, choking up.

"Come on kids, let's get you washed up before bed," Marc announces into the yard. "Do you want to come in," he asks, looking at me.

"Not just yet." I take a sip of broth, attempting to slow my worried heart.

"How did I end up here...in Van Buren? Is that what you said the name of this was?" I ask Marc, still sitting on the porch, now wrapped up in a blanket that he brought out for me after he put the kids to bed.

"Right, Van Buren. Well, actually, we live in Cyr Plantation, but it's considered part of Van Buren," he confirms. "When your parents died, you and your sister moved in with your aunt in Portland—"

"My aunt Jan?" I interrupt.

"Yes. Your dad's sister. We met while we were both interning at the mayor's office in Portland." He pauses, biting on his lower lip.

"So, we didn't meet—um, well, bump into each other—in the JFK airport?"

He lets out a chuckle. "No. I've never been out of the state or on an airplane."

I swallow. "I thought I interned in my mom's office in New York City?"

"No…you told me your mom was a housewife," he stutters with a flash of uncertainty.

"So, my mom was never the mayor of New York City?"

"No. No, she wasn't." He shakes his head.

"Did I go to Columbia University?"

"No, you went to Southern Maine University."

"For Political Science? Or something else?"

"It was for Political Science," he confirms.

I raise an eyebrow. At least I recall something correctly.

"Where do I work now?"

"Well, let me tell you our story," he states calmly. "When we met at twenty-one, we instantly fell in love. How could you resist me after all?" He smiles. "We got married twelve days later. You got pregnant two months after that. And when we graduated from college, you were eight months pregnant. You were the one that convinced me to move back home."

I wrap the blanket tighter around me, feeling like I'm about to fall apart.

"I got a job at the city clerk's office in Presque Isle. After Abby was born, you immediately wanted another. So, thirteen months later, we had Jacob. You wanted nothing more than to be a mom," he declares. "And you're the best mom," he adds. "You loved this particular spot of land because it faces East and has the best view of the sunrise, so we bought this plot and built this house."

I'm left without words because he's describing a person who's the opposite of who I remember myself being.

"You loved it here so much that you convinced your sister to move here as well," he continues. "We introduced her to my brother, and they hit it off." He clears his throat, choking up. "My brother died five years ago."

There's silence for a long moment before I'm able to speak. "I'm sorry," I offer, unsure how else to respond.

He nods and then clears his throat.

"Anyway, my dad passed a week before my brother. He was the town manager here. The people loved him. I took over the position from him. But you're really the one that does so much for this town; you've molded it into what it is today. While I may take care of the politics, you give so much of yourself to the people. I'm certain I wouldn't be able to hold this position without you."

We sit there a while longer. I'm scared that I'm no longer the person he remembers me being. I don't feel like that person. I already miss the busy streets of New York, and I can't stop thinking about the party life that I remember having in college. I don't feel thirty-four and I certainly don't feel like a mom.

"I think I'm going to head to bed," he announces, standing from the rocker.

"All right. I don't think I'm ready yet. I'll be in soon."

He bends down and then freezes in place, realizing what he's doing is unknown to me.

Slowly, he extends his head toward mine and kisses my cheek.

"Je vais vous faire tomber en amour avec moi," he whispers before pulling away.

Chapter Four
— Small-town USA —

"Is she sleeping?"

"Maybe she's dead."

"No! Look at her stomach. She's breathing, stupid."

"Should we wake her up?"

"Who cares. I'm out of here."

"Mama?" a tiny voice whispers so closely that I feel a warm breath tickle my ear.

I open my eyes to be welcomed by three faces standing over me.

"Mama! Why are you still sleeping?"

"Why are you sleeping on the couch?"

I contemplate pulling the blanket over my head and staying like that until the tiny humans get bored and run off, but instead I blink the sleep out of my eyes and offer a half-hearted smile.

"Come and eat your breakfast before the bus gets here," a voice calls out.

"Are you driving me to school today?" a girl, who I presume is the oldest of the kids, asks.

I scrunch up my face and shrug. "Do I normally?"

"Yeah, of course." She rolls her eyes and crosses her arms in front of her.

"I'll drive you today. Just eat your breakfast," the round-bodied woman from the hospital—my mother-in-law—announces, sauntering in from the kitchen.

"I'm not hungry. I need to finish doing my hair," the girl states, turning and bolting up a staircase.

"How are you doing today?" my mother-in-law questions. "Are you hungry?"

"I'm okay."

"I made your favorite. If you want a chance of having any, you better get up before the kids eat it all."

I nod. "Thank you."

When I sit up and put my feet on the cold floor, it's as if it awakes my senses and I immediately smell coffee.

I get to my feet and walk in the direction of the smell. As I approach the kitchen another smell fills the air—a not so appealing one—and my stomach turns.

"I rolled a ploye for you, Mom," one boy proclaims. "I put some extra creton on it, just how you like it." He smiles at me, looking for my approval.

"I poured your coffee for you," the littlest girl states, beaming. "I even put the cream and sugar in all by myself," she squeaks in delight.

"Thank you." I pull a chair out at the massive dining room table that sits between the kitchen island and the living room.

The moment I lower myself into the chair, the little girl leans over the table to me. "I told Jacob you weren't dead," she whispers, looking up through her eyelashes to the boy sitting at the end of the table.

The boy glares at her before getting up, taking his unfinished breakfast with him and throwing it in the trash.

"Come on kids, it's time for school. Austin and Jacob, get your schoolbag and head outside to wait for Mr. Beo," my mother-in-law advises, gathering the plates from the table. "Emma, go get Abby upstairs. I'll drop you both off at school, but we have to leave now."

"Should I be doing something?" I ask her.

"You need to eat and rest. I'll make sure they all get to school today. And then I'll pick them up from school and make supper. I don't want you to do anything. Marc left for work already, but he said he'd be by after his meeting this morning. And Megan stopped by before she left for work, but you were asleep. She'll be by for supper."

I press my lips together, offering her a small smile before taking a sip of coffee. The instant the hot fluid hits my taste buds, I swallow hard and the woman notices.

"There's more coffee in the pot. I told Emma she was putting too much sugar."

"That's all right," I mutter, pushing the cup away.

"After I drop the kids off at school, I could drive you into town so you can get your Starbucks if you're feeling up to it."

"Starbucks?"

"Yeah. You always go to Joe's Restaurant in the morning and Madame Cecile has your coffee ready for you."

The sound of a loud horn blares from outside and my mother-in-law rushes to the back door. "Austin and Jacob, leave those chickens alone, Mr. Beo's here."

Through the window, I see the two boys running toward the house.

My mother-in-law scurries to the front door. Opening it, she offers a wave.

And after a moment, I hear the bus drive away.

"Girls, come on, we have to leave," my mother-in-law calls upstairs before returning to me. "I'll drop the girls off and then come pick you up. It'll give you time to eat your breakfast, shower, and change. Okay?"

I shrug and nod.

After they've all left, I remain sitting at the dining room table. I feel like an intruder. Looking around, it's evident that this home is filled with love. Colored pages and notes scribbled by tiny humans plaster the refrigerator, toys and books are scattered throughout, and homemade trinkets are displayed among primitive decorations around the living room.

I walk over to the hallway where large photographs line the walls. Running my fingers across the glass, I take in each picture, hoping that one of them will help to spark my memory—any memory. They are all the four kids, Marc, Megan and what I assume is her own family, and a few other individuals that I don't know. And I'm in most of them. I don't recall any of these moments that are snapped in these photographs. Not a single one.

An overwhelming feeling of sadness fills me. I don't know if it's because I remember a different life or if it's because I don't remember *this* life. I look genuinely happy in each picture. We all do.

I see a telephone hanging on the wall. Approaching it, I notice it's a rotary phone with the receiver attached by a cord. It's just like the one that I recall my grandma having in her living room in Connecticut when I was little.

I lift the receiver and put it to my ear. The moment I hear a dial tone a thought fills my head: maybe this is my chance to contact Tom—my real friend, the one that I remember. If only I could talk to him, he could help me figure out what's going on.

I place a finger in the number one slot and turn clockwise. After letting go of the wheel, it returns to its original position. I continue to dial the rest of Tom's cellphone number and wait for the signal to catch up. Once it does, I anticipate the line to begin ringing, but instead a loud recording blares into my ear: *"We're sorry. You have reached a number that has been disconnected or is no longer in service. If you feel you have reached this recording in error, please check the number and try your call again."*

A sinking feeling fills my chest, and I return the receiver in its position.

Before I can stop myself, I remove the receiver again and begin to dial my parents' phone number.

My eyes widen when a voice answers, "Hello."

"Mom!" I exclaim with anticipation, my heart racing.

"Excuse me, who is this?" the woman replies, and I realize that it doesn't sound anything like my mom.

"Is this Theresa O'Reilly?" I ask with a slim glimmer of hope.

"No. I'm sorry, but you must have the wrong number."

My chest tightens. "Sorry." I swallow back tears before returning the receiver to its home and wiping my eyes.

After steadying my shaky legs, I make my way upstairs and observe four doorways lining the hallway. Peering into the first one, I see a bunkbed and walls painted in blue and red, with baseball posters scattered across them. A familiar sound can be heard coming from a small television; it's connected to a video game console—Nintendo—and the music to Mario Bros plays repeatedly.

I step into the room and turn the television off.

Exiting, I see a second doorway across from this room. It's a bathroom with towels scattered across the floor, and a curling iron is plugged into the wall.

After unplugging the curling iron, I walk down the hallway to the next door. Inside is a bedroom painted in bright pink and purple and decorated in butterflies. A beautiful canopy bed sits along one wall. And a white wooden desk sits along the other, with a pegboard above it that's filled with photographs.

In the last room sits a twin-sized bed with Strawberry Shortcake sheets. A large dollhouse is displayed in the middle of the floor, surrounded by Barbie dolls dressed in a variety of sparkling outfits.

I go back downstairs and walk down the long hallway, looking for the master bedroom. I pass by one door, and when looking in I see a large, mahogany desk sitting in the center of the room. The desk is covered in papers and folders, and off to one side is a clunky tan computer.

I stroll into the room and around to the other side of the desk. I pull out the chair and lower myself in it, staring at the computer screen.

After looking around, sensing someone watching me, I press the power button and a loud, whirling fan starts up. Moments later an image pops onto the screen, with the words *Microsoft WindowsNT*.

After waiting a few minutes, when the image doesn't disappear, I click the mouse, hoping to wake it up, but nothing happens. I decide I should turn it off before my mother-in-law returns, but the image finally fades, and the home screen comes into view. There are only four icons on the screen: an image of a computer labeled *My Computer*, an image of a trashcan labeled *Recycling Bin*, an image of a folder labeled *My Documents*, and the last image is of a triangle with a large O in the center with the label *America Online*. Reading the words, I spell out A-O-L in the back of my mind. *AOL*, that must be the internet.

I double click on the icon and a pop-up box shows with a button labeled *Connect*. I click it and a loud, screeching sound fills the room.

Panic sets in. *What if my mother-in-law should walk in?* She'll see me snooping. But I so desperately want to search for Tom, and even my mom or dad—actually, anything that I remember.

The screeching sound doesn't stop.

"Come on," I bellow, growing anxious. "Hurry up."

A car horn blasts outside, and it makes me instinctively press the Cancel button on the screen. I swing around in the chair to look out the window, but all I see is a car driving up the street.

I remain panicked so I decide to turn off the computer and find the master bedroom so I can get changed before my mother-in-law returns.

After showering in the master bathroom, I search through the massive walk-in closet for something presentable to wear. Thumbing through the many shirts neatly hung up along one wall, I find the only blouse that doesn't look like it's from the nineteen-seventy's era. On the other side of the closet, I find a complementing blue miniskirt and a pair of strappy sandals.

"Sara, I'm back," I hear my mother-in-law call out.

"Okay. I'm in the bedroom getting changed. I'll be out in a second." I rush to the door and push it shut, realizing that I'm stark naked.

Staring at myself in the long mirror, I wrap my arms around my stomach. My body looks ragged, sagging, and old. I run my fingers across the roadmap-like stretch marks lining my belly and scrunch up my nose. I turn to the side and regard my sagging breasts, belly pooch, and cellulite that cover my butt and thighs. While my face doesn't look much different than I remember, the rest of my body looks nothing like me.

I slip into a pair of floral, lace underwear that I found in the dresser. And strap on a matching bra. At least I have good taste for lingerie. I can't say the same for the rest of my wardrobe. I slide the skirt up my legs and throw the blouse over my head. Both fit snug, but they'll have to do.

I saunter to the kitchen to find my mother-in-law leaning into the refrigerator. "I got the eggs from the chickens for you," she states without turning around. "I see you didn't eat your breakfast. I placed it on the top shelf so you can warm it up later."

She closes the refrigerator door and turns around, and her eyes widen. "You look wonderful. You haven't dressed up that much in a long time."

I shrug and feel my cheeks blush. "I look silly, don't I? I couldn't find anything in the closet."

"No. No. Don't be embarrassed, you look beautiful."

I clear my throat, unable to wash away the embarrassment. "You don't need to drive me to get coffee. I can drive on my own." I'm unsure of how much more time I can spend with her while feeling the awkwardness grow between us.

"Of course not. I'm happy to take you. Plus, I'd love some bread pudding."

My mother-in-law opens the door and a small bell chimes, signaling our entrance. Chatter fills the room.

"Sara!" a sweet voice exclaims, and the room goes silent. Every head in the restaurant turns to us. "Oh, la fille est ici," she announces, walking out from behind the counter. "When did you get out of the hospital?" I take note that she too has a thick molasses accent.

"Um. Yesterday," I respond.

"Viens. Viens avec moi, ma fille." She takes me by the wrist and walks me to the counter, and a gentleman stands up from a shiny metal stool.

He waves his hand in the direction of the stool, directing me to sit. "It's so good to see you," he says, wrapping his arms around me, and before I can even react, he envelops me in a big bear hug. He smells of Old Spice and cigarettes.

"Comment va-t-elle?" another older gentleman questions.

"Bien," my mother-in-law says to him. "Mais elle ne se souvient pas beaucoup."

"Ah. C'est okay. Elle se souviendra. Il va juste prendre du temps."

"Oui. I hope."

I look around the restaurant, which looks more like a nineteen-sixties diner with booths lining one wall, and on the opposite side sits a long countertop with shiny metal stools. A small opening overlooks a kitchen where the smell of bacon and eggs fills the air. The place and the people have a very "Mayberry" feel.

"La fille est ici," the sweet lady tells the gentleman flipping something on the grill. He quickly turns and looks my way, a smile filling his face.

Before I know it, he's out of the kitchen and standing beside me. He places a bowl on the counter in front of me. "I made it every day that you were gone. I was hoping you'd be in for some." He leans down and plants a kiss on my cheek.

I look down at the bowl and observe a heaping portion of some kind of bread or dessert with what I think are raisins peeking out, and the smell of cinnamon filling the air. I must admit this is the first thing I've smelled so far that makes my mouth water.

The sweet lady places a white disposable coffee cup in front of me and the gentleman returns to the kitchen. "Here's your Starbucks, la fille."

Unsure of if I want to try a spoon of the bread concoction or take a sip of my highly anticipated Starbucks first, I grab at the cup. Raising it to my lips, I take a large gulp. I narrow my eyes, staring at the white cup. This coffee tastes nothing like I recall. I press my lips together, offering a polite smile, trying to hide my distaste.

Wanting to mask the un-Starbucks taste, I spoon a large piece of dessert and place it in my mouth. I just about melt in my seat when the flavor hits my taste buds. It's absolutely divine. I make quick work of the rest of the bowl while my mother-in-law and the others in the restaurant chat in French around me.

As I scrape the final crumbs from the bowl, the sweet lady remarks, "You sure missed the bread pudding, huh?"

I raise an eyebrow in confirmation while licking my spoon clean.

"We should get going," my mother-in-law announces. "I think Marc will be home soon. He said he should be out of his meeting by ten-thirty."

She reaches into her wallet and slides a ten-dollar bill across the counter. When she does, my eyes are drawn to the wall next to the cash register where photographs of men dressed in military uniforms are taped up.

My mother-in-law takes notice, and she points in the direction of one of the photographs. "That's Marc's pepere," she states.

"Who?"

"His grandfather—my dad. And that one is Marc's dad—my husband—when he was in the Navy," she explains, pointing to another photograph. "And that one is Marc's brother—Megan's husband," she adds, her voice dropping with a hint of sadness.

"Did he die in the military?" I question before realizing that I probably shouldn't have. I should maybe have left that question for Megan.

She shakes her head. "No. He had been out of the military for six years before he died."

I want to ask her how he died—I want to know more—but I choose not to question any further.

After promising to return tomorrow morning, we leave, the door chime signaling our exit.

Pulling open the door to my mother-in-law's car, I see a woman from the corner of my eye leaning out of the doorway of one of the businesses. "Sara," she calls, waving her hands frantically in the air. "La fille is back!" She takes long strides in my direction.

My mother-in-law walks around the car to me, and I look to her for guidance. She smiles.

"Oui, elle est sortie hier," my mother-in-law says to her. "She got out yesterday," she translates, looking at me.

"I'm so happy," the woman proclaims. "I just wanted to let you know that I made sure to bring over your weekly flowers while you were in the hospital." She grabs my hand.

"Flowers?" I scrunch up my face in confusion.

"Yes. I brought them both and placed them in the pots next to their pierres. And I removed the old ones. You'll really like this week's flowers. They're the purple tulips that you loved the last time I had got a shipment of them."

I nod, not wanting to give away my complete confusion.

"You can just let me know if you want to collect next week's flowers or if you want me to bring them. I don't mind doing it until you feel better." She squeezes my hand and then leans in, hugging me. "We're all so happy you're back, la fille," she utters, rubbing my back.

"Thanks."

"Thank you, Madame Irene," my mother-in-law echoes.

"Oh! Claudette, I got that magazine with the different flags for the festival. Do you want me to get it for you?"

"Ah, non. I'll stop by later today. I have to drop Sara home and then I have an appointment to get my hair colored. I'll stop in when I drive by."

"Okay, sounds good," the woman tells her. "Feel better, fille," she adds, smiling at me.

We arrive back at the house and my mother-in-law tells me that she'll pick up the girls from school and bring lasagna for supper. I thank her and hop out of the car.

The moment I step foot inside the house, I release a long breath. My quest for Starbucks turned into a fanfare event. I've heard of Mayberry, but I never knew it actually existed. I miss the city, where you're just a passing face on the street. I could surely use that Starbucks now.

I'm startled out of my moment of meditation when the phone rings, echoing throughout the house. I contemplate not bothering with it, I don't think I could deal with another person welcoming me back, but there's a slim possibility that the person on the other end of the call could take me out of my misery so I rush down the hallway.

"Hello!"

"This is a collect call from an inmate at the Connecticut Wargate Correctional Institution," a recorded voice comes through the phone.

"Robert O'Reilly," a voice—a *very* familiar one—adds.

"That's my dad!" My heart speeds up.

"Do you accept this call?"

"Yes, yes, yes!" I answer much louder than I know is needed.

A click is heard and then a long pause.

"Dad? Dad, are you there?"

"Amanda. Oh, honey! I'm so happy I was able to get through to you. I got worried when you never showed up or answered my calls."

"Dad, where are you?"

"I'm still here, honey. They haven't gotten rid of me yet."

"Where? What do you mean? Are you in prison?"

"Yes, I'm still here. But I tried calling you many times the past couple of weeks. Are you all right? Did something happen?"

"Daddy. I'm so lost. I...I don't know where I am. I was in some kind of accident. I'm somewhere in Maine. I have no idea what's going on. Why are you in prison?"

"Honey, what do you mean? My execution date isn't until next week. But what happened to you?"

"Execution?" I gasp.

"Baby girl, what is going on? Why do you sound so confused?"

"What year is it, Daddy?"

"It's still ninety-three. Amanda, what's going on?"

"No, Daddy. No. I...I..." I inhale and tears form. "I don't know."

"What do you mean?"

I tell him about waking up in the hospital room and all that has happened in the last couple of days. He remains silent until I'm done—until I can no longer speak because I'm crying so hard.

"Two-minute warning," a recording interrupts our call.

"Why are you in prison, Daddy?"

"Honey, I've been here for nearly seventeen years. You've been there for over twelve. I don't know what happened to you, but you're where you belong. Marc is a good man. His family are good people. I trust that they will take good care of you once I'm gone."

"*Gone?* What do you mean, Daddy?"

"I'm sorry that you don't remember any of it. And I'm sorry that I have to break the news to you again, but I'm scheduled to be executed in seven days."

MY ANYWHERE

My lungs cease working. I stand there, mouth agape, in complete shock. I'm left unable to move.

"One-minute warning," the recording announces.

"Baby girl, I promise to call you again if they'll let me. I just wish I didn't have to hang up with you while you're feeling like this. I'm so sorry, Amanda. Did you get the latest letter that I wrote to you this week? I love you so much, baby girl."

"No, Daddy, don't go. Plea—"

The line goes silent, cutting me off.

I fall back against the wall and drag myself down to the floor.

Chapter Five
— Scrawled Notes and Swamp Things —

Lifting my head from the pillow, I squint in the direction of the alarm clock, struggling to see what time it is.

After my phone call with my dad this morning, Marc came home and found me in a heap on the floor in the hallway. He questioned what I was doing there, but I was able to play it off, telling him I started to feel lightheaded. He bought it. Once I found my feet under me, he led me on shaky legs to the bedroom, and I told him that I wanted to lie down. I couldn't calm the anger and confusion that was raging through me.

How could my "sister" claim that my parents are dead? Regardless of what my dad said, I don't believe a single word any of these people—these strangers—tell me. I don't know who they are or what their agenda is, but I want no part of it. I need to get my dad out of prison. And I want my life back.

When I was finally able to convince Marc that I was fine, he reluctantly went back to work, and I got up, knowing exactly what I wanted to do: I needed to get out of here and to my dad, *immediately*. I rummaged through the closet and found a piece of luggage tucked away on the top shelf. After stuffing it with a few items of clothing and toiletries, I took it outside and placed it in the back of the van. Realizing that I should at least leave a note so they wouldn't send a search party for me, I made my way back to the house just as my mother-in-law pulled into the driveway with a carful of kids. Within seconds, I had kids hanging off every limb, all excited to see me up and out of bed.

My plan foiled.

For now.

Sitting up on the edge of the bed, I take note that it's nine-twenty-three. Marc snores from the other side of the bed.

I slip on the sandals that rest on the floor by me and stand, the floorboard creaking under my feet.

"Shit," I whisper, standing still. But the snoring continues.

When I'm sure that the coast is clear, I rush through the next step of the strategy in my head. I took full advantage of the time I had between dinner and bed to devise my escape plan. I almost gave myself away when I got so wrapped up in thought during dinner that Claudette, Megan, and Marc had to keep repeating their questions to me. Even at one point, I may have missed something one of the kids said to me because the oldest boy threw his fork, transporting it into the lasagna casserole in the middle of the table, sending the girls in a fit of laughter. He stormed off from the table and went outside to the backyard, slamming the door behind him. But when I pushed aside my mostly uneaten piece of cheese lasagna that Claudette had made just for me—which was surprisingly appetizing— and told them I wasn't feeling good and needed to lie down, they simply thought that I was tired. Little did they know that I needed silence from the little voices chattering around the table; they were distracting me from being able to mentally strategize how the hell I was going to get out of here.

First on my to-do list: Get up.

Second: Leave a note.

I must write a note.

MY ANYWHERE

I tiptoe out of the bedroom and down the hallway. In the kitchen, I flick on the light above the stove and find a pencil. Taking it, I turn to the dining room table that houses stacks of the kids' schoolwork. I rummage through it and find a blank piece of notebook paper. Quickly, I scribble a note:

> I left. This isn't my life, and I want no part of it. Don't try to find me. I'm not coming back. I'll return your van.

Getting ready to sign it, I realize that one of the kids might find it, and as much as I don't want to play "mom" to them, I don't want to be this cruel either. They all appear to be innocent bystanders in this messed up situation.

I crumple the paper and place it in my pocket.

I pen another note:

> Went for coffee
> Be back later
> ~~Mandy~~ Sara

They'll never know what time I left so they won't think about sending out a search party for me until at least mid-morning. That'll give me time to make it far enough so they can't find me. Once I make it to my dad, I'll devise a way to return the van.

    I toss the note onto the kitchen island. When I do, I notice a stack of mail. My dad mentioned that he wrote letters to me, so I quickly flip through the envelopes, but come up empty. Maybe, just maybe, Marc or another one of these imposters confiscated it. I wouldn't put it past them.

    Glancing one more time at the clock, I realize that I've already wasted ten minutes. I have to get out of here.

    Next on my escape plan: Keys.

    I look around the room. If I owned a house like this, where would I leave my car keys?

    I hurriedly tiptoe to the front door. *Bingo!* On the wall above the kids' school bags and stack of shoes is a shelf lined with hooks that house three separate rings of keys. Noticing the dealership tag hanging on one of the rings, I know that the key attached must be for the van—my new "chariot" that Marc acted to present to me so proudly at the hospital. *Blech.*

    Only two more items left on my escape plan.

    Up next: Make a quiet getaway.

    I put my hand on the doorknob and pause. The house remains in complete silence. I turn the knob and slowly pull the door open enough for me to squeeze through. I can't risk the door making any kind of noise or my plan will be foiled for a second time. And I couldn't possibly explain that I'm headed to find coffee at this time of night. It's not like I'm in New York City where coffee shops are open all hours of the day and night. I'm almost certain the entire town goes to bed at nine p.m. *Do adults really go to bed that early?* Especially on a Friday night. Apparently, those in Mayberry do.

Once I'm out of the house, on the porch, and have the front door closed behind me, I hop down the stairs two at a time, headed straight for the van parked in the driveway.

Grabbing the handle to the car, I pull it in a slow, controlled motion. And when it's open enough for me to squeeze through, I hop in behind the wheel, pulling the door closed so that it latches shut, quietly.

Last step: Put the van in reverse and roll back down the driveway.

Placing my foot on the brake, I grab hold of the stick shift attached to the steering wheel and drag it down to the reverse position. Slowly releasing my foot on the brake and glancing in the rearview mirror, it's as if the van makes a pact with me; it rolls backward down and out of the driveway, as if saying, *"We're in this together."* These people may be colluding against me, but this van is on my side tonight.

I let the van roll a few feet down the street before I press the brake and turn the key in the ignition. Music blares through the speakers, making me jump and look around. *Damn it!* That's certainly loud enough to wake not only the neighborhood, but the entire town. With a flick of my fingers, I turn the volume knob completely down. *What kind of music was that anyway?* This place just keeps getting more bizarre.

I look up at the house and notice a curtain from an upstairs bedroom move. That's the boy's bedroom, if I recall correctly. I don't want to sit around much longer; I need to get out of here while I can.

The car idles in the street while I fidget with the controls, attempting to find the switch to turn on the headlights. It's pitch-black around me, without a single streetlight to be seen.

After accidentally turning on the wipers, I find the switch. Twisting it between my fingers, the road ahead of me illuminates in a warm glow. I squint, trying to adjust my eyes before I look in the rearview mirror at the pair of lights that approach.

Just as I put the van in drive, a car swerves from behind me and, in a flash, it passes me, horn blaring. *Fuck!* If I didn't already wake everyone, they are likely wide awake now. "Damn idiot," I groan through clenched teeth.

I press my foot down on the gas pedal, not wanting to stick around a moment longer in case Marc was, in fact, woken up.

Driving a distance in the dark with both hands on the wheel, in the opposite direction of where Marc's mom drove me to town, I take notice that I'm only driving ten miles per hour. I can barely see five feet in front of me. *How could there not be any streetlights around here?* This certainly can't be safe.

I see a pair of lights approach—very bright, blinding lights; I have to turn my head away. The lights dim as they get closer and pass. Another car, not far behind, nears and the driver flashes the headlights. What does that mean? Is that a way of saying "Hello" around here? What a weird place. Really weird.

Glancing in the side-view mirror, I raise my middle finger in the air. "Hello, asshole. And goodbye!"

The moment I return my focus to the road in front of me, my eyes widen, and my breath catches in my throat. I stomp on the brake and jerk the steering wheel, sending the car into a tailspin.

I squeeze my eyes shut until the car screeches to a stop, giving one last shake. Afraid to open my eyes—to see where the van landed—I cover my face with both hands.

When my heart slows, I peek through my fingers. Just then, I hear a loud horn blast and lights flash, making me grasp the steering wheel. My attention is drawn to the passenger side window, and I'm welcomed by a massive animal—a creature, swamp-thing—staring down at me through the window. The beast stands well over seven feet tall, nostrils flaring, with eyes pinned open, the size of grapefruits.

After we make eye contact, the creature turns his head in the direction of the horn that continues to blast through the darkness. He lets out a loud, exaggerated huff through his nose and takes one step in that direction, challenging the noise. When he does, I get a full view of a set of antlers that sit upon his head, about the size of the van I'm currently held hostage in.

A loud crack sounds, and I instinctively cover my ears. The creature slowly redirects his gaze back in my direction and nods, before turning and calmly walking into the woods.

What. The. Hell.

A knock on the driver's side window takes me out of my trance, my entire body trembling. "Are you okay?"

With a shaky hand, I roll down the window.

"Are you all right? Are you hurt?" the young man repeats, cradling a rifle in his arms like it's a newborn baby.

"I…I don't think…I think I'm okay," I breathe out, eyes peeled on the gun. He takes note of my terrified expression and shifts the gun in his arms. I'm not sure if I'm more afraid of the massive creature that I possibly created a bond with or the young gunslinger I just rolled down the window to.

"That was a close one. He wasn't easy to scare away either. The moose are out in full force lately. Someone hit one just up a ways a couple of hours ago." He glances inside the van. "So, I'm not sure where you're headed, but, if you'd feel safer, I can lead you out of this stretch of woods, back toward town."

"Back toward town?" I repeat. It's a statement more to myself than a response. I don't want to go back in that direction. I want out of here. Somewhere *extremely* far. But if there's any chance of running into those creatures again, I'm not sure this direction is the right way out.

"Are you sure you're all right? Do you want me to get you an ambulance?"

I shake my head. "I'm fine. I...sure...I'll follow you back to town."

"Okay," he responds, sounding relieved. "Stay right here. I'll pull up in front of you. We'll drive slowly, but follow close, and keep your eyes peeled."

I stare at him, panicked.

"You never know when those fuckers will come darting out. But I'm sure we'll be fine."

I grip the steering wheel so tightly with both hands that my knuckles turn white, and my fingers begin to ache while we crawl our way out of the wooded area. We drive past the house—my house—and down the road where streetlights suddenly shine overhead.

The young gunslinger pulls over to the side of the road, directly across from a building with a sign out front that reads "Riverview Nursing Facility."

I pull up behind him.

He exits the car and walks over to me. "We're safe now. He was a big one. I haven't seen one that size in a while. That was enough to shake anyone up. Are you sure you're all right?"

I nod, a sense of relief washing over me. "Thank you."

"Glad I was able to help. Have a good night's rest." He spins on his heels.

"Hey!" I call out. He turns back. "Is there another way out of town besides the direction we just came from?"

He presses his lips together in a tight line and narrows his eyes, looking at me quizzically. "Well, it depends on where you're headed. I suppose you could go through Hamlin and Limestone up there a bit," he directs, pointing toward downtown.

"Ah...yeah, Hamlin," I confirm, trying to sound like I know the area.

He gazes at me, nodding, a confused expression on his face. "You might want to wait until morning." I get a sense that he knows about my plan to get the hell out of here. "Get some rest. Things will be better in the morning."

He tips his baseball cap, nodding. Then he turns back toward his car, leaving me feeling ashamed and guilty.

Chapter Six

— Where the Lights Will Lead You —

With both hands on the wheel, leaning forward, I glance through the windshield, looking to my left, and then right. If I go left, I'll end up downtown. I remember that from earlier today. If I go right, well, I don't know where that takes me. The street looks dark in that direction. It's like this town only had enough streetlights to line the way to downtown and back. To hell with the rest of the streets once the moon comes up; you all are stuck at home. Maybe it's a way to enforce curfew for the rowdy teenagers, or maybe even those who carry rifles in their car. That must be it.

I can't go right. I just can't. I'm still shaken up by the events of the last twenty minutes, and heading back into darkness almost confirms to me that I will meet up with another swamp animal. There must be a way out of here in the direction of the lights.

I lean back and release my foot from the brake, just as the gas light starts to blink in the console. *You have got to be kidding me.* This can't be happening right now. How did I not even think about making sure there was enough gas in the tank while I was devising my getaway? It must have been that kid at dinner that distracted me from that step. What am I going to do now? I have barely enough gas to make it out of town, let alone all the way to my dad.

Now turning in the direction of town, I happen upon a gas station as I round the corner. It's like God made me drive in this direction, knowing. But does God also know that I need money to pay for the gas? "Do you, God?" I question, looking up.

I turn into the station and pull into a spot near a gas pump. Looking down between the seats, I notice the cup holder is filled with coins. I can't possibly fill the tank with coins alone. I peer down further between the seats, and my eyes are drawn to a purse laying on the floor behind the passenger seat. I grab it in haste, reaching into it and removing a wallet. "Thank you, God." What do they say? *God always provides*—or something like that. Who are "they" anyway? How would I know? I haven't been to church since I was confirmed as a kid.

A tap on the window startles me and I let out a shriek, my hand clutching at my chest.

A young man raises his hands in surrender and mouths, "Sorry." I roll down the window.

"I'm sorry. I didn't mean to scare you, Sara." He lets out a chuckle.

"You know me?" I ask before I can stop myself. *Way to play the part, Mandy.*

He laughs some more. "Yup. But I'm sorry, it's ten o'clock so we just turned off the pumps."

"Are you serious?" I blurt out a bit too quickly and loud.

He takes a step back. "I...I could see if Marie could turn them back on for you." He shrugs and gives me that *I really am sorry* kind of look.

I puff out my cheeks and let out a long, exaggerated huff. "I don't even know if I have any money anyway," I announce, opening the wallet.

"We do take checks," he states, eyeing the checkbook peeking out of the wallet. I direct my focus to the checks, flipping them over in my hand. I can pay for gas with a check? A check decorated with those little Hummel figures. No, wait, they're not Hummels, they're Precious Moments figures. I remember those. My grandma had them in a hutch in her dining room when I was a kid. She kept all the boxes for them in a spare bedroom closet as well. She had over a hundred of them. And she used to tell me and my sister that they'd be ours someday. "They will be worth a lot of money, especially with the boxes," she'd tell us every time we went to visit. Whatever happened to those anyway?

"I've got this," a familiar voice takes me back to the present. I look up and it's the young gunslinger.

Suddenly, I feel embarrassed again, like he just caught me with my hand in the cookie jar. *But wait, is he following me?*

"I promise I'm not following you." He raises a bag in the air. "I was just inside getting some things when I saw you pull up."

Great. Now he reads minds too.

"No...I can...it's fine. He said that they take checks." I shrug.

"Sure, we do. And if it bounces, I know where you live." He laughs, the young gunslinger joining him. Are they serious? Don't stalkers or kidnappers say, "I know where you live"? Creepy!

"Let me tell Marie to turn the pump back on," the gas attendant states before walking away.

I fumble through the purse—the gaudy-looking, oversized, fake purple leather bag that has a few too many rhinestones—and find a pen. The young gunslinger doesn't move; he continues to stand by the van, looking at me, making me feel more uncomfortable by the minute. I decide to get out of the van. That might give him a clue that his services are no longer needed. I offer him a pursed smile before I unscrew the cap to the gas tank. He remains unmoved.

Turning around to the pump, I'm unsure of how to proceed. *Do I have to slide a check in the machine to get it to turn on?* I don't see anything to indicate that I can pay with a check. "You have to select American or Canadian before you can do anything," the young gunslinger chimes in. *American or Canadian what? Check?*

I run a hand over my face. He takes a step closer and presses a button, awakening the machine.

"Where do I put the check?"

He lets out a small chuckle. "You give that to Nolin once you're done."

I nod, biting down on my lower lip so hard that I wince in response.

"Are you sure you're okay? You seem more than just a bit shaken up still."

"I'm...yes, I'm fine." I dismiss him, waving my hand in the air.

He takes a step forward, making me take one back. He presses a few buttons on the pump and inserts the nozzle into the gas tank. He doesn't move, leaving me to continue to feel uneasy. He waits until the tank fills and returns the nozzle to the pump. "So, you headed home now?"

I eye him with furrowed brow. "Home?" I repeat.

He nods. "Um...I'm sorry. I don't mean to poke my nose in your business. I was just thinking maybe we could grab a drink before calling it a night. It might help to settle you, and I could use one myself. Plus, it's the least you could do since I did save your life earlier tonight."

I laugh. He cocks an eyebrow, turning his head to the side. "I don't even know your name. And, I don't have any money."

"How could you forget *my* name? You sure you don't want to go get checked by a doctor?"

"I...I didn't mean that I didn't know your name. Of course I do. I was just joking with you."

I attempt to smile. *Who is this guy anyway?*

"Thank goodness. I was starting to get a complex," he quips. "And The Shipyard takes checks," he adds, waiting for a response. "I'm just kidding with you. I've got it covered."

The gas attendant—Nolin—returns, interrupting our conversation. I was happy to see him; things were starting to get uncomfortable. I sure wish I did know his name though. He thinks that I should.

"Who do I write the check out to?" I ask.

"You can—"

"I got it," the young gunslinger interrupts, handing the now confused gas attendant some money. The gas attendant hesitantly takes it.

"Have a good night, Sara," he says, smiling. Passing by, he taps the young gunslinger's shoulder. "Marc is going to kill you," he whispers.

The young gunslinger clears his throat. "Good night, Nolin."

"So, you ready for that drink?" he asks once the gas attendant is gone.

"I don't know, I really should—"

"Come on! Just one. I promise," he begs with a pitiful look on his face.

"Fine." Once he's had a drink in him, maybe I can coax him into telling me how I can get out of here. This might not be a bad plan after all.

He slides into his car and takes off. He thinks I know where I'm going, but I haven't a clue. I pull out of the parking lot, the lights of the gas station turning off behind me. I drive in the direction that he headed but press on the brake when I see his car in front of me. He's going at a snail's pace, not even five miles an hour. *Did he see yet another creature in the road?* I look around and see nothing. We pass a grocery store and the post office, both of which have their lights turned off, closed for business. Then we approach a movie theater; a few teenagers are huddled in front and a couple is making out against the wall. We continue down and I recognize the flower shop that the woman from earlier today came out of and then the restaurant we had breakfast at—the one with my Starbucks and the incredible bread pudding. I could use another piece of that right about now, but I'll pass on the coffee. Across the way is a small building with a sign out front that reads "Town Hall." That must be where Marc works—or claims to work. I still don't believe a thing these people tell me. For all I know, this young gunslinger is in on the plan to keep me hostage.

Driving down a bit further we pass another gas station and then I notice a row of cars all facing the street. Some people are sitting atop the hood or leaning up against the car; others are sitting behind the wheel with their windows rolled down. They all appear to be waiting for something, like a parade or show. They have front-row seats to whatever's about to happen. I overhear one of them yelling something to someone walking on the sidewalk across the way, and the person waves a middle finger in the air in response.

The young gunslinger turns on his blinker and pulls over, parking along the curb. I pull up behind him. While grabbing my purse, I see the young gunslinger get out and he starts a conversation with a woman leaning up against a building, with a cigarette in hand.

When she sees me approach, she drops the cigarette to the ground and stubs it out with her shoe.

Without warning, she leans in and wraps both arounds around me, drawing me in for a hug. I'm frozen in place. "Cris! I'm so glad to see you're alive. We sure were getting worried," she slurs into my ear in a raspy voice like she's had one too many cigarettes, not pulling away. The stench of alcohol and tobacco practically chokes me.

The young gunslinger taps the woman on the shoulder. "Come on, Beatrice, give the girl some room." He cocks an eyebrow at me, and I offer him a weak smile as a thank you.

"Sorry, I'm just happy you're okay," she croaks. "We were all so worried. I don't know what we'd do if you died. Did you know that they started a prayer group while you were in the hospital? I wanted to go, but I couldn't get a ride and my back's been hurting more than usual lately so I couldn't walk there."

"All right, Beatrice. You all can catch up some other time." The young gunslinger offers her a light tap on the shoulder.

"Bien wayon, Dean, just let me talk to her…Wait, are you guys out on a date? Where's Marc? Are you not with Marc anymore?" she questions with a hand over her mouth, shocked.

Dean, aha, that's his name!

"No, we're not on a date, Beatrice. Don't you go on starting any rumors now," the young gunslinger—Dean—advises. "Sara just needs a drink."

She redirects her attention to an older gentleman wearing a driving cap who approaches. "Welcome back. Je suis heureux de vous voir bien," he says, looking at me, smiling.

"Thanks." I smile, trying to decipher everything he just said.

"You coming in for a game?"

I look to the young gunslinger for guidance.

"No, we're headed to The Shipyard for a nightcap. Sara here almost had another run in with one of the biggest moose I've seen yet," he tells him. "The rack on that guy was huge." He spreads his arms in the air to demonstrate.

"Oh oui?" The gentleman whistles.

"Those fuckers are everywhere. Thank goodness you didn't hit it. You sure would be dead this time," the drunken woman chimes in.

The gentleman in the riding cap rolls his eyes. "I think it's bedtime, Beatrice," he warns.

She glares at him but doesn't say anything. And then she walks away, dragging her feet, and mumbling something about red pillows.

"Maybe I'll stop in for a game later, Marcel," the young gunslinger says.

The gentleman tips his hat, nodding. "C'est bon, Dean."

He nods to me before turning and walking into what I now see is a game room. Pool tables line the center of the room, and a few arcade games are scattered about. Kids—teenagers—push out of the door in a mound.

"You can't kick us out, we're leaving," one hollers back as the door closes behind them.

"Let's go find Gretchen and Tracy. I hope they were able to sneak out. They better be at the club," another says, putting an arm around his friend's shoulders. They look barely thirteen, but clearly drunk.

When I turn back to Dean, I see him staring at me with a grin on his face.

"What?"

He shrugs. "Nothing. Let's go have a drink."

We make our way to the bar, and Dean pushes through a crowd of people. They all stop chatting and look our way.

"Sara?" a female voice questions. "Sara's back!"

"Sar...ra, Sar...ra, Sar...ra," a group chants.

"Wait, what is she doing here?" someone questions.

"And with Dean?" another one adds.

Dean continues to push through the crowd, unfazed. I feel a hand grab at mine, and I instinctively grasp it as it pulls me forward. Once through the mass, I look down to see it's Dean's hand I'm holding a bit too tightly.

We pass through a group of men dressed in military fatigue and make our way through the doors. Once inside, Dean pauses, letting out an exaggerated huff. "Had I known there'd be so many drunks out tonight, I'd offered to take you to Saint Leonard instead." He shakes his head. "I think I now need that drink as much as you do."

He looks down at our hands clasped together, and pulls away, offering me a forced smile. He motions for me to walk ahead.

We enter a lightly dimmed room, a cloud of cigarette smoke looms in the air. I spot the bar in the middle of the room, and as we approach, I take in the faint smell of pot. It's clear that some people are having a good time tonight.

Dean tugs on my arm. "I see two seats at the end of the bar," he says, leaning in and pointing to the far-left corner. My eyes are drawn to a band playing, and people scattered around the dance floor, all moving out of rhythm, but clearly having a great time.

We pull out a couple of bar stools and sit. The bartender approaches, placing a drink napkin in front of Dean. "Hey there, Dean." She stands a bit straighter, puffing out her double-D chest. She runs a hand along her collarbone and smiles a bit too wide, clearly smitten with my new friend. "What can I get you?" she sings.

"Whatever she's having." He tilts his head to me.

She looks my way and offers an exaggerated gasp. "I had no idea you were here. Where's Marc?"

"Um…he's—"

"Wait…a…minute. Just wait a minute. Are you two?" She wags a finger, pointing between me and Dean, her mouth hanging open.

"Don't get any ideas, Tammy. We're just here for a drink. Nothing more. Don't you start anything."

Her smile disappears. She pushes a drink napkin in front of me. "What can I get for you?" She looks from me to Dean. Dean's gaze doesn't leave mine, waiting for me to respond.

Suddenly, I feel like I need a drink. A strong one. "How about a couple of shots of tequila and then a gin and tonic to wash it down," I order with a confident look on my face.

"Wow. Okay," she says, surprised.

When she turns away, I look at Dean who wears a smug grin, clearly amused by my answer. "I guess you really do want a drink tonight," he quips. "I might end up regretting asking you to come out. I'm not sure I can keep up."

The band announces that they're taking a break and the music dies. Everyone on the dance floor disperses.

The bartender returns with two shot glasses in one hand and two drinks in the other, placing them on the counter in front of us. She turns back without a word.

Dean grabs the saltshaker from the counter and offers it to me. I grab the shot glass, and without another thought, down it, straight. I slam the glass on the counter and wince. The liquid burns my throat, far worse than I ever recall it doing so.

"Whoa," Dean lets out. "Damn! Even I can't do that."

"Come on, you wimp," I retort, attempting to look like that didn't just kick my ass.

He stares at me, wide-eyed, shaking his head. Then brings his hand to his mouth, biting down on his fist. He closes his eyes a brief second and then quickly grabs the glass and downs it. "Whoa. Fuck!" he yells, jumping off the barstool.

Now all eyes are on us, and I'm left feeling embarrassed once more while the tequila warms my insides.

Dean leans forward with both hands pressed down on the bar. He lets out a cough. "Damn, girl, I'm too old for this," he manages. And then he takes a swig of the gin and tonic. I can't help but laugh. There's no way that made it better.

He pulls the bar stool back toward him, sitting back down on it. Resting his elbows on the counter, he lowers his head in his hands. After a moment, he turns my way and just stares at me, mouth agape. "That was better than an orgasm," he proclaims after a beat. "You've got some catching up to do." He pushes the glass of gin and tonic toward me.

I hesitate. I'm still recovering from the tequila. He darts a thumb toward the glass. After swallowing hard, I bite down on my lower lip before raising it to my mouth. Pausing, I tip the glass and when the concoction reaches my tongue, I notice that it tastes like straight tonic water so I down it in one swift gulp. I take a piece of ice between my teeth and let it sit on my tongue, enjoying the extreme cold while it extinguishes the burning sensation that radiates through me.

"Tammy, get us another round over here," Dean orders, raising a hand in the air.

"No!" I quickly add. "I can't drink anymore. I have a long drive ahead of me."

He cocks an eyebrow. "Long drive? You're acting like you're just traveling through town. Cyr Plantation ain't more than a couple of miles from here. You can handle another drink after the show you just put on."

"I...I mean..." I stumble on my words. "It's just, the last shot did me in. I think I've had enough." I push myself off the stool and stand.

"Don't go. I'm just playing with you." He rests a hand on my arm.

The bartender returns with our drinks, setting them down.

"We've changed our mind," he tells her, not looking away from me.

"Well, someone's gotta pay for these." Her response is blanketed with annoyance.

Without removing his hand from my arm, or his gaze from mine, he reaches into his jeans pocket with his other hand and slides a few bills across the bar. "Keep the change."

"I really should get going," I announce, feeling a twinge of something grow between us. I pull out of his hold. I grab the shot glass and down it, the liquid burning all the way down to my toes. I take a sharp breath. Not looking back, I round the bar. When I get to the door, I excuse myself as I squeeze past a couple making out.

"Let's go upstairs," the guy mutters to the girl before reaching down and adjusting himself in his pants. They dart past me and run up a staircase, pausing midway to make out some more.

Once outside, the cool air awakens me.

"Sara," Dean calls from behind me, exiting the bar. I don't stop, I keep walking in the direction of the van. This isn't how I planned for the night to go. I only wanted to get information from him, instead we end up throwing a few back like old friends. And I still don't know how to get out of here. I feel him approach, our shoulders brushing. "How about we go to St. Leonard for coffee. Just coffee. I promise."

"Coffee?" I stop mid-step. "Saint Leonard?"

"Yeah," he draws out the word. "Tim Hortons in New Brunswick. You know, in Canada." He points to his left.

"How far from here is that?" He furrows his brow and looks confused.

"I mean...what time is it? Won't that take us a while?" I clarify, trying to redirect the conversation.

"No, it's only about eleven o'clock or so," he announces, looking at his watch. "It's just across the border a bit. I promise to have you back home before midnight, before you turn into a pumpkin." He smiles.

I let out a chuckle. "You do know that it wasn't Cinderella that turned into a pumpkin. It was the horse-drawn carriage that did, right?"

"No, but same difference," he retorts without skipping a beat. "Come on, the Sara that I know can't refuse a good cup of coffee."

Apparently, they all know me better than I know myself these days.

"No. I really shouldn't even be out right now. I need to get home." I attempt to sound convincing, but mostly just want to get away from him. He smells of trouble.

When we reach his car, I turn to him. "Thank you for the drinks." I offer him a smile.

With a defeated look on his face, he presses his lips together and nods. "You're welcome. You sure you don't want that coffee?"

I scrunch up my nose, shaking my head. "I don't think that's a good idea. Thanks though. Maybe next time."

He nods again. "You gonna be all right to get home?"

I put on a brave face. "I'm good. Have a good night. Thanks again." Stepping off the sidewalk, I saunter to the van.

Dean hops into his car, takes a quick look in his rearview mirror at me, and then drives off.

Feeling antsy, I tap my fingers on the steering wheel. "Canada. There has to be a way to the nearest highway from there. Everyone from New York goes to Canada, so everyone must be able to come back," I mutter to myself in a hushed tone, afraid someone might hear me. My head feels a bit loopy from the shots. When did I become a lightweight?

I bring a hand up to my mouth and I bite down on a fingernail. A crowd of people on the sidewalk look my way, talking—likely about me.

I put the van in drive and pull out of the parking spot. I decide to turn down the first street on the right that I come to; Marc did point in this direction when he mentioned Canada. Once I round the corner, I see a group of kids huddled outside the basement door of The Shipyard. The door is propped open, music booms and lights flash to the rhythm from within. It's obviously a dance club. Here I was thinking that everyone in the town goes to bed with the sun, but I'm mistaken; it's clear that this town never sleeps.

I drive down the street and quickly happen upon a large bridge. Slowing the car, I lean forward, questioning if this is the right direction—the way to Canada. Before I can discourage myself from finding out, I press my foot on the gas pedal and direct the van up and over the bridge.

Once on the other side, I slow down and notice a car ahead of me, stopped. A gentleman in uniform converses with the driver, waving his hands in the air, laughing. A moment later, he waves the driver goodbye and turns in my direction, waving a hand, directing me to pull forward.

With anxiety building, unsure of what's to come, I inch my way toward him. Lowering the window, he leans down so we're eye level. "Bonsoir. Où allez-vous ce soir?"

"Um…I'm sorry, what?"

"Ah, excuse me. Good evening, ma'am. Where are you headed tonight?" he asks in a thick accent. He leans in so close that his cologne stings my nose, and when he talks, he smells of onions.

Butterflies flutter in my belly and sweat slathers every inch of me. "I'm…I'm going to Canada for coffee." I feel like I'm going to pass out. I blink my eyes and plaster a fake smile, feeling my hands shake in my lap.

He narrows his eyes and nods slowly. "Have you been drinking tonight?"

"No. Well, yes. I had a drink, but…I'm fine to drive, if that's what you're asking."

"Mmm hmm," he hums. "And you say you're going for coffee?"

"Yes. A guy I just met said there was a good coffee shop in Canada. He said that it was just over the border," I answer, waving my hand in front of me. "I…I thought maybe I could grab a cup before…going home," I add, now waving both hands in the air in all directions. I quickly return my hands back to my lap when I realize what a maniac I must look like. Play it cool, Mandy. Swallowing, I offer another fake smile.

A car approaches behind me, and I let out a quick breath, hoping that he'll now wave me forward, wanting to keep the traffic moving.

He pays no mind to the other car; he keeps his gaze fixed on mine. "Are you from around here?"

"I'm from New York City," I blurt out. "No...I mean, I'm from Van Buren. You know, Maine. That's...where I'm from," I correct myself. *Shit!*

His brow creases. "Can you pull the car over to the side, right there." He points to a parking spot off to the side.

My face reddens and my heart pounds in my chest. "It's all right, I don't need to go get coffee. I can just...turn around and go back." I try to act cool, but even I am not buying it.

"That's okay, ma'am. Please just pull over and I'll be right with you."

I'm tempted to slam on the gas pedal and make a break for it, but my subconscious tells me it's not a good idea. I shift the van in drive and pull forward, parking in a spot off to the side.

The gentleman waves to the car that was behind me, signaling them to drive through. He walks inside a brightly lit building, and he starts a conversation with another gentleman, both looking my way.

In my head, I chant, "I'm *not* Mandy. I'm Sara. I'm *not* from New York. I'm from Van Buren, Maine. I'm *not* trying to run away. I'm just going for coffee. I had only *one* drink. With a guy named Dean...something-or-other. Whatever, just Dean. At the bar across the bridge...Shipwreck? I'm *not* a virgin. I'm married, with four kids. I'm married to a guy named Mark, no wait, it's Marc. I must practice rolling my 'r'."

I take a minute to do just that, until I realize the officer is standing by the van, staring down at me. I close my mouth tight, accidentally biting the inside of my cheek. I raise my hand to my cheek and wince.

"Do you have some identification on you?"

"Ah...I think so." I dart my eyes around the van. I grab the purse on the passenger side seat and reach in for the wallet.

"You said your name was?" another voice questions. I look up and see the other officer has joined us.

"Hi. I'm Mandy O'Reilly...no, I mean...I'm Sara," I correct, darting my eyes back to the wallet in my lap. *Shit, shit, shit, shit, shit!* Way to go, Mandy.

"So...you're not Mandy. You're Sara. Did you say your last name was O'Reilly?"

"Right. Well, I mean, I'm Sara, not Mandy. My last name is...well, it's not O'Reilly. Um. It's..." I flip open the wallet and the checkbook stares directly at me. Reading the names on the top left, I sound out the last name, There-e-alt. "There-e-alt," I shout a bit too excitedly.

"There-e-alt?" one of the officers mimics.

"Yeah, that's right. See." I raise the checkbook so they can read the name.

"Tat-e-o," he enunciates in his thick accent. "You mean, Tear-e-o, right?"

I nod frantically.

The officers look at one another.

"I think we're going to need you to step out of your car, ma'am."

"I can find some ID," I slur, rummaging through the purse in a panic.

"Ma'am, just step out of the car." He swings open the door.

"See, I found it!" I bellow, raising a driver's license in the air.

"That's great. Thank you," he says, taking it from me. "Now, please, exit the car, ma'am."

On trembling legs, I stand outside the van.

"Do you give us permission to search the vehicle?"

"Um...sure."

"And is there anything in the vehicle we should know about?"

"Anything you should know about?" I echo.

"Yes, ma'am. Any weapons. Or drugs, maybe?"

"Um, no...Not that I know of anyway." I shrug.

"Okay. Officer Laplante, here, will take you inside while I do a quick search of the vehicle."

The other officer clutches my elbow, directing me inside. Once through the doors, he leads me to a desk and has me sit in the chair. He lowers himself in the other chair, facing me.

"I have to tell you guys something," I utter before he has a moment to speak.

"Okay." He nods. "But first let's wait for Rosaire to return."

"You see, I was in a car accident a couple of weeks ago, and I woke up from a coma. I lost all my memory. The doctor tells me that I dreamt of another life. You see, that's why I said my name was Amanda O'Reilly, instead of Sara...There...There-oh?" I stutter. He puts a hand in the air, signaling me to stop. I pause, and then it hits me. *Why am I lying?* This could be my chance to get away from here. This officer has a civic duty to follow up on any suspicions, right? I lean in toward him. "Okay officer, listen, they're keeping me hostage. There's one guy named Marc, a lady named Claudette, and another lady Megan, who says she's my sister. Now even if she looks like me, she's not. People can look like one another without being related, right?" I look to him for confirmation. He doesn't say anything, so I continue. "Anyway, my mom is the mayor of New York City. I just graduated from college, and I was off to Bermuda with friends. The plane crashed. And then when I woke up, I was in a hospital, and they said I was in a coma. I was in a plane accident. I remember it. But listen to this, they're telling me that I was in a car accident, and that I'm married, have four kids, and I was pregnant and lost the baby. Do you want to know the kicker? I'm a virgin." I purse my lips and cock an eye. The officer rubs his chin, leaning back in his chair.

"So, you're telling me that you've been kidnapped, huh?"

"Yes! Yes, that's exactly what I'm telling you." Finally, someone believes me.

"Hmm. Okay." He stands. "You stay here, and I'll be right back."

He walks over to the other officer, who enters the room. "Est-ce vous avez trouvé quelque chose?"

"Non, mais…je ne sais pas, il y a quelque chose d'étrange à son sujet."

"Elle m'a juste raconté une histoire d'être kidnappée."

"Kidnappée?"

They continue to talk, periodically glancing my way. And I offer a wide smile, feeling proud of myself and confident that I've finally found someone to help me.

They both walk to me. "So, let me get this straight," the other officer says. "Jean-Claude just told me that you're being held against your will by people you don't know. Right?"

"Yes! Yup, he's right," I confirm, nodding to the other officer.

"The man you say is keeping you hostage is Marc Theriault?"

"Right. Yes!"

"The same Marc Theriault who's the town manager of Van Buren?"

"Yes! That's right. That's what he said," I exclaim. "He told me his dad was the town manager, but he died. And then he became the town manager. Crazy story, huh?"

"Well, I don't know if it's crazy. What he told you is true."

"Wait. What?" My expression fades and my stomach aches.

"That's true. His father, Jean, was the town manager for many, many years. When he died, his son did take over," the other officer explains. He pauses. "I know that Marc does have a wife. Although since I moved to New Brunswick myself, I don't know her, but I remember seeing her. And, well, you do look like her."

"No. No, it's not me. I'm Amanda O'Reilly. You can call my dad or my mom, they'll clear this up...Well just call the prison and ask to speak to my dad. He'll tell you that I'm Amanda, his daughter. I just spoke to him today."

"Son père est en prison?" one officer mumbles to the other.

The other officer shrugs. "À Van Buren?"

"Je ne sais pas. Je pense que c'est Clarence de service ce soir. Peut-être devrions-nous l'appeler?"

"His name isn't Clarence," I interrupt. "His name is Robert O'Reilly. My dad is Robert O'Reilly."

They both look my way, but quickly return to their conversation. "Nous pouvons essayer d'appeler, mais je ne sais pas s'il est hors service maintenant."

"We will call. Have a seat," one officer instructs, walking around the desk. I sit and he takes the receiver in his hand, dialing a number.

"It's the—"

He raises a hand in the air, cutting me off. He runs his tongue along the top of his teeth and waits. Moments later, he hangs up. "No answer. They must be off patrol already."

"How did you know which prison to call? How did you know the number? How can there be no answer? They can't be off patrol, it's a prison," I assert, baffled.

"Elle sonne comme si elle était droguée," the officer standing utters.

"Are you sure you didn't have something other than one drink tonight?" the other officer questions.

"No. I told you, I had one drink...well, really it was two shots and a gin and tonic, but have you seen how small those shot glasses are and that gin and tonic tasted like straight tonic water, so it was just one drink.

I was with a guy named Dean at that bar across the bridge. Did you know that he saved me from being killed by a swamp-thing earlier?"

"Appelle son mari."

Chapter Seven
— Dear Sara —

Hearing the bedroom door creak, I open my eyes. Marc walks to the side of the bed and sits. He places a hand on my back, rubbing it, making me feel uneasy. "I have to go out for a bit. Sister Mabel is getting out of rehab tomorrow so we're going to build the ramp for her at the rectory. I'm going to drop Abby and Jacob off at the bowling alley, they have their meet this morning. On the way, I'm going to drop Austin and Emma off at Megan's house. She's going to take them to Rachel's birthday party. I'll have someone pick up the van and bring it by later. So, you just rest, and we'll all be back around three o'clock to get ready for mass."

"Church?"

"Yes. We go to the four o'clock mass every Saturday."

"And...I go too?"

He smiles. "You sure do."

I press my lips in a tight line and nod.

"I left something for you on the kitchen counter. I hope it'll help you to remember some things," he reveals, still with a hand on my back. "You do know that I love you, right?" he expresses in a hushed tone.

Unsure of how to respond, I sigh. And then, I close my eyes, trying to hold back the tears.

The officers ended up calling Marc last night. They had to keep calling a few times before he answered. He didn't hear the phone ring until it was about four o'clock in the morning. By that point, I had fallen asleep and awoke when Marc came for me. I felt so defeated, and despite my pleas, they refused to let me drive, stating I was drunk, and they would arrest me if I tried. So, I had no choice but to go with him. Marc confirmed to them that I had been in a coma and lost my memory. But he didn't seem pleased when the officers told him that I was with another guy earlier that night. He probably thinks that I slept with him, not that I really care.

Once Marc exits the bedroom, I pull the covers up under my chin, and feeling the exhaustion set in, I let my body sink into the mattress.

Moments later, the bedroom door creaks open. Feeling annoyed, I glare at the small figure standing in the doorway. Peeking in is the smallest girl, wearing pigtails and a wide smile. Her eyes light up when she sees me awake. After throwing the door open, she skips to me, her floral party dress bouncing with every step and her white patent leather shoes clattering on the floor. "Mommy, it's Rachel's birthday today! Are you coming to the party with us?"

I shake my head, my annoyance dissolving. Offering a small smile in return, I tell her, "I'm not feeling so well, sweetie," and watch disappointment flood her face.

"Come on, Emma, let Mommy rest," Marc calls from the doorway.

She looks at me with a pout. Turning away, she slumps and pads out of the room.

The moment I hear the front door slam and the house take on a calming silence, I'm left alone, but unsure of what to do next. Deep in thought, I'm startled when the phone rings. At first, I don't have any interest in answering it, until about the third ring when I realize that it could possibly be my dad. He did say he'd try to call back.

I jump out of bed and sprint down the hallway to the phone. My heart racing, I answer it. "Hello?"

"Good morning, sunshine," the voice on the other end answers.

I puff out my cheeks and roll my eyes, sadness taking over me.

"Sara? Are you still there?"

"Yeah," I reply, disappointed, snatching a runaway tear from my eye.

"I'm calling to see how you're doing. Would you be up for a cup of coffee this morning, maybe?"

"I'm sorry...but, um, who is this?"

He lets out a chuckle. "Please forgive me, it's Father Tom."

Ah, it's *my best friend*.

"Sorry, but I think I'll pass on the coffee today." There's no coffee around here that's worth having to spend some time with my "good friend" the priest. "Thank you though," I quickly add.

"All right, maybe some other time. Will we be seeing you at mass this evening?"

"Ah...yeah, sure."

After we hang up, I decide to rummage in the kitchen for some food, my stomach growling. I find a stack of Ziploc bags, all stuffed with some leafy greens. Opening the first one, I reach in and grab a handful, realizing that it's kale. It not only looks good but smells fresh. Glancing around the kitchen, I see a blender and immediately know that I want to make a smoothie.

Leaning further into the refrigerator, I find a container of yogurt, a package of pineapple, and a bowl with fresh strawberries. I place a handful of all the ingredients into the blender, adding a bit of water, and can barely wait until it's finished before pouring some into a cup and downing it.

I cringe when the concoction reaches my tongue. Raising the glass in the air, I stare at it. This smoothie tastes nothing like I remember. I've always started my day with a green smoothie, after my coffee, of course. Even this smoothie's betraying me.

I dump the liquid down the sink and grab the bowl of strawberries, stuffing one in my mouth, enjoying the sweet juices.

Turning around, I see a card propped up in the center of the kitchen island, with Sara scrawled on the front. Taking it in my hand, I flip it open and read:

My sweet Sara,
I know you're having a difficult time trying to piece together your life. I thought maybe if you watched this video, it would help to bring back some memories you've lost.
Love, Marc

After putting the card down, I take the video in hand, flipping it over back and forth, trying to make sense of it. I recall my parents having these tapes when I was little, but do they still even exist? Then I read the label affixed to the side: *Sara and Marc's Wedding*

I read it a few times, letting it sink in. Then my curiosity grows. Clearly, if I'm really married to Marc like they claim, it'll be me I see on this tape. But what if it is me on this tape?

Anxiety builds. I put the tape down, staring at it. While holding the bowl of strawberries tightly in one arm, I shove another in my mouth. Smelling the aroma of coffee, I redirect my attention to the coffee maker on the counter, filled with a fresh pot. It's as if it beckons me. I dart my eyes between the video and the coffee.

After pouring a cup, I grab the video and walk to the living room. Sitting on the shelf below the television is a VHS tape player, just like the one I recall having as a kid. Taking a sip, I insert the tape and turn the television on, standing back and staring down at it, waiting for it to come to life.

The moment that it does, I take another couple of steps back and lower myself onto the couch. With both hands grasping the coffee mug, I take sips and stare.

The video starts out of focus, and once the image becomes clear, Marc comes into view. He's standing at an altar, in a small, quaint church. He's dressed in a simple black tux, and he looks so young, but it's most definitely him. An older gentleman dressed in a military uniform stands by his side. Both are looking in the same direction, focused. Music begins to play and the video pans across the room, displaying rows of wooden benches, filled with people all dressed up in their Sunday best. A little girl and boy walk down the aisle, tossing rose petals in front of them, lining their path. The camera then zooms in on a young woman and man, and a lump forms in my throat, causing tears to surface. She looks just like my sister—the sister that I remember—Rebecca.

I feel like I can't continue to watch, but also can't move; I'm left frozen in place, eyes pinned to the television. The young man at her side also wears a military uniform. She threads her arm through his, and they make their way down the aisle, stopping to hug Marc and taking their place at the altar.

The music changes and everyone stands, turning to the rear of the church. I catch a glimpse of a woman in the front row who is dabbing a tissue to the corner of her eye. It's Claudette.

The video pans down the aisle and then stops, the camera resting on a pair of wooden doors. A few seconds later, the doors open and a young woman in a wedding gown appears in view, with a gentleman at her side. When the camera zooms in, I let out a cry—a wail. The gentleman is my uncle, the one that I'm told that Rebecca and I went to live with once our parents died.

He leans over and plants a kiss on my cheek—there's no mistaking that the girl in the wedding gown is me. The me, at the same age that I recall last being. That simple, yet elegant, wedding gown opens a door in my mind—a memory, perhaps.

With the coffee cup gripped tightly in my lap, a steady stream of tears flows down my face. I continue to watch myself on the video, motionless. And when the priest announces that it's time to recite our vows, a string of words come into thought: *"You know me better than anyone else in this world and somehow still manage to love me. You're my best friend and one true love. There is still a part of me today that cannot believe that I'm the one who gets to marry you. I remember how I told you I didn't believe in soul mates. That is until you came along. Your love made me believe. I call you 'My Anywhere' because you're my everything."*

The coffee cup crashes to the floor, and I follow it, crumbling in a heap when I hear myself echo those exact words on the video.

How could I know? If that wasn't me that I'm staring at, how could I remember?

I watch in a trance right through to the end where Marc and I kiss and then wave goodbye to everyone before we hop into a horse-drawn carriage and ride away.

The phone rings, and I don't know how long it's been since the video stopped and I've been staring at the blank screen.

So many questions flood me while the ringing goes on. If my parents are supposed to be dead, then how could I have spoken to my dad just yesterday? Could this gentleman who claims to be my dad, instead be an imposter? I've heard of sickos in prisons who create a connection with women outside of the prison walls. Would I be that foolish to fall for such a thing? *Have I forgotten practically my whole adulthood and this is really my life?*

The ringing goes on, so with trembling hands I lift myself from the floor. I feel a prick on my finger and notice that I've cut myself on a shard from the coffee cup.

Willing my feet to move, I make my way to the phone.

I answer it and a gentleman responds. "Hello. Is this Sara?"

"Yes."

The way I looked at him makes me ache for such a love. The way he looked at me confirms his love.

"Hi, Sara. This is Dr. LaBrec. Do you remember me from the hospital a couple of days ago?"

"Yes."

If we were that in love, how could I forget such a thing?

"I'm just calling to see how you're doing."

"I...I guess I'm fine."

Why am I grasping onto a dream world, where the parents I remember aren't real, and the person that I was, isn't me?

"Good. And has any of your memory returned?"

"Ah...well...I...well, I don't know...maybe...I think it just did," I answer, lost in thought and dumbfounded still by what I just watched.

If that isn't my dad on the other end of that call yesterday, then who is it? Why does he sound so much like him? I've heard of women writing to men in prison. Would I have been so stupid to be one of them?

"Are you sure you're all right?" he questions, catching the confusion in my voice.

I clear my throat. "Yes, I'm fine. You just caught me at a bad time." I stare at my blood-stained hand.

That was my dad. I just know it. Letters—he mentioned a letter he's written. Where is it? What does it say?

"Oh, I see. I apologize. Don't let me keep you any longer. I'm glad to hear that you're doing well. Please don't hesitate to call me if you need to talk or have any questions, okay?"

"I will. Thank you." I hang up, my insides shaking.

I pace the hallway, regarding the blood trickling down my fingers, my mind numb, my heart racing.

"Sara? Hi Sara, it's just me."

I peer down the hallway and see Claudette leaning in the doorway to the house. I open my mouth to speak, but nothing comes out. I don't know how long she's been standing there, but she has a puzzled look on her face.

"I'm sorry to disturb you, but we brought by the van. I'll leave the keys on the hook." She hesitates and then takes a step inside. "Is everything all right?"

I can only offer a nod.

"Would you like me to stay? Do you need anything?" She appears to want to take a step in my direction but doesn't.

I clear the frog from my throat. "No, I'm fine. I just...I dropped my coffee cup and cut myself while cleaning it up. I'm fine though." I straighten up and offer a broken smile, pointing to the living room.

"Oh non, fille! Are you sure you're not hurt?"

"No...no, I'm fine. Really. I—I was just headed to the bathroom to get a band aid."

"Okay," she says, offering an unbelieving look. She hangs the key ring on the hook and looks out the window. "Dean vient d'arriver." She regards me again. "I left my car at the border patrol's office. Dean is here to pick me up. Do you need me to pick up anything downtown for you?"

"No, that's really kind of you, but I'm fine." I wave her off. "I appreciate it though."

She offers a tight-lipped nod and hesitantly walks out the door and down the stairs.

I peak through the window, eyeing the car in the driveway. As I thought, it's the same Dean from last night. This town sure is small. I see tiny flakes of snow fall. *It's supposedly the end of May, and it's snowing?*

Once they've spun out of the drive, my thoughts immediately return to the letters. Something tells me that they're the key to figuring out some of my life that I've evidently forgotten. *Maybe I wrote to this guy to feel connected to my dad somehow?* That thought instantly sounds foolish…in a way, so I try to dismiss it. But a yearning to find those letters builds.

Looking down at my hand covered in blood, I make my way to the master bath and get washed up, bandaging up the cut and brushing my teeth. I feel a chill in the air, so I go to the closet to find a sweater. I grab a grey wool cardigan that hangs on a hook. Wrapping it around myself, I scan the closet, still in a daze, deep in thought. High up on the top shelf are cardboard boxes. I count two that are labeled "Pageant stuff," another is marked "Kids' School Paperwork," and the last one reads "Sara's College Books." I reach up and take hold of that one, intrigued, hoping it might help spark a memory.

I shuffle to the bed and plop it down. Opening it, one by one I remove two large textbooks: *Political Science, An Introduction to American Government and Politics Today, Book One and Book Two*. They've both been used and read over many times. Flipping through the pages, they're filled with highlights, notes written in the margins, and pages earmarked. Neither give any indication as to which school they're from nor offer any memories.

I rest them on the bed and reach into the box, removing another book: *American Justice and Civil Procedure, Volume One*. This book doesn't look like a textbook, but more of a reference book. When I flip it open, a stack of papers falls to the floor.

Gathering them, I see that it's a phone bill with yellow highlights throughout. All the calls highlighted are labeled "Connecticut Wargate Institution." The date on the bill is August 1, 1992, to August 31, 1992. That was just last year. Evidently, I've been speaking to this person for at least nearly a year now.

I turn the book upside down, fanning the pages to see if any other phone bills or papers are tucked inside, but there's nothing.

Peering into the box, I see a large brown Pendaflex folder. When I open it, my legs begin to tremble uncontrollably. The folder is filled with well over twenty or so envelopes, all addressed to: *Sara Theriault, P.O. Box 302, Van Buren, ME 04785*. And with the return address, *Connecticut Wargate Correctional Institution*. Some envelopes are bundled together with an elastic band.

Feeling frantic, I grab the box and toss it to the floor, making room on the bed to sit. In a rush, I rip through one of the envelopes lying on the top of the folder. The instant I unfold the letter I recognize the handwriting—it's without a doubt my dad's scrawling. We always joked that he should have been a doctor because his penmanship was practically illegible.

I run my fingers across the page, feeling the indentation of the words penned across it. A tightening forms in my chest. This letter was written by my dad. I'm certain of it. I scan it, looking for any clues that would possibly spark a memory or two. But nothing. I flip through a couple more letters, but they're filled with small talk, my dad missing me and feeling the need to stay in touch.

Crushed, I grab the stack of envelopes bound by the elastic and pull out a tri-folded piece of notebook paper on the top. Unfolding it, my eyes grow wide, and my breathing quickens the moment I recognize my own handwriting.

Timeline of Events:
- Tuesday, March 23, 1976: Jack Wilson, the head of the Crimes against Connecticut group, approaches Dad for the first time, requesting he investigate Mom's family
- Wednesday, April 21, 1976: Dad finally agrees to take on the investigation
- Over the course of the following two weeks, Dad analyzes the thirty or so boxes of evidence, and finds a few things similar with most of cases: the same branded image on each of the victims; the letter that each of the victims' families received after the body was uncovered; and the black Cadillac that was spotted at twenty-nine of the crime scenes
- Wednesday, May 5, 1976: the day after Dad receives word from Detective Donovan at the Broward County Investigative Unit that he has enough evidence to charge them, Dad confronts Mom
- Thursday, May 6, 1976: Mom goes to the Broward County Police Station where she makes a

statement to Officers Clarmont and Baxter. The day Mom dies.
- Monday, May 10, 1976: Dad is arrested, and Timmy, Becca, and I are placed in a safe house
- Friday, June 25, 1976: Becca and I go to live with Aunt Jan and Uncle Mike, and Timmy goes to live with George
- Monday, April 5, 1977: Dad's trial begins
- Friday, April 29, 1977: Dad is found guilty of killing Mom and sentenced to death

Wiping the tears from my face with the sleeve of the sweater, I flip the paper over in my hand, trying to make sense of it, the words "jump out" playing over and over in my mind like a broken record. In a trance, I picture myself standing on a sidewalk, watching a car go up in flames, my mom behind the steering wheel, panic flooding her face, screaming and hysterically trying to pry open the car door.

Chapter Eight
— The Old West —

I pound on Megan's door so hard that my hand tingles and becomes numb. I need answers and I need them now. I pace the length of the porch, rubbing my hand. No one answers the door and the only car in the driveway is my own. The town is small enough that I will find her, and when I do, she will come clean with everything.

I jump back into the van, on a mission. I glance over to the passenger seat and stare at the stack of envelopes, fixating on the address that reads: *Sara Theriault, P.O. Box 302, Van Buren, ME 04785.*

After peeling out of the driveway, I head toward town, paying close attention to the cars that pass by, in case one should happen to be Megan. I slam on the brakes and honk the horn the instant I come upon a large green tractor—not your run-of-the-mill garden tractor, but one whose tires are the size of this van—going barely three miles an hour in front of me. This cannot be legal. A tractor, driving down a main road. *Is this the Old West?*

The gentleman driving the tractor peers into the side-view mirror and, smiling, waves to me like we're old pals. "What the hell? Come on, buddy, get out of the way," I bellow, raising my hands in the air, agitated. I can't stay behind him any longer; I'll never get to where I'm headed.

I look for any oncoming traffic, and when I don't see anything, I lay on the gas pedal and swerve past him. When I return to my lane, I look into the rearview mirror and shake my head in annoyance.

As I redirect my attention to the road ahead, sirens blare, and a police car pulls behind me, lights flashing. *Damn it!* Of all the times for the one police officer in this town to be out, exactly where I am, it must be now.

I slump back into the seat and pull the van over to the side of the road. I lower my window and reach down to grab the driver's license from the purse on the passenger seat.

"License and registration?" the officer requests, my back to him.

With wallet in hand, I sit back in the seat.

"Oh, it's you...Mrs. Theriault," he stutters. "I apologize; I didn't recognize your new van." He takes a step back, looking it over.

The tractor from earlier passes us, the word *Oliver* imprinted on the side. The driver looks at me with an expression that suggests, *"That's what you get."*

I look away, still feeling exasperated, but now also feeling a slight bit embarrassed.

The cop waves to him and then turns back to me. I remove the driver's license from the wallet and offer it.

"No need, Mrs. Theriault. Please just remember to slow down. Have yourself a good day."

Before I know it, he's pulled away, driving on down the road behind my good friend, Old MacDonald.

When I get to town, I pull along the sidewalk and enter the post office. A tall gentleman with salt-and-pepper hair stands behind the counter, handing stamps to the lady in front of me.

"What can I do for you today, Mrs. Theriault?" he asks in the same thick accent that I'm grown accustomed to hearing around here.

"I hope you can help me. You see, it seems as I've lost the key to my P. O. Box." I scrunch up my face, attempting to express disappointment.

I'm not really lying. The key may not be lost, but it's true that I don't know where it is. And I'm convinced that there are letters awaiting me. Why I have a P.O. Box when I also have a mailbox at the end of the driveway remains a mystery to me, but there must be a good reason that I will get to the bottom of. It appears that "Sara" has something to hide…from her husband, maybe?

"Ah," he draws out. "Hmm. Give me one minute."

He walks over to a woman toward the rear of the room. "Elle a perdu sa clé. Comment en faisons-nous un autre?" I overhear him mutter to her.

I don't understand what they're saying, but please let it be that I do in fact have a post office box here and that I can get to it.

I realize that I'm staring at them with a pained expression. Stop staring, Mandy. Act natural. I stand up straighter and paint a smile on my face, but the weariness builds inside regardless of my attempt.

"Ah, c'est Sara—Madame Theriault." She looks my way, offering a friendly nod. "Obtenez son identifiant et remplissez ce formulaire pour en faire un autre. Nous pouvons ouvrir la boîte jusqu'à ce qu'elle reçoive la nouvelle clé."

The gentleman returns, with a paper in hand. "I just need your ID, and we'll get a new key made for you. Did you need to get your mail today?"

I nod. "Yes, I'd like to, if I can." *Thank goodness.*

"C'est bon. I can open the box for you until you get your new key. It shouldn't take longer than a day or two."

"Thank you." I hand him the license.

A few minutes later, I leave the post office with a new unopened letter, the envelope's address in my dad's handwriting.

Chapter Nine

My Sweet Baby Girl,

I hope you get this letter. I'm so worried. You never showed up and I haven't been able to get through to you on the phone. A part of me is happy you decided not to come, but now that I haven't been able to get in touch with you, I'm worried something happened. The last time I called your house, one of the kids answered the phone. I wanted to ask them about you, but I didn't want to scare them. I keep thinking that something awful has happened to you, but I hope I'm wrong. I tried calling Bruce, but he didn't answer. I was hoping he'd know something about where you are. It's at a time like this that I wish your sister would speak to me.

It looks like my execution date is final and all I want is to get to see you or speak to you one last time. I hope you didn't in fact come to see me and something happened to you along the way. Instead, I hope you changed your mind and are just busy.

If you get this letter, please try to call the prison. I know they won't allow me to come to the phone, but leave a message for me so I know that you're all right.

I love you so much, baby girl. I will keep trying to call, hoping you answer.

Dad

Chapter Ten
— Milkmaids and Penny Candy —

I round the corner of Main Street, headed straight for my sister's house, anger, confusion, and sadness coursing through my body, tears prick the corners of my eyes. It's been over five hours since Marc left with the kids, and it's almost two o'clock now so they should be either home or headed back soon from the birthday party.

Megan knows so much more than she's letting on. What is she trying to hide? And why?

As I get over the hill, I see a blue Pontiac approach from behind. Taking a closer look, I notice that it's Rebecca—Megan—whatever name she may go by these days. I pull to the side of the road, hoping she too will stop. I want her to pull over, I need to hash this out *now*.

She passes, slowing to wave, but continues. I pull back onto the road and lay on the horn.

The kids sitting in the backseat turn around, looking back at me. Their faces light up. They smile and wave. Megan offers another wave, peering in the rearview mirror. I flash my headlights and honk the horn some more.

The kids continue to smile and wave, making funny faces at me, thinking that I'm playing a game. And my sister glances back at me in her mirror again.

The moment she returns her attention to the road, she slams on the brakes. I stomp on my brakes, stopping within inches from her car. *What the hell?*

Luckily, we were only going about fifteen miles per hour, but the sudden stop leaves me feeling a bit dazed.

After a moment, Megan exits the car and jogs over to me. Seeing her sends rage coursing through me again, the current situation at hand forgotten.

I swing open the door and get out. "We need to talk," I demand, standing within inches from her.

"I'm sorry, I had to slam on the brakes, or I was going to hit the cow," she announces in a panic.

"What?" I glare at her, my attention redirected.

"It looks like Mr. Cyr's cows got loose again." She points to the road ahead.

Scanning the street, I see it's littered with cows of all colors and sizes. Well over ten or so of them. One lets out a long, drawn-out *mooooooo,* and a chill inches up my spine, not from the nip in the air, but from the realization that I'm within feet from a giant cow—so much closer than I've ever wanted to be. The cow cranes his neck and starts to munch on some grass on the side of the road, not amused by our disruption.

Oh, hell no! I jump back into the van, feeling safer, but still needing to talk to my twin sister who gazes around, assessing the situation, unfazed by the large creature at her side.

After reaching over to the passenger seat and grabbing the letter, I roll down the window. "You're a liar." I shove the letter into her chest.

She looks at me, confused. "What are you talking about?"

A car approaches from the other side of the street, and after pulling over to the side, a man exits. "I just told Martin where they are. He should be here in a minute to get them," he hollers from his side of the cow barrier, his hands cupped around his mouth.

First a swamp-thing, then a tractor, and now cows? *What the hell is this place?*

Megan waves to the man in recognition, and then redirects her attention to me. Looking down at the envelope, she swallows hard and pales. "We can't do this right now," she warns under her breath as the man approaches. She hands the envelope back to me.

"Can you believe they got out again?" the man exclaims.

Megan plasters a smile on her face. "I know it. Mr. Cyr said that he hired a new helper at his dairy farm two weeks ago. I think he accidently forgot to close the gate again."

After about an hour, the cows are all transported back to their home and the crowd that formed around us go on with their day like this is a natural occurrence around here.

My sister gets into her car without another word.

When we arrive at her house, she seems surprised when I pull up behind her in the driveway. "Kids, make sure not to get dirty. We're going to church in less than an hour." The kids file out of the car one by one. "Go in the house and get a snack. There are some berries in the fridge. We'll be in, in a minute."

The littlest girl runs over to me, hugging my leg. "I got this My Little Pony in my goodie bag, Mama. And this scratch and sniff sticker too." She extends her hand for me to sniff the sticker smelling of cookies and cream.

I offer a smile, pushing her strawberry blonde hair out of her face.

When our eyes meet, I'm taken aback, she has my same piercing hazel eyes and dimples that pucker her cheeks. It's like looking at a childhood photo of myself.

Before I can pull my hand away, she trots over to the other kids, leaving me awestruck.

A car pulls into the drive, dragging me out of my trance.

"We can't do this now," Megan whispers, her eyes pleading. "He doesn't know anything."

Marc exits the car and saunters over to us. "I heard Martin's cows got out again." He laughs.

Sitting in church, our family that includes Claudette and Megan and her kids take up an entire row. People file in, tapping me on the shoulder or offering a wave of recognition. "Everyone's happy to see you back," Marc leans in whispering, taking my hand in his.

I look over at my sister and offer my own look of recognition, reminding her that she's not off the hook. Not in the slightest. This might not be the right time, but the right time will come, and soon—like right after this.

The service begins and everyone plays their part, the priest recites, and the people respond, all in unison. I follow suit. Giving and taking, offering and returning, standing and sitting, and occasionally kneeling. Like an age-old dance that everyone knows the moves to. And I fall right into step with the rest. Like an old pro. Despite the fact I don't recall being in a church since I was a teenager, I go through the motions, not skipping a beat.

It comes time for the priest to make his final announcements and he goes into detail about a Memorial Day Festival happening next weekend. He is asking for prayers that Mother Nature cooperates, willing her to bring us sunshine instead of snow flurries like she did today. "If she decides not to cooperate, we'll all board the nearest plane and take our celebration to a beach in Florida," he jokes, sending everyone into a fit of laughter.

The moment he utters the words *a beach*, an image of Marc and I walking barefoot along a sandy beach plays in my mind. Me in a pastel, striped sundress with spaghetti straps and trimmed with satin, and him in a pair of tan cargo shorts and light blue linen button-down shirt, walking hand in hand. I look like me—the self that I last recall being. Young, thin, with hair down the middle of my back, and most definitely happy. Marc lowers himself onto one knee and presents to me a ring box, proposing, asking me to be his lifetime partner. I drop to my knees and take him in a long, passionate embrace before he slips the ring onto my finger.

I twirl the diamond ring on my finger around and around, pausing to run a finger across the row of diamonds.

I feel a hand grab mine, making me snap out of my thoughts. Looking around, I notice that everyone has left, except for Marc.

"Are you all right?" he asks, squeezing my hand and rubbing my back.

Confused, I stare at him for a moment. "Did you propose to me at a beach?"

His eyes sparkle in recognition. Smiling, he nods. "I did. At Old Orchard Beach. You remember?"

My lip quivers and my chest feels heavy. "I think so."

He leans in and kisses me softly on the corner of my mouth. "I've missed you so much, Sara," he proclaims through tears. "I couldn't bear losing you. Not for a single moment."

With his hand nestled in my hair, he rests his forehead against mine and I have to close my eyes because the rush of affection that my heart currently feels is too much to handle. It's a feeling so foreign to me; being this in love is not something I ever recall experiencing.

Our reunion is broken up when little feet stomp down the aisle toward us. "Can we go to Rosie's to get some penny candy, Daddy?"

Marc clears his throat, sniffling before turning to the little ones. He reaches into his pocket and hands each of them a dime. "You guys better be sure to stay together and listen to Abby. Don't go running off without her. And hold her hand to cross the street. Okay?"

They all nod in unison.

"Don't take too long. We need to get home, Memere is getting supper ready."

"We won't. I'll bring you some Tootsie Rolls," the oldest girl tells him before they all run back down the aisle and disappear outside.

He redirects his attention to me, smiling. He bites down on his lower lip, appearing to want to say something. "I have something to ask you, but please don't get mad."

"Okay," I reply, unsure.

"I caught word that you were out at The Shipyard last night with Dean. Is that true?"

All in a moment, I feel flush and guilt courses through me. "Yeah." I swallow. "He took me out for a drink after my encounter with that large creature he saved me from. It was nothing more than that," I affirm, feeling the need to justify myself, but unsure why. "Should I not have gone? I mean, is there something with him that I should know about?"

He presses his lips together, taking in a breath through his nose, and shaking his head.

"You may not remember it right now, but he's been wanting to get too close to you for some time now. I don't know what his motive is, but it doesn't come across as innocent. Everyone in town's been talking about it." He offers me a sideways glance. "I just want to be sure to protect you during your weakest moments until you regain all your memory."

The door to the front of the church opens and Father Tom strides through. "I thought I heard voices." He walks toward us.

"We were just reminiscing," Marc tells him while I replay his last words to me.

When we arrive back home, Claudette is placing the last of the dinner plates on the table. "Kids, go wash up," she announces, and they all file down the hallway to the bathroom.

There's a knock on the door. "It's open," Marc hollers from the kitchen sink, washing his hands.

Father Tom saunters in, wine bottle in hand. "It smells amazing, Claudette." He plants a kiss on her cheek. Megan peers from behind, hugging a casserole dish.

"I brought over a broccoli salad," she announces, resting the platter in the middle of the table.

I eye her before taking my place at the sink.

"I have to apologize, Sara," Claudette says. "I made your favorite, but then I realized that you aren't eating meat right now. I'm sorry." She frowns.

"That's okay."

"I did make a salad and fresh rolls to go with the pate chinois though. And Fred brought over some fresh fiddleheads this morning." She shrugs.

"That sounds great." I feel a sense of appreciation for all the efforts she's made for me—not just for this meal, but what seems like forever. "Thank you, Claudette."

Hands washed and bellies growling, we all gather around the table. Father Tom offers grace and then everyone digs in. I can't seem to keep my gaze off my sister across the table from me, making her squirm in her chair.

The phone rings and Marc gets up to answer it. Within minutes he returns. "It must have been a wrong number. They hung up," he announces, shrugging.

"You guys sure do get a lot of wrong numbers," Claudette says.

An uneasy feeling rises from the pit of my stomach. Could that have been my dad? What if I just missed his call? What if he needed to talk to me? It had to be him.

"Sara?"

I look up and notice all eyes are fixed on me. "What?" I try to play it off.

"You dropped your fork on the floor and your face paled. Are you feeling okay?"

"Um…yeah, I'm fine."

One of the boys slams his fist down on the table. "Why do you always have to ruin things for us?" he barks. "If you don't love us, why are you still here?" He jumps from his chair, causing it to topple back, coming to a crash on the floor.

He storms out of the dining room and up the stairs, a door slamming moments later.

The room goes silent, everyone looking at each other. "I'll go talk to him," Marc announces after a beat.

"No," I interject, pushing myself from the table. "I'll go. I think it's best if I talk to him."

After willing my feet up the stairs, I knock on his bedroom door. I have no idea what I'll say to him, but it's evident that he's angry at me for something. It's not like I've been the best mom to him lately—well actually, I haven't been a mom at all.

When he doesn't respond, I turn the handle and open the door a crack. He's lying on the bed, crying into his pillow. When he sees it's me, he grabs hold of the nearest stuffed animal and throws it my way. "Go away," he mumbles.

"Please just let me come in." I take a step into the room, closing the door behind me.

"You don't love us. You had that accident on purpose. Just go away. Leave us. I hate you," he booms, through gritted teeth, large tears streaming down his face.

After I take a cautious step in his direction, and then a couple more, I lower myself next to him on the bed.

He pushes at me with his hand. "Go away, I said. You didn't want us, so why are you still here? Go away. Go to New York City like you keep talking about. Just leave us alone."

Each word he speaks squeezes around my heart tighter, crushing my soul.

I swallow back the golf ball-sized lump in my throat.

"Jacob, I know I haven't been myself lately."

He raises his head from the pillow and looks up at me. "You said my name. You remember me?"

"I...I guess...yeah, I do," I answer, equally shocked.

I also know that he loves to do tricks on his skateboard. I know that he's a straight-A student at school and his favorite cartoon is Tom and Jerry. And when he was four years old, he broke his arm when he fell from the large oak tree in the backyard, and it had to be in a cast for two months. I know that he hates peas, but he loves root beer floats. And I know that he and I share a special bond, that I can feel right down to my core.

"It doesn't matter. In the hospital you said you didn't want us." He turns away from me.

"I know I said that, and I'm sorry. I don't remember everything from before the accident, but I don't believe that I had that accident on purpose. And when I woke up from the coma, I was thinking I was somebody else. I promise that I'd take back those hateful words if I could, because they're a lie." And as I utter those syllables, I know they're the truth. And I also know that I love this kid.

"You would?" he asks hesitantly, rolling onto his back, turning toward me.

"Yes, most definitely, for sure," I tell him, my heart bursting with every word. "You're my little buddy, and I love you."

"You always called me your little buddy," he proclaims, gleaming.

I lie down next to him, and he snuggles into me, and it feels so familiar.

Chapter Eleven

— Deep Family Secrets —

I slip into the rain boots sitting next to the front door and grab a jacket off the hook.

The night is overcast, only the full moon illuminating my path through the long grass that runs between my house and Megan's. The chill in the air is crisp, and I breathe out puffs of smoke with each exhale. Wrapping the jacket tighter around me, I make my way through the trail to her house, being careful not to slip on the thin layer of frost that covers the stone pathway when I reach her front yard.

"I can't believe it's this cold," Megan calls out through the darkness, startling me. "I have something to keep us warm though."

She's sitting on the wooden swing hanging from the porch, and as I make my way up the steps, I can see she's wrapped in a quilt, holding a large mug with both hands.

"I didn't think you'd still be awake." I take a seat next to her, grabbing the extra quilt folded neatly on the swing.

"I knew you'd be by."

I made my way here, on a mission to get my sister to confess, to tell me why she's been lying and to find out the reason we've taken on a new identity, but after my conversation with Jacob, who missed me—his mom—the past few weeks, and my few bursts of recollection earlier in the day, a feeling deep in my belly tells me that there's a logical reason for it all.

Resting the mug on the table beside her, she reaches over and grabs another cup, handing it to me. Then, opening a thermos, she pours some coffee into it, the aroma awakening my senses. After returning the thermos, she grabs hold of a bottle, and raising it in the air, she smiles.

"This is the good stuff," she proclaims. "This will be sure to keep us warm." She pours a generous amount of Baileys into the mug.

A few moments pass; we just sit, swinging and sipping, the drink warming my insides. Finally, she breaks the silence.

"Are you still in contact with him? Or is that an old letter?" she questions, holding the cup to her mouth, staring into the night.

"I guess I don't know. I don't remember. But I think I've still been in contact with him. I spoke with him on the phone a couple of days ago."

She turns to me, fixing me with a look. "What?"

I swallow hard, feeling like I'm six years old, caught stealing a piece of gum from the local convenience store.

Scrunching up my face, I shrug and nod. "What's going on? Why did you say that our parents were dead, and claim to have a past that's different than I remember?" A feeling of defeat fills me. "Please, just tell me. What's going on?"

"You really don't remember anything?"

"Becca, I promise you I don't—"

"Megan…you mean Megan. You can't call me Becca, Sara. You just can't."

"Fine. Megan." I huff. "Anyway, I did find a timeline that was written in my own handwriting. I don't remember writing it and I don't recall much of what's written on it, but it states that Mom died. And when I read that part, an image of her trapped in a burning car came to mind. The words 'jump out' play over again and again, but I don't know why."

She closes her eyes and passes a hand through her hair. "I don't even know where to start. I can't believe that I'm having to recall any of it again."

"I'm sorry." In this moment, feeling her anguish, I do feel sorry that I'm having to put her through this because it seems like it's something she doesn't want to remember. Maybe even something I, myself, am better off not knowing.

She clears her throat and takes a sip from her cup.

"Two weeks before we were to graduate from high school...Mom died in a car explosion, and Dad was charged with capital homicide. We ended up in a safe house for three weeks before you and I went to live with Aunt Jan in Portland and Timmy went to live with his dad. A month or—"

"Timmy's dad? What do you mean?" I interject, confused.

"Timmy wasn't Dad's son. He was the son of Mom's assistant, George."

My eyes shoot open. "What?"

"Dad knew, but to protect Mom's political status, he remained quiet about it. It's apparent that he did a lot for Mom, a lot more than you and I will ever know."

"You and I never knew about Timmy's dad?"

She shakes her head. "Neither did Timmy."

"Anyway, a month or so before that, Dad was approached by an independent crime investigation group that was examining a string of murders in the state, and they believed it included the killing of Grandpa and Uncle Matt. They had evidence to prove that Mom's family was part of the Irish Mafia, and they wanted Dad to investigate it. The leader of the group, his name was Jack I think, claimed that he had collected enough evidence, but wanted Dad to dig further, to strengthen their case. At first, it left Dad unsettled, he didn't want to do it. He knew that it was likely that Mom's family had some kind of involvement in the mafia—there were clear signs pointing to it, even you and I knew that," she confirms, nodding. "But he didn't want to believe that they were the ones that had killed his own father and brother, or that Mom would have let that happen. Anyway, somehow, they eventually convinced Dad to take on the case, and after a few weeks he decided that they were right. Not only was Mom's family part of the mafia, but her dad, Grandpa Don, was said to be the leader."

She goes silent and pours another cup of coffee, taking a long sip and swallowing. I'm too astounded to speak.

"When Dad found out, he approached Mom, telling her everything that he uncovered and that he was thinking about going to local detectives with the information. While it was clear that she knew their involvement and had hidden it from him, she threatened to leave him, stating it would ruin her campaign for mayor of New York City and as a result crush his own career. She left the house in a rage and never returned that evening. The next day, she went to the police and made a statement, claiming that Dad was involved in a hoax to break up her family, that he wanted to have them sent back to Ireland. She told them that Dad was the one behind the thirty-six unsolved murders, stating evidence to link him. Much of that evidence she detailed was information Dad had told her just the day before, but it was obvious that she had spoken to her family as well."

She wipes her eyes and inhales. "Upon leaving the police station and starting the car, it exploded with Mom inside. When the first burst went off, she tried to unlatch her seatbelt, but she was struggling. There were two police officers in front of the station who ran to help her, they had just enough time to open the car door, and everyone around was yelling at her to jump out. But before she could get her seatbelt unfastened, a second blast went off, causing the car to erupt into flames, taking her life and that of the two police officers. It was believed that her family thought Dad was the one at the station that day since her car was in the shop and she had used the spare car that Dad often took. Dad was arrested; the police claimed that she presented enough evidence to pin him to all the murders, including his own dad and brother, as well as Mom and the two police officers. After the trial that we were both called as witnesses for, we had to change our identities because we were getting death threats by the families of the victims. They didn't care that we were only kids, they saw us as one of the bad guys protecting Dad. It was scary for a while. We had security following us everywhere because we were receiving threats just about daily. The jury did find him not guilty of the thirty-six murders, but guilty of killing Mom and the two police officers. Since it involved the death of two cops, it was considered a capital offense, so he received capital punishment, which was death by lethal injection in the state of Connecticut."

She runs a finger around the rim of the mug. "I had no idea that he was still alive."

I'm dazed by what I'm hearing. "So, he's been in prison all this time?"

"I guess so. It's been seventeen years."

"Do you think he did it? Do you think he killed Mom?"

She shakes her bowed head. "I know he didn't."

"Has he ever filed for an appeal?"

"Yeah, twice. But he lost."

She pulls the blanket tighter around her and blows out a puff of smoke before continuing. "Fifteen years ago, Grandpa confessed to the string of murders. He only served five months on death row before he died of liver cancer. The bastard knew what he was doing. He took the heat for the rest of the family who all fled the country. He knew he was going to die anyway. The least he could have done was take the heat for Mom's death too. But he wanted nothing more than to see Dad go down. He knew if Dad got out prison, his family would be found out. The rest of the family may have fled, but they still have power over us. I'm surprised you were still in contact with Dad. That is not good, Sara," she utters, looking at me with a worried expression.

I suddenly become even more lost, unsure of what she could mean. "I don't follow. He's our dad, and you did just say that he's innocent. What do you mean?" I inquire, creasing my brow.

"I thought we had made a pact five years ago, when Marc's dad and Luc died," she questions, her tone littered with a hint of anger.

"What does Marc's dad have to do with any of this? And Luke? Who's that?"

"Luc," she corrects, pronouncing it like *Look*. "He was my husband."

So, this is where I learn what happened to him.

"We're convinced, you and I, that they were both killed by Mom's family."

"Are you serious?" I become dumbfounded. It sounds absurd to think that two men totally unrelated to our father or his family, living in a small town on the edge of the universe, could be targeted by the mafia. *Honestly?*

Silence hangs between us while I wait for her to elaborate, but she appears to be lost in thought, affected by what happened to her husband, so I don't press.

My mind races, a string of different scenarios play like a slideshow, unsure if any are real—maybe memories coming back to me, or maybe they're the result of my vivid imagination.

She stands. "We're going to need more coffee." She grabs the thermos. "And maybe we can retreat to the house where it's much warmer."

"And with all that coffee, I need to use the bathroom." I stand, thankful for the potty break.

We enter the house and remove our shoes. Pointing, she says, "The bathroom is…"

"…The second door on the right," I finish for her.

She shoots me a knowing grin. "You remember."

I nod, thinking. I do remember. I recall a lot about this house, for some reason.

"This is Marc and Luc's childhood home. You lived here for a couple of years when you moved here and while your house was being built."

"I remember," I confirm, the memories of large Sunday dinners and Abby crawling on the living room floor playing out in my mind.

She walks in the direction of the coffee maker in the kitchen, and I make my way down the hallway. Flicking on the bathroom light, I'm stopped in my tracks. It looks nothing like I remember. The walls that were once covered in mint green tiles are now a stark white. And the sink and toilet that were pink, so bright that they looked like they belonged in a pack of Bazooka bubblegum, now are a charcoal grey. It feels open and airy, unlike how I recall.

When I return to the living room, I notice a large, framed photo on the main wall. Leaning in to take a closer look, I see that it's of Megan and her husband on their wedding day, and they're standing in front of a large, white, perfectly square home that looks familiar.

Megan walks over to me, handing me a cup. "Do you remember *that* house?"

"I think so," I answer, shrugging.

"That was the house Claudette was raised in. Her family's home," she reminds me.

"They were farmers, right?"

"Yes, potato farmers."

I nod, knowing.

She walks to the sectional in the corner of the room, and sits, bringing her knees up to her chest and wrapping a blanket around herself. I follow her, sitting on the other end, facing her and mirroring her pose.

"I miss him so much." She frowns, looking up at the portrait. She says it in a way that causes my chest to ache—my heart to hurt for her.

She sniffles and clears her throat.

"I need you to make me a promise," she pleads, eyeing me. "If you are in fact still in contact with Dad, you *have to* stop."

"I...I'm so confused. I don't get it."

"We both remained in contact with Dad until about five years ago, when Marc's dad was killed and then Luc's accident."

"Do they think that Dad is the one that was behind their deaths?"

"No. No, not that. We—me and you—strongly believe that Mom's family were behind their deaths. And now that I know that you've still been in contact with him, they may have even been behind your car accident." She reaches over and places her cup on the coffee table and then pulls the blanket tighter around herself.

"What?"

She shrugs. "Maybe not, you did hit a moose. But...I don't know. Everyone whose gotten close to Dad—who has tried to help him—has been killed." She pauses, her eyes still fixed on the portrait hanging on the wall.

"You were close to Marc's dad and once we found out that Dad had lost his appeal, you felt helpless. We both did. Against your better judgment, you approached his dad and told him the whole story—everything. You even wanted to tell Marc, but his dad persuaded you not to. He spoke a few times with Dad's attorney on the phone, convinced that he could help him, and even took a trip to visit Dad in prison. But...he never made it back home." Her voice is flat. "On his way back, he stopped overnight at a motel in Portsmouth, New Hampshire. He had called Claudette when he got there, telling her that he'd be home the following day. He had told her that he was going to a convention in Boston. It wasn't out of character for him; he often went to conferences for mayors and town managers, so no one ever questioned it. But when he never arrived home the next day, Claudette called the motel, and they told her that he hadn't checked out yet. They called his room and when he didn't answer, they went over and found him dead, a single gunshot to the head."

She pauses, a sob forming. "He was branded with the same Celtic cross symbol as the other victims."

I recall the mention of branding in the timeline I'd read.

Beginning to feel weak, I reach across the sofa and take her hand in mine, giving it a light squeeze.

Feeling her body shudder against mine, she goes on. "Because that case had long since been closed, and Grandpa had already passed, the police never made the connection. But we sure did."

A rush of guilt fills me. "So, ultimately he died because of me?" I mutter in a low tone.

She squeezes my hand. "No. Don't start feeling guilty for that again. You were finally in a good place; don't you dare start to think about that again. Marc's dad is the one that made the decision to go see Dad, despite our pleas for him not to. I promise, his death was not your or my fault. While we knew that he had been in contact with Dad's attorney, he hadn't even told us that's where he was going. We had no idea until after he died."

"What happened to your husband? Was he with him too?" I question, hesitating before I add, "I'm sorry to ask. I wish I remembered so I didn't have to."

She looks pale and tired, like she's been carrying the weight of the world on her shoulders for decades. I feel her grief.

"No. He died nine days later." Her voice breaks, quivering.

I slide across the sofa and rest my head on her shoulder. She lays her head on mine.

"He loved hunting. One early morning he left to go deer hunting, but by nightfall he hadn't returned, and no one had heard from him. Marc and his friend went off looking for him in all the areas of the woods that he was known to go, but there was no sign of him or his truck anywhere. The next day, many of the people in town joined in on the search. And the game warden was called as well. By mid-afternoon, they found him. The animals had gotten to him overnight and there wasn't much left—" she cries, unable to continue.

I wrap both arms around her, squeezing her. "I'm sorry. I'm *so, so* sorry."

It feels like hours go by, but it's mere minutes before she speaks again.

"Three days before, Luc had walked in on you and I arguing. We had gotten scared that Mom's family was coming for us next that I wanted us to break all ties with Dad, but you didn't want to. You were still convinced that we could get him freed. Luc heard everything, so we couldn't deny it. We told him what had happened, and he was angry; he was determined to get justice. The next day, he called an attorney in Caribou, stating that he wanted to have his dad's death investigated. And then the next day…he was killed." Her voice starts to falter.

"Did he have that same branded image on him too?" Feeling her anguish, words get caught in my throat.

"No. Well…we don't know. His body was so mangled that there was no way to tell."

She looks me square in the eye.

"They did it, though. They murdered him. We know it, deep down, right here," she declares, laying a hand on her chest.

Chapter Twelve
— Gravel Roads and Revelations —

I rummage through the refrigerator, famished.

Exhausted from the day and the emotion-filled conversation, my sister and I fell asleep on the couch. Either my subconscious was playing tricks on me, or it was a result of a dream, but I awoke at three twenty in the morning in a panic. I sat up from a dead sleep, convinced that I was late to get the kids off to school. After realizing where I was and that today is, in fact, Sunday, I sent Megan off to bed and made my way back down the path toward my house.

I can't stop my mind from racing. All the details about my past life feel like a jumbled mess, so surreal that not a single soul would believe me if I were to confess.

With alcohol still in my system and not having eaten much the last few days, I feel weak and unsettled with hunger. Popping grapes into my mouth, I pull out containers of food, opening each to see and smell what's inside.

I remove the leftover dish from dinner—shepherd's pie—and grab a spoon from the drawer. Scraping the spoon across the top, being certain not to scoop any of the meat, I take a heaping dollop of cold mashed potatoes. And when it reaches my tongue, I savor it like it's the first thing I've consumed in years.

Hugging the dish in one arm, I continue to rummage through the fridge between bites, pulling out a bowl of boiled potatoes and carrots, a macaroni salad, and a large block of cheese. I lay everything out on the kitchen island, a buffet for one. I spoon, fork, and cut into everything. I can't eat it fast enough to satisfy me.

In my haste, I take a bite of something that is both unfamiliar and surprisingly delicious. I grab hold of the pie plate in both hands and smell it. The strong scent of meat fills my nostrils, making me cringe.

I stare at the plate, and without a second thought, I fork another piece out of the dish and scoop it into my mouth.

As I devour it, I'm convinced that it's this pie that ended my days of not eating meat. If all the vegetarians in the world knew how delicious this tasted, they'd convert for good, too.

Clasping the pie plate in one arm, afraid that if I let go, I'll die from starvation, I slide myself along the open door of the refrigerator, sitting on the floor. Leaning back, I continue to fork mouthfuls of this incredible pie concoction into my mouth while the stress of the day washes away.

"Don't do that! Stop poking her."
"What is she doing? Did she faint?"
"Is that food in her hair?"
"Ew!"

I open my eyes to four tiny faces staring down at me.

"Mama, why are you sleeping in the fridge?"

"And why do you have a spoon hanging out of your mouth like that?"

I reach up and pull a fork out of my mouth, staring at it, trying to make sense of the current situation.

"Wait, did you have a seizure? Mrs. Cormier puts a spoon in Todd's mouth when he has a seizure at school."

"She didn't have a seizure, kids. Give your mom some room." Marc rounds the corner into the kitchen, a smirk on his face.

I blush, realizing that I've been caught with my hand in the cookie jar, as it were.

There's a knock on the door, and I give thanks for the welcomed distraction. All four kids run to answer it, fighting over who will get there first.

Marc extends his hand to me. Still embarrassed, I take it, unable to look at him. He pulls me to my feet.

"I see that you found the tourtière." He reaches up and picks something out of my hair. "And I'm glad to see it's still your favorite," he adds, smudging a thumb to the corner of my mouth.

"I guess...I was hungry," I retort.

"Mama, Madame Madore is here for some eggs," one of the boys announces, walking into the kitchen.

"Eggs?" I'm confused. She wants some eggs from the fridge? Is that like neighbors borrowing a cup of sugar? I shrug. "All right."

I turn to the open refrigerator and grab a couple of eggs.

"Not those. Some fresh ones."

I lean back, looking around the refrigerator door to Marc for guidance.

"We have chickens in the backyard," he tells me.

"Oh."

He grins.

"I'll help you, Mama." Emma, the littlest girl, takes my hand and leads me to the back door.

When we step outside, my jaw drops open.

The backyard not only has a couple of chickens, but it's also a full-fledged farm. To the right is a row of coops, with countless chickens roaming within a fence. There's even a rooster perched, overlooking everything, the king of his castle. And there's a pink pot belly pig, oinking as if he's happy to see us.

Over to the left is a large garden, with rows upon rows of freshly planted fruits and veggies, enough to feed the entire town.

"You're going to need your boots. That mud might be a bit slick from the morning dew," Marc warns over my shoulder.

I slip into the dirt-stained boots that sit at the top of the stairs and follow behind Emma as she leads me straight to the eggs.

After we've collected a dozen eggs, Emma counting out each one by one, I take a step back…and the pig lets out a loud oink as I fall over him, landing on my backside right into the mud.

I sit there, unmoving, the ice-cold sludge soaking through my clothes.

A burst of laughter erupts within me. I've gone mad. I've seriously gone completely mad. I sit here, in a pile of mud and God knows what else, and all I can do is laugh until tears stream down my neck.

Emma looks at me with her big hazel eyes, mouth agape, in shock. And then quickly, she too bursts into a full belly laugh, bending over and losing her balance, landing directly into my lap.

"Oh my God, what happened?" Marc shrieks from the door. A series of gasps follow.

Glancing over my shoulder, the audience looks back in shock, making us both cackle even harder.

By the time we compose ourselves and make our way back into the house, both Emma and I are covered in caked on muck and the distinct farm smell has set in.

We both head to our respective bathrooms for a much-needed shower.

Upon exiting, I slip into a pair of underwear, and then wipe a towel across the bathroom mirror and grab my hairbrush.

"I helped Emma take a bath. And the kids ate breakfast, and they've started their chores. I have to leave now for the festival meeting. My mom will be by soon to get the kids to help her with her weekly grocery shopping in Caribou. Abby has to go over to Katie's house for ten o'clock to work on the parade float. Do you want me to come back to pick her up or do you want to drop her off?"

Before I can register that I only closed the bedroom door, forgetting to close the door to the bathroom and I'm standing here stark naked from the waist up, Marc saunters in.

Why would he be deterred by a closed door? It's his bedroom as well, after all. And, to him, I'm his wife. And he's my husband. I did, in fact, watch us get married on the video.

When he sees me, he pauses, taking me in. And then he takes a hesitant step in my direction, unsure. When I don't stop him, he continues toward me, an eyebrow raised, a playful expression forming on his face.

"Well now, there's the woman I married. You sure clean up nicely." He leans in and plants a kiss on my shoulder, sending a tingle down my back.

While I am embarrassed and it even feels as if he's invading my privacy, I get the sense that this is a natural occurrence for us. As it should, I suppose. Married couples see each other naked. That's part of the deal of marriage. *Then why do I still feel like a virgin on prom night?*

He wraps both arms around my waist from behind, and I stiffen in his hold, my stomach clenching.

"You're so beautiful," he whispers in my ear before kissing my neck.

I suppose I should respond—do something—move, even—but he has me completely enthralled.

I take in his scent and it's familiar. It's comforting. It makes me relax in his arms. A moan escapes my lips, unbidden.

A desire to rip off his clothes bubbles up inside.

Before I can will my body to respond, he pulls away, running a gentle hand down my hip.

"So, can you drop Abby off?"

I nod.

"I'll be back soon." He looks at me from the doorway. He runs a hand through his hair and swallows, his Adam's apple visibly bobbing hard, leaving me with a deep sense of wonder.

"I love you," he states before turning around.

I want to call him back, to ask him to hold me again, to feel his body pressed up against me, but my feet feel like they're melting into the floor, taking my voice with them.

I hear Claudette's voice as I exit the bedroom.

"Good morning," she says, greeting me when I enter the living room.

The kids gather around her, hugging her. It's evident the love they have for this woman. She seems to be the glue to this family, the one that picks up all the random pieces that need gathering. And it's evident that she enjoys it.

"I can't go with you this week, Memere," Abby tells her.

"That's okay, sweetie. Are you working on the float today?"

"Yeah, Mom's dropping me off. Katie and I have to finish it."

"That's good. Madame Lily said she finished your dress. I'll pick it up later."

"Okay! Thanks, Memere."

"Oh, Sara, could you pick up some potatoes from Jackie's stand on your way to dropping Abby off? We'll need some for supper." She reaches into her pocket and hands me a couple of dollar bills.

"Um, sure…can you remind me where Jackie's stand is?" I push the money back toward her.

"It's about four houses down on State Street here," she explains, pointing.

"I'll show you, Mom," Abby chimes in.

Once Claudette and the kids leave, Abby and I jump into the van and head toward town.

"The potato stand is right there," Abby directs, pointing to the end of a driveway where a wooden stand sits, holding rows of white paper bags. A sign reads "New Potatoes $1.50."

I slow and pull over.

Grabbing my purse, I remember that I don't have any cash. Abby hops out of the van.

"Wait, you need some money," I mutter, not looking up from the bag, hoping that money will magically appear at the sound of my voice.

"Memere gave me the money on her way out," she announces, walking up to the stand.

I look up to see her grabbing two bags of potatoes.

She returns to the van and places them on the back seat, and then sits back in the passenger seat and closes the door.

I stare at her. "Did you forget to pay?"

"What do you mean? I left the money." She narrows her eyes.

"Where? I didn't see you give it to anyone."

"I put it in the can. I promise, I'm not lying," she explains defensively.

"You don't have to give the money to a person? You just leave it there?"

She furrows her brow and then laughs. "Yeah, of course. We just leave it in the can."

"All right…and it's safe there in a tin can on the side of the road?"

She shrugs. "I guess. We always do that. Everyone does."

People sure are trusting around here. The only money I ever recall leaving in tin cans was to the homeless folks on the street corners and the subway. I suppose there are benefits to living in a small town.

Abby directs me to her friend's house, down a long, winding, pothole-filled dirt road. When we arrive at her friend's house, I observe a group of men building a new home next door.

She opens the door and begins to exit the car.

"Is there a bank around here where I can get some cash?" I'm craving coffee and maybe some of that bread pudding at the little restaurant on Main Street.

"Of course, Mom," she huffs, rolling her eyes. "There's the credit union in front of the high school."

I recall passing the high school on the way to church yesterday, which I believe is also on Main Street, down further through town.

"Sorry, I forgot. Thanks. Do you need me to pick you up?"

"You're not staying?"

"Oh, I'm sorry. Am I supposed to?" I ask her, dumfounded and feeling remorseful.

"You don't have to. It's just that you usually help out with my pageant stuff...But it's all right, you can go to the bank and then come back if you want."

"Okay. I'll do that...I'll be back in a bit."

She pushes the door closed and a few of the construction men wave and acknowledge her. One of them—an older gentleman, the foreman perhaps—says something to her, making her laugh.

He offers a wave to me, and I return the gesture.

Once she's headed inside the house, I feel lost, alone. Looking around, none of the surroundings feel familiar or trigger any memories.

I decide to head in the opposite direction from where we came, hoping that it'll lead me to a paved road at the very least. The car buckles and bounces along the pothole laden path, tossing up dirt as it does. Then, I happen upon a stop sign at a three-way intersection. The paved street directly ahead seems to veer off into a U-shape, leading to the right, in the direction of town.

The moment I press on the gas and the tires begin to turn, a drumming noise plays from below. The constant knock goes on, the van pulling to the right a bit, as I direct it along the road. After driving a few feet more, the sound doesn't subside, so I decide it best to pull over. I steer the van over to the side, into an empty, unpaved lot.

Exiting the car, I immediately see the front tire is on its way to being flat. *Damn it!* I haven't a clue as to how to change a tire. I don't know if I have a spare and the proper tools needed to attempt it even.

I kick at the tire in frustration.

Glancing around, I see a house across the street, and two little girls are riding their bikes in the driveway. The older girl has long light brown hair tied in a ponytail. And she rides a bike with training wheels and a sparkly blue banana seat, and in her blue and white basket tied to the front sits a stuffed bear. She guides the bike in a circle around the manhole at the end of the driveway. The smallest girl has two curly, strawberry-blonde pigtails on each side of her head that bounce as she peddles her little red tricycle, following behind the other girl. Around and around they go, in a circle.

The oldest girl looks at me and waves, smiling wide.

Her smile quickly fades when she hears her mom call from the porch, "Evelyn, I told you to watch your sister. You're not supposed to go into the street. Come inside!"

"I told you not to follow me. You got me in trouble," I overhear her murmur to her sister as she makes her way up the driveway.

The littlest girl simply smiles at her.

After a moment, they both pedal toward the house and then run inside, and I return my attention to the issue at hand, bending down to assess the damage.

I suppose I should see if that woman can help me or call someone who can. I don't have many other options at the moment, without a cell phone or the know-how needed to do it on my own.

"Ah non, you got a flat?"

I look up, startled, and I'm welcomed by an older gentleman sitting behind the wheel of a taxicab.

"Yeah. Looks to be the case. I have no idea how to change it though."

He pulls the car over to the side and exits. When he approaches, I notice that he's missing most of his right arm.

"Do you have a spare?" He points to the back of the van.

I shrug and remind myself to stop staring. While he's missing his right arm from the elbow down, his left hand is large and looks strong. I'm sure he has a good story to tell about how he lost his arm. I become intrigued by this gentleman.

"I don't think I have a tire in the garage that would fit." He bends down, examining the flat, running his hand along the treads of the tire. "Je peux appeler Conrad pour voir s'il a un tire."

I offer him a blank stare.

"Do you want me to call Conrad at the garage to see if he has a tire?" he translates.

"Ah, sure. That would be great. Thank you."

"C'est bon," he replies, walking across the street to the little girls' house.

A few minutes later, he returns. "Il 'tit Dumond…Conrad is sending the Dumond boy to bring a tire over in a few minutes. I'll let him do the dirty work." He laughs, his smile crinkling the corners of his eyes.

Sprinkles of rain begin to fall. I look up at the sky, frowning. If I didn't have bad luck, I'd have no luck at all.

"I need to head to a call, but do want to go in the house? My wife can make you some coffee while you wait for him," he asks just as a tow truck pulls up behind the van. "Well, on second thought, here he is."

I'm surprised when Dean—my drinking buddy—hops out and walks toward us.

"I see you're still causing a ruckus around here," he says to me, grinning.

"You! Of course it has to be you. Why is it that I'm always bumping into you the past few days? Are you stalking me, or something?" I retort.

The older gentleman and Dean laugh in sync.

"This boy's been causing trouble ever since he moved here," the older gentleman jokes, punching Dean on the shoulder. "I have to go, but if he's not good to you, you tell me, and I'll fix him." He points a large finger at Dean in warning.

"Thank you for helping me. I really appreciate it."

He nods, offering me a warm smile, and then gets into the cab and drives away.

"What kind of trouble did you get yourself into this time?" Dean asks, kicking at the flat. "Let me guess, you drove by the house they're building on Lincoln, right?"

"I think so. The house over there?" I answer, pointing a thumb over my shoulder.

"Yup. You're the third person in the past two days who fell victim. You'd think with the cost of nails these days, they'd take better care of them." He shakes his head. "I'll be sure to send them the bill for your new tire."

By this point, the rain has picked up to a steady stream. I push a few wet strands of hair out of my face.

"How about you sit in my truck while I change out the tire? It shouldn't take me long."

I don't refuse the offer. In fact, I'm more than happy to oblige.

"So, I hear you tried going to Canada on Friday night without me." He leads me to his truck and opens the driver-side door.

"Wow, news travels fast in a small town." I hop in behind the wheel.

"Especially when it involves the drunk wife of the town manager," he declares, smirking.

"I wasn't drunk." My cheeks flush and Marc's warning about Dean rings loud in my head. I clear my throat, attempting to find my composure.

"That's not what I heard," he sings, closing the door.

The rain slathers the windshield so hard that I can barely see out of it and there's a chill in the air, making me shiver. I fumble with a few knobs, making warm air burst through the air vents. Music plays low on the radio, a gentleman in a deep voice sings about having friends in low places. At the moment, I can't help but think maybe Dean is that friend the past few days, coming to my rescue time and time again.

Feeling bad for him stuck in this downpour out there, I flick the wipers on to clear the windshield. When I do, my focus is directed to the key in the ignition. It's not so much the key, or the other group of keys that accompany it, but the keychain attached to it.

I take it in my hand and bend down close to examine it. The image is familiar, very much so. I run my fingers across the top and get lost in thought.

I'm startled when the passenger side door opens, letting go of the keychain and folding my hands in my lap.

"I'm almost done. I'm glad you found the heat in here. I shouldn't be more than another couple of minutes."

I smile at him, tight-lipped.

He pushes the door closed and then begins to load the flat tire in the bed of the truck.

When I return my attention to the keychain, I remember where I've seen that exact image before. In a haste, I remove it from the ring of keys, while keeping my eyes fixed on Dean who's currently walking my way.

"All set," he announces when I open the door and hop out.

"Thank you," I reply, rigidly, walking past him.

I see him staring at me from the corner of my eye.

"You're...welcome."

When I realize where I'm at, I don't recall how I got here. I look around and the street seems quiet, peaceful. I notice the doors to the church are open.

Without a second thought, I exit the car.

While I was just here yesterday, when I walk in, it's like I'm seeing it for the first time. It's massive, with rows upon rows of wooden benches facing the altar. The walls and woodwork are ornate, and all the windows portray detailed religious images in beautiful stained glass. The ceilings are so high that they appear to reach the heavens.

"Sara!" Father Tom exclaims when he sees me, his voice echoing. "You're just in time. We need your opinion. We can't seem to agree on which flowers we should put at the foot of the altar."

"Hey, la fille," the florist lady that I met last week acknowledges me as I walk down the aisle to them. "Do you like the lilies or the mixed arrangements?"

"Mixed arrangements," Father Tom whispers to me when I approach.

"Ah, ah, ah," she scolds, wagging a finger at him. "Don't tell her what to say…The lilies sure are nice though," the woman jokes.

"Lilies."

"Hey! I thought you were on my side," Father Tom quips, bumping his shoulder against mine.

"See, I told you," the woman states, smiling at him.

She arranges the lilies in a row and leans back to examine them. "Perfect," she declares. "Thank you for coming to my rescue." She wraps an arm around my shoulder, giving me a squeeze.

"Okay. So, I need to go get the rest of the flowers at the shop and I'll be back," she announces. "Oh, and I have the flowers pour la pierre de Jean et Luc. I'll bring them for you, and we can go put them on together." She points a finger in the air before turning. "And you better not touch the lilies while I'm gone. You watch him, Sara," she warns, making me smile and Father Tom laugh.

"So, what brings you here on this rainy Sunday?" Father Tom asks once she's gone.

My chest feels heavy. "I'm not sure."

He looks at me with narrowed eyes. "Come sit." He directs a hand toward the front bench.

I lower myself on the seat and he sits, resting an arm across the back of the bench, bringing a leg up, facing me. "Is everything all right?"

I shake my head, unsure how to answer that. Technically, I'm fine, but something in the pit of my stomach doesn't feel right.

"I've been hiding something from Marc."

"I see. What is it?"

I decide that if I'm going to seek help from someone, I'm in the right place. "Do you know anything about my past? I mean, have I ever told you about what happened to my family?"

He swallows and nods. "Yes. Are you just now remembering it?"

"Kind of." I bite the inside of my cheek. "I confronted Megan last night and she told me about it. But it's eating at me that I haven't ever told Marc. He's my husband and I've been keeping a huge secret from him. I know that it's ultimately for his own protection, but it doesn't feel right. I don't know if I've always felt this guilty about it."

"You have always struggled with it, Sara. We've talked about it many times over the years in confidence. I can't tell you what the right thing to do is, but you need to do what feels best in your heart. You can't keep carrying this heavy burden."

ISABELLE VAN BUREN

I reach my hand inside my jacket pocket and take the keychain in the palm of my hand, running my fingers up and down and side to side over the embossed cross-shaped image.

"Who's Dean?"

Chapter Thirteen
— The Tie That Binds —

I drop Abby off at the high school and head back toward downtown. When Emma directs me to turn up a street on the right, my attention is drawn to the large white building on the corner. *Conrad's Garage*, the sign reads above the large double doors. Dean's truck sits off to the side of the building, next to a set of wooden stairs that leads up to what appears to be an apartment above the garage. Either he starts work early or this is where he not only works but lives as well.

I continue up the street, past a funeral home and a row of houses, and then round the corner to a small grey building: Kindle School.

I help Emma out of the van and walk her inside. I'm greeted by a nun wearing a habit and a warm smile.

"Good morning, Mrs. Theriault. It's a pleasure to see you again. How have you been doing?"

"I've been fine. Thank you," I respond, returning the smile.

"And you, Miss Emma. You sure look pretty in that dress today."

"Thank you, Sr. Constance," Emma exclaims, twirling. "Mama, come, I want to show you the new baby dolls we got." She tugs on my arm.

She leads me to the corner of the room where a play kitchen is set up.

"Look at this one, she has blonde hair just like me," she announces, raising the doll up in the air so I can get a better look.

"She's beautiful."

"And this one's a boy," she states, grabbing another doll. She cups a hand around her mouth and reaches up on her tiptoes to me. "He has a pee-pee," she whispers, her cheeks flushing.

I hold back a smile.

I feel a hand on my shoulder, so I turn.

"I just wanted to remind you about the kindergarten graduation in two weeks," another nun says, holding out a paper. "They've been practicing their presentation with The Letter People, and I think you'll enjoy it."

"I'm Miss E, for Emma and Exercise," Emma proclaims, beaming.

"That's right, Emma. Good job," the nun confirms.

"Nice work, Emma," I chime in.

"And Jacob told me E is also for Enema, which rhymes with Emma," she adds, stone-faced.

I bite my top lip to stop myself from bursting out laughing. This girl is undoubtedly my daughter, and her brother, without a doubt, is my son.

The nun looks terrified.

"Thank you. We'll be here." I take the paper from her, trying to deflect the current uncomfortable situation.

She nods and walks away.

I tell Emma goodbye and that I'll be by after school to pick her up. I head back toward downtown, to the auto body shop.

Yesterday when I left the church, I drove by the garage, hoping that Dean would be there, but the *Closed* sign hung on the door and his truck was nowhere to be found. Father Tom told me that he's only lived here for about six years, that he moved here to be closer to his ailing father who lives in Madawaska. Conrad gave him a job since he knew a lot about cars. But that's the extent of what Father Tom knew of him.

He said that Dean keeps to himself, but always attends the four o'clock mass on Saturdays, sitting in the back row.

With the keychain in my possession, I know there's so much more to Dean that I plan to find out about. No one just happens to have a keychain with the exact image that was branded into those people that were murdered by my mom's family all those years ago. Photos of bodies flash through my mind, all of them with this same Celtic cross branded on the chest, directly above their heart.

A chill runs down my spine at the thought of who he could possibly be and what he's doing here, in the same town as me and my sister.

When I reach the bottom of the street, I notice that Dean's truck no longer sits in the same spot it was not ten minutes ago. *How could he have gone so quickly?* He can't be far.

I turn onto Main Street and pass the pool room and a barber shop, and a string of other businesses. Cars line the street, but none are Dean's.

I continue through downtown, passing by the Town Hall and seeing Marc's car in the parking lot. I decide to turn onto State Street, heading back home. I only have a few hours before Emma has to be picked up from school, so I decide it best to return to speak to Dean later. While it's still early I want to try to call the prison to see if I can talk to my dad. Something tells me that he can give me more information about this keychain. I could ask my sister, but she seems to be adamant about not wanting to be involved. And now that I know why, I can't say I blame her.

When I get home, I'm met with a truck in the driveway; it looks like an ice cream truck without the little service window on the side. *Schwan's Ice Cream and Finer Foods* is printed in its place.

I park the van and get out, noticing a gentleman knocking on the front door.

"Hello, ma'am," he greets me when I walk up the stairs to the front porch. "I was just in the neighborhood and thought maybe you'd like something. We have a special on pork chops this week. And I have some of those ice cream pops in stock that the kids like."

"Um…sure. So…I normally buy food from you?" I ask, narrowing my eyes.

"Yes," he states, matter-of-factly.

"Okay…Oh, oh, oh, wait, do you have those pies that have the meat inside? I *really* like those," I ask, practically salivating at the thought.

"Well, we have chicken pot pies. But I don't have any with me today."

"No. Not those. Um, they have some meat other than chicken in them."

"Hmm. The only other pies we have are blueberry, lemon meringue, cherry, coconut cream, and chocolate. We hope to have rhubarb pie next week."

"That's all right," I tell him, disappointed. I was looking forward to devouring another of those delicious pies. "I guess I'll take...pork chops? Is that what you said?"

"Yes ma'am. And the ice cream pops for the kids?"

"Sure...and throw in a chocolate pie."

After I write out a check and he leaves, I place the food in the freezer and pour myself a cup of coffee. I head straight for the phone, gripping the chocolate pie pan in one hand and the coffee in the other.

After laying the pie plate and coffee mug on the table, I dial 4-1-1 and wait.

"Directory Assistance. How may I direct your call?"

"Hi, can I get the phone number to the Connecticut Wargate Correctional Institution?" I request, twisting the phone cord between my fingers.

"Please hold one minute," she states, followed by a long period of silence. The silence lasts so long that I think I've gotten disconnected.

"Hello," I call out into the silence.

"Yes, ma'am. You said, The Connecticut Wargate Correctional Institution, correct?"

"Yes," I answer, annoyed.

"All right, thank you for waiting. I have the number. It is 860-249-6500."

I scribble it onto a piece of paper.

"Thank you."

"Can I be of further assistance to you today?"

"No, thank you."

I hang up and dial the number, my hands shaking with anticipation.

The line rings, and just as I get ready to hang up, someone finally answers.

"Wargate Correctional Institution."

"Hi. May I speak with Robert O'Reilly?" I ask, butterflies aflutter in my stomach.

"Please wait a minute," the gentleman says, and then adds after a moment, "I'm sorry, I can't seem to find Mr. O'Reilly in the directory. What department does he work in?"

"Oh, I'm sorry. He doesn't work there, he's *in* prison," I clarify, it sounding more like a question than a statement.

"I'm sorry, ma'am, inmates cannot receive incoming phone calls."

"This is Amanda...um, I mean, Sara. I'm his daughter and I really need to talk to him. It's...kind of an emergency," I declare, desperate.

"*Well*, Amanda Sara, this isn't a vacation club, this is a prison," he responds, irritated. "Like I said, under no circumstances are inmates allowed to receive incoming phone calls. There's nothing I can do to help you."

"Can you give him a message?" I ask, my own annoyance growing. *How can they not let a daughter speak to her father?*

He chuckles and lets out an exasperated snort. "Sorry, we can't do that either. We're not an answering service. You'll have to wait until he calls you."

"Well, you suck!" I shriek, slamming the receiver.

I scoop large forks-full of chocolate pie into my mouth and savor the silky goodness while I calm myself.

A moment later, the phone rings, startling me out of my self-pity party. I quickly answer it, hoping that the prison has told my dad to call me after all. "Hello," I answer, muffled, through a mouthful.

"Hi. Sara?" an unfamiliar male voice questions.

"Yes, this is her."

I take a swig of coffee.

"This is Bruce. I'm happy I finally caught you at home."

I slump, disappointed that it's not my dad or the prison calling back to apologize.

"I'm sorry, who is this?" I ask, assuming it's some kind of sales call.

"It's Bruce—Bruce Barnam," he clarifies. "I've been looking into Dean Dumond for you, and I think I've found some information that you'll find interesting."

My eyes fly open wide. I swallow hard. "You...did?" I try to play it off, unsuccessfully.

"Yes, it looks like your hunch may have been right. There's something about him that I haven't fully uncovered yet, but I'm hoping you might be able to help me out."

"O-kay," I drawl out cautiously.

"He was a tough one to crack. I ran Dean Dumond through all the connections that I had and nothing. Not a single thing. Then, I ran his social security number that you had given me, and not surprising, it belonged to someone who's been deceased for fifty years. Normally when that's the case it's because the person who now has that social security number has changed their identity. I was determined to figure it out, so I had my guy run Dean's photo through some programs, and just when we thought we hit a wall, we finally got a hit. It appears that our boy, Dean, was born in Connecticut in nineteen sixty-eight. His parents on record are George Delany and—"

The receiver drops out of my hand and onto the floor.

When I arrive at the auto body shop, I see the large double doors of the garage are open. I pull up my van next to Dean's truck. Clutching the keychain tightly in my hand, I hop out of the van and rush toward the garage, my feet barely touching the ground. I storm into the garage and then pause to look around, my eyes eagerly searching for him.

"I sure hope you came to return my keychain. Or, at the very least, came to offer me a proper thank you, unlike yesterday." Dean rolls out from under a car.

I take a step back to make room while he pushes himself up from the ground. He doesn't look at me. He grabs a rag from his front pocket and slowly wipes his hands.

"Timmy," I blurt out. "Timothy Daniel O'Reilly," I proclaim with even more conviction.

He pauses slightly, but enough for me to know it's registered.

He walks around to the side of the car, his back to me, and leans over into the open hood of the car.

"What are you doing here? And why do you have this keychain?"

He shoves the rag into his back pocket and takes the wrench resting on the car. "I don't know what you're talking about. I heard that you got amnesia, I think you're taking me for someone that I'm not."

"Don't you dare play it off," I spat with so much fury raging inside, I feel like I'll either punch him or collapse from exhaustion.

He continues to tinker with the car.

I nudge him on the arm. "Are you the one that killed Marc's dad and brother?"

"I didn't kill anyone," he states flatly. There's not a hint of annoyance, no sign of anxiety or remorse in his voice.

He straightens and faces me for the first time. "Do you go around accusing everyone without finding the whole story first? Or do you just do that with me?" His eyes—his familiar eyes, Timmy's eyes—look directly into mine.

"What am I supposed to believe after I find you with this keychain," I declare, holding it up to him. "I'm going to ask you one more time: what are you doing here?"

He swipes the keychain out of my fingers and shoves it into the front pocket of his jeans. Then he runs an arm across his forehead, leaving streaks of grease smeared on his brow. "You weren't supposed to find that. I'm here to protect you."

"*Protect* me? *You* are here to protect *me*?" I laugh. "Protect me from *what*? Swamp things?"

"Like I said, you don't understand."

"Well then, Timothy Daniel O'Reilly, please explain."

He shakes his head, tight-lipped. "That bastard killed our mother. There's no way in hell I will let him walk free," he groans through clenched teeth.

My heart ceases to beat for a second. That wasn't what I was expecting him to say.

"Who? Who do you claim killed our mother? Dad? My dad...Robert?"

"That bastard needs to rot in hell."

"He didn't do it, Timmy. He didn't kill our mother. Her very own father did."

"Bullshit," he blurts out. "That's bullshit," he says even louder.

"No. No, it's not bullshit, it's the truth. I don't know who's been feeding you lies, but Dad did not kill our mother. Just like he didn't kill those other thirty-six people."

He's silent. And just when I think he won't speak, I see his lip quiver. "He left me." His face crumbles. "Because of him, I had to go live with strangers. I was a twelve-year-old boy, torn away from my family—the only family I knew, completely uprooted and placed with a man I knew nothing about. George—my father—ended up drinking himself to death. I was forced out on the street at only sixteen, with nothing but the clothes on my back. All because *your dad* wanted nothing more than another notch on his belt."

I'm stunned by what I'm hearing. I had no idea.

"So, yes, because of what he did, Mom ended up dying and I died along with her."

My heart breaks for him. It does. But it's clear that he knows as well as I do that my father—our dad—is innocent. He never killed our mom.

"Timmy," I say, resting a hand on his arm. "I didn't know. And I'm sorry to hear that you had a rough life. But blaming Dad for Mom's death is not right. You know it. Her own family did that. Dad did what he knew was right."

"He's not my dad." He pulls away from my hand. "I don't have a dad."

"He was more of a dad than your own father ever was. He was the guy who took you as his own all because Mom didn't want her reputation spoiled. He was the one who covered up for our mother time and time again. Who brought you to baseball practices, who was sitting in the bleachers at every game, and who was there to pick you up from school every day? Could you say that much about our mother, who was so caught up in her job to see what her true priorities were?" I pause. "Timmy, he not only fed you, but he also loved you like his very own."

'Get out," he shouts. "Get the hell out of here." He points to the door. Large tears stream down his face. He turns away from me. "I love you, Timmy. I always will. But it terrifies me to think that you're wrapped up in the mess that is our mother's family. I'm scared for you," I admit, my voice cracking.

Chapter Fourteen

— Road Maps and Stolen Kisses —

I sit in the van, clutching my stomach. It feels like I'm going to fall apart. I don't know how long I sit here when Dean—Timmy—comes bolting down the wooden staircase, a collie dog running behind him. They both jump into the truck and peel out of the driveway, tossing up gravel.

I feel a sudden urge to see Marc, to tell him everything.

"Hi, Sara," a woman greets me when I enter the Town Hall. "How have you been?"

"I'm good. Thank you," I answer—my usual response these days.

"I'm happy to hear that. We've sure missed you around here."

I offer a smile.

"You here to see Marc, or are you here on some other business?"

"I was hoping to see him, if he's not busy, of course."

"He's just in a meeting with Donna." She rolls her eyes. "They're going over the plans for renovations to the old mini mall. I'm more than certain that he'll be happy for the distraction. I'll let him know you're here," she says. "Come in." She pulls open the small swinging divider door leading behind the reception desk.

Walking to the back of the large room, she props open the door to Marc's office.

I glance around the room. The walls are covered in wood paneling and various large photos. I notice a framed map of the United States, so I walk up to it. Squinting at the many gold star stickers that are scattered about on the map, I find New York and place my finger on it, running it up through Connecticut, Massachusetts, New Hampshire, and Maine, coming to rest at the tip of the state, where a gold star and the word *Home* is handwritten next to it. I notice just how far New York is from here.

"Marc says you can go right in," the woman announces, walking to me. "Can you believe his dad traveled to all those places? He always thought that while it was nice to travel, it was even nicer to return home. There was no place like northern Maine, he'd always say."

We exchange smiles and I make my way to Marc's office.

When I approach, I glance in and see a woman, about our age, with long black curly hair stretched as wide and as high as it'll go, fanned out like a peacock, no doubt enough Aqua Net sprayed to deplete the ozone layer. And she wears a white scoop neck top, low enough to show a good serving of cleavage and thin enough to see her red satin bra underneath, skin-tight, high-waist, stone-washed jeans, and a pair of red patent leather high heels. She giggles and taps Marc on the shoulder, like he just told her the funniest joke. Or maybe she's flirting? I feel a hint of jealousy in the pit of my stomach.

He continues talking with a serious expression, flipping through a stack of papers on the desk, not taking notice of her possible advances. When he glances up and sees me in the doorway, he continues to speak but stands and rounds the desk and walks to me, smiling.

"Have Roger call me after you're done with the edits. I'd like to go over the final plans with him directly," he shoots over his shoulder to the woman. He doesn't take his eyes off me, and while it should make me uncomfortable, it doesn't. He makes me feel wanted. And it's a welcome feeling.

She clears her throat and grabs the stack of papers from the desk.

"C'est bon," she utters, walking past us. She doesn't look at me, instead she bows her head and walks straight out of the room.

"You're both a breath of fresh air and sight for sore eyes. You look stunning today. How is it possible for you to be more beautiful with every passing day?" He pulls me to him. I take in his scent and it's intoxicating. He kisses me on the forehead, letting his lips linger a few seconds, and I close my eyes. "Ah, ma belle femme," he whispers.

He leans back, running a hand along my arm. "What brings my beautiful wife to the office today? Is everything okay?" He looks at me with a suspicious eye. He takes my hand in his and raises it to his lips.

"I...I need to talk to you."

"You do?" He walks me to the chair behind the desk. He directs me to sit, and he leans back on the desk, crossing his legs at the ankles and folding his hands in front of him.

I glance at the items scattered about the desk. There are photos of us, of the kids, and various handmade trinkets obviously made by little hands. There's one photo of me that brings me back to the moment it was taken. I'm standing on a six-foot snowbank next to a road sign that reads "Bump Ahead." Megan had taken the photo, and I surprised Marc with it; it was my pregnancy announcement to him. He was so ecstatic; we both were. It's a recent photo, not more than six or so months old. And, I now remember, it's the baby I lost in the car accident.

He catches me staring at the picture. "That was a really good day." He swallows hard, seemingly holding back tears.

He clears his throat. "You want some lunch?" he asks, changing the subject. Grabbing a bag and a soda can, he raises them in the air.

I glance at them, furrowing my brow. "Chips and soda for lunch?"

He shrugs. "Not just any chips and soda, but Moxie and Pork Rinds!" He wiggles his eyebrows in exaggeration.

I scrunch up my face. "That does not sound appealing."

"Hey, you never know, your taste buds may have changed. Give it a try," he suggests, offering the bag for me to take.

I raise my hand in his direction. "I think I'm all set. I'll stick with coffee, thank you."

"One of these days, I'll get you to love the good stuff," he quips, popping a pork rind into his mouth, followed by a long swig from the soda can. "Mmm," he moans, closing his eyes, waving his head in the air, like it's the most delicious thing to ever touch his lips.

I let out a laugh. He's adorable and funny, and he's apparently mine, and clearly in love with me.

"So, what do you want to talk to me about?" He rests the bag and can back on the desk and crouches down in front of me, our eyes meeting.

"He doesn't know." Megan's words ring loud in my head. *"They murdered him. We know it, deep down, right here."* What if I tell Marc everything and they come for him next? *"They found him dead, a single gunshot to the head."* I look deep into Marc's eyes. *"He was branded with the same Celtic cross symbol as the other victims."* In this very moment, something tells me that I couldn't live without this man. I feel like he's my world—him, the kids, my sister, Claudette: they're my life.

I shake my head. "I was just...well, I was just thinking that I feel like I should be doing more. You know, um, well, you said that I used to do a lot for the town. I haven't been doing much the past week. I feel like I should be doing something," I fumble.

"All right." He reaches both hands up, cradling my face. "I wanted you to get well. That's why I didn't push you to do anything. Nothing is more important to me than for you to get better. I *need* you. I need you *so* much, Sara. The kids need you. This town needs you. We all do. I don't even know how I've managed to function the past few weeks without you. I don't want you to feel pressured into getting back to your daily hectic routine of life until you're one hundred percent better. And if you don't want to go back to doing everything that you did before the accident, I'll understand. It was a lot on you. You held this town in the palm of your hand. If that was too much, I get it."

His words reach deep inside of me, right to my heart.

Before he can murmur another word, I lean down and press my lips to his.

I feel his warm breath against my lips as he exhales.

Later that evening, I accompany Marc and Claudette to a Memorial Day Festival planning meeting. We sit at a large table outdoors, with a group of others, at a place just on the outskirts of town called The Acadian Village. It's like a village all its own. And while it includes seventeen buildings, none of them are currently occupied. They haven't been for many years. A woman—Madame Annette—is like the mom of this place. And after about an hour of discussion regarding the various activities and events planned for the weekend, she sits down with me and tells me about the history like it's the first time I'm being told, even if I've supposedly visited this place on a few occasions.

Madame Annette speaks with a molasses-thick accent just like Claudette, and I find her simply intriguing. When she talks about the settlement, she makes it sound like it's the greatest place to be. And as I look around, I feel she might be right.

"The seventeen buildings overlook the St. John River," she explains, pointing across the street. "And it retains the cultural heritage of the Acadians who settled in the St. John Valley during the mid-eighteenth century, our family heritage. The settlement reflects the traits inherent to the Acadians, like fishing, lumbering, and ship building. A number of these homes are significant because of their distinct Maine Acadian construction, like what they call 'ship knees,' which are used for supports in the construction." She points to two buildings behind the fence. "All of the buildings have been moved to the village or were built on-site. The first building was moved here in February of nineteen seventy-five, and many more buildings were added since then. Even Claudette's family home is here."

"I remember that house," I chime in.

"Oui. Megan and Luc had their wedding reception there before it was transported here," Claudette confirms.

Annette continues talking about some of the buildings in the settlement, some of which are staged with the original furniture and décor. There's a small schoolhouse that her own grandmother, who was a teacher for thirty-one years, taught in. There's even a church, a post office, barns, and farming equipment. And while some of the homes may not be massive, they housed large families, some even as many as nineteen kids. "If those walls could talk," she says. And I can only imagine that most of those homes, filled to the rafters with children, must have entertained many laughs and memories.

Marc rests his arm on the back of my chair and runs his hand through my hair and down my back. And when they announce that supper is ready, I'm sad that he must stop. He has a way of making me feel loved in a manner that I don't ever recall feeling, that I never thought possible.

"We can take a tour after we eat," Annette tells me.

"I'd love that," I say, excited to find out more about Marc's heritage.

We get up from the table and form a line. Marc places his hand on the small of my back and rests his chin on my shoulder. "Did you see what they're serving? My favorite," he beams.

I investigate the large buffet trays at some kind of one-pot meal, but it doesn't conjure up any memories. I shrug. "What is it?"

"Patates fricassées!" he answers, with an expression of sheer joy. He looks like a small boy who was just offered a second helping of dessert. I smile and kiss him on the nose. There's no mistaking that he loves food.

When we approach, the aroma of the meal intensifies. And while I don't recall ever seeing it, the scent makes me remember.

"Wait a minute, is this what we served at your thirtieth birthday party?"

His face lights up. "Yes. Yes, it sure is! I knew that no one could ever forget patates fricassées. Definitely not my girl, that's for sure."

He scoops a heaping serving onto both of our plates and we continue through the line.

"And now, here's your favorite," he declares.

I recall these. Claudette made them for breakfast the morning after I got out of the hospital. They look like pancakes, but they are a bit thinner and have a different texture.

"Combien de ployes puis-je recevoir pour cette fois?" a gentleman holding a pair of tongs asks.

I look to Marc.

"He wants to know how many ployes you want," he translates.

"Oh, I'm sorry. I'll take one. Thank you."

"Juste un? Es-tu malade?" the gentleman questions, wide-eyed.

Marc chuckles.

"He's wondering if you're sick because you only want one. Let's just say, you're known around town for your love of ployes. And coffee, of course."

When we sit at the table, I notice that everyone is slathering their ployes with butter, and then they roll them up and dip it into their patates fricassées. So, I follow suit. And I must admit that Marc has good taste. The dish may not seem appealing, but it's quite tasty. It's not as good as the meat pie I tasted—well, devoured—but I would say it comes in as a close second. And there's no question as to why I love these ployes so much. They practically melt in your mouth. Now I regret not eating them that other morning for breakfast. I sure didn't know what I was missing.

I go back for seconds, and Marc laughs when he sees what I'm doing.

"Ah, ça c'est ma fille," the gentleman from earlier mumbles between bites.

As I return to the table, someone comes over and taps Marc on the shoulder. "I just heard on the scanner that someone put bubbles in the fountain again."

Marc shakes his head. "Ronald might have to turn it off for good this time. Whoever it is, they keep doing it."

"Either that or he sets up a camera so they can catch who it is."

"I suppose he could. I'm not sure it's worth all the trouble, though."

"Oui, c'est vrai," the gentleman agrees.

Marc turns to me. "Some kids, or I think it's kids anyway, keep putting dish soap in a fountain that the owner of an apartment complex has. It makes so many bubbles that they run directly into Main Street. We thought that the novelty would die down after a while, but it's been about a year now and they keep doing it."

"That's crazy."

"It is, and I guess we need to find some other things to keep the kids busy or they'll just keep finding creative ways to entertain themselves. The new indoor playground and arcade will hopefully do just that. It'll not only create jobs and bring in some business for the town, but it'll keep the kids from wreaking havoc. When my brother and I were younger, we were too busy helping Grandpa in the potato fields to get into much trouble. I suppose we would have done the same thing if we hadn't been."

"How did you go from helping out in your grandpa's potato farm to wanting to get into politics?" I ask, genuinely interested.

"I didn't really care for farming, that was more Luc's passion. I just did it to help the family. I didn't really know what I wanted to do out of high school; I didn't think I wanted to follow in my dad's footsteps. All I knew is that I wanted out of this town, and I couldn't get out of here fast enough. It wasn't until I started college and got through my first year of basically just partying, that I figured out that I was interested in politics. So, I changed my major to Political Science. Then, I interned in the mayor's office and met you and knew right away that I had made the right decision," he says, winking. "And then, as much as I wanted to move away at eighteen, I wanted to move back just as badly at twenty-two after you fell in love with it here. I knew, without a doubt, there was no place else I ever wanted to be."

Listening to Marc tell his story, while watching the sun go down at this place that is so rich with history and family, I feel myself relax for the first time today—for the first time in a while. And I sense myself falling in love with him all over again, like it's the first time.

Chapter Fifteen
— Skipping Town —

I drop the girls off at their respective schools and drive by the auto body shop. The doors are closed, lights off, and parking lot bare. I didn't sleep much last night. While unsure what I'll say, I feel the need to talk to Timmy again today. He was so broken—angry, but yet, sad—when I left him yesterday. I'm not certain of his specific involvement in "the family business," but I need to get him to realize his choice isn't the right one. Something tells me, it wouldn't take much convincing.

I pull up along the curb in front of Joe's Restaurant. I need a cup of the strongest coffee.

When I make my way inside, all heads turn in my direction.

"Elle est ici," someone calls out.

"Sara's here," I hear another person announce.

I smile and offer a nod to the crowd of eyes on me.

"Sara, here. C'est Beverly à Gateway on the phone for you. She tried calling you at home," the woman behind the counter explains, waving the phone receiver in the air to get my attention.

I narrow my eyes, confused. "Who's on the phone?"

"Beverly, the secretary at Gateway School," she clarifies.

I reach for the receiver, still confused.

"Hello?"

"Hi, Sara. I tried calling you at home, but then remembered that you drop the girls off at school and go for your morning coffee. I'm glad I caught you. There's been an incident here at school with Austin. He got in a fight with another kid. Would you have time right now to come in to talk with Mr. Deschaine?"

"Um, yeah, sure."

"Great, thanks. I'll see you in a bit then."

I hang up the phone, feeling a wave of panic, but also still confused because I haven't a clue as to where Gateway School is.

"Is everything all right?" the woman behind the counter asks, resting a cup of coffee and bowl of bread pudding in front of me.

"I guess Austin got in a fight at school, and they need me to go in."

"Austin?" She gasps.

The bell chimes on the door, signaling someone's entrance. Everyone again looks to the door in unison, and I join in. A rush of relief washes over me when I see that it's Claudette.

After she approaches and I fill her in about Austin, she assures me that everything will be fine and that she'll drive me.

Taking our coffee and bread pudding to-go, we leave in a rush.

When we pull up at the school, Austin is sitting on the bench outside the main office. He sits, hugging his legs up to his chest, his face buried in his knees, crying.

Claudette lowers herself down next to him, draping an arm around his shoulders and drawing him into her.

I go to the front desk to notify them I'm there. The secretary tells me that it'll be a minute, that the principal is currently talking with the other boy's mother. So, I go join Austin and Claudette on the bench.

When Austin sees me approach, large tears pool in his eyes. "I'm sorry," he mutters through sobs.

I lean in. "What happened?" I swipe the tears from his cheeks.

Before he can answer, the other boy and his mom exit the office, the boy red-faced and glaring at Austin. He holds an ice pack to his face, his eye swollen.

"I'm sorry," the mom says to me, coming to a stop in front of us.

I nod, offering a smile of thanks.

She exchanges a look with her son, and he frowns, turning to face Austin.

"I'm sorry," he mumbles barely audible, and then looks back up at his mom.

"I don't think he heard you," she advises, causing him to scrunch up his face, offering a look of anger.

He huffs and looks at Austin again. "I'm sorry for saying that about your mom," he declares louder this time.

Austin doesn't look at him; he keeps his gaze fixed to the floor.

I nudge him and he looks at me. "Tell him you accept his apology," I whisper to him.

He shakes his head. "No," he growls steel-faced. "He's a liar."

"It's okay," the mom says. "It was Joshua's fault, and he knows he shouldn't have said what he did. Right, Josh?" She looks at her son.

The boy crosses his arms and looks away. "Yes," he murmurs.

"I just wanted him to apologize."

"Mr. Deschaine will see you now," the secretary interjects.

The mom mouths a sincere *"I'm sorry"* over her shoulder as they walk away.

We're escorted to the principal's office, and I'm surprised when I see Megan sitting at the table with another woman.

"What are you doing here?" I ask her when we take a seat.

"Austin was in Mrs. Bellefleur's classroom when the incident occurred." She gestures toward the woman sitting next to her. "And since my class is next door, I went in to help break up the fight."

I furrow my brow. "You're a teacher?"

She laughs. "I've been the French teacher here for the last nine years."

I don't remember Megan ever speaking or learning French. I sure have forgotten a lot, it seems.

When the principal asks Austin to recount what happened, Austin starts to cry again. I take his hand in mine and give it a squeeze.

"Josh said you were cheating on Dad. He said that people saw you kissing Dean at The Shipyard on Friday night," he drones, between sobs. "I told him that he was a liar."

"And then you punched him?" the principal questions.

"Yes. He wouldn't stop talking about it."

I swallow hard. Now that I know the truth about Dean, it's a disturbing thought that people think he and I would ever have any kind of romantic relationship. But it does appear to be the consensus around town, based on my own observation on Friday night. I look at Megan's sorry expression and think that I have to tell her what I've learned about Dean.

"I understand that Josh was wrong to say those things about your mom, Austin, but what should you have done instead of punching him?" the principal asks.

"I should have told Mrs. Bellefleur," he answers, his head bowed.

"Correct. You know, Austin, I've never once seen you in my office. And this was certainly out of character for you. Which leads me to believe that what Josh said really upset you. I commend you for sticking up for your mom, but you know what you should have done instead of punching him. If you had told Mrs. Bellefleur, she could have taken care of the situation for you, and you wouldn't be in my office right now. Right?"

Austin nods.

"So, because I know you'll never do this again, my punishment will be light. But you have to promise me that you'll seek the help of a teacher in the future."

Austin nods again.

"How about you take the rest of the day off from school to cool off. You go home with mom, and I want you to come back to school tomorrow ready to be friends with Josh again. You'll have to forgive Josh for what he said, and he'll have to forgive you for the punch you threw. Okay?"

It takes some coaxing, but Austin finally agrees.

Claudette drives us back to my van, and after I thank her for helping me yet again, Austin and I get in the van. I lay the take-out container of bread pudding on his lap. He opens it and his face lights up.

"Can I have it?" He looks up at me, uncertain.

While I shouldn't be rewarding him for what he did, I can't help but feel bad for him. He was only sticking up for his mom. And, well, just a week ago I didn't even remember that I was a mom, so I think I'm handling this "mom thing" pretty good, considering.

"Yes." I offer him the disposable fork.

When we arrive home, I take note that it's just about lunchtime. I ask Austin what he'd like to eat.

"Anything but tomato soup like we would have had at school again today."

He rummages through the pantry and takes out a can of Spaghetti-Os.

"Can I have this?" he asks. "Pleeeassse?" he begs.

"Sure."

His mouth drops open. "Really? You're going to let me have it?"

"Sure. Why not?"

"Because you never let us eat this stuff. Only grandma does."

"Well...I guess, just today then."

"Thank you!" He hugs me.

He pulls away, screwing up his lips. "Are you and Dad going to get a divorce?"

"Why do you think that?"

"Well, if what Josh said was true, then wouldn't that mean that you don't love Dad anymore?"

I crouch down so I'm eye level with him and take his tiny hands in mine.

"Dad and I aren't getting a divorce, and what Josh said wasn't true. Dean and I were at The Shipyard on Friday night, but we're only friends. People sometimes make up stories when a girl and boy are friends, and that is just what this is. I promise you, sweetie, your dad and I are not getting a divorce."

"Okay," he replies, content with my answer. "Can I go play video games until lunchtime?"

I smile, his innocence is refreshing. And, again, while I should probably be punishing him for what he did, I can't help but say yes.

I take a pot out of the cabinet and open the can of Spaghetti-Os, dumping it in and placing it on the stove.

Then, I turn the coffee maker on, getting ready to make a fresh pot when the phone rings.

I rush down the hallway, and answer it, willing it to be my dad.

After a moment of silence, I hear the familiar recording, and my heart thumps in my chest.

"Dad!" I exclaim when I hear his voice. "Yes, yes, yes, I accept the call."

"Sara," he calls out when the line connects. He sounds different—sad, maybe even, crying.

"Dad? Are you all right?"

He clears his throat, and I hear him sniffle. "Yes. I'm happy you answered, baby girl," he says, his voice cracking.

"Wow, Dad, I have so much to tell you."

"Me too."

"Are you sure everything's okay?"

"Well…not really." He huffs. "Today's the day…I have until six o'clock."

"What do you mean?"

There's a long pause, but I hear his labored breathing through the phone.

"It's my day of execution."

My insides shake uncontrollably. My fingers begin to tingle, the sensation running down my body in waves, reaching all the way to my toes. I collapse to the floor, my legs no longer able to support me.

MY ANYWHERE

"Sara?" my dad calls out into the receiver. "Baby girl, are you there?"

I have to force my hand to keep its grasp on the receiver. The weight of it feels like a brick. I need my daddy. This cannot be happening.

"No...no, no."

The room spirals around me and my vision blurs.

"Mama."

I blink open my eyes. Austin hovers over me and a loud sound blares in the background.

"Mama, the fire alarm is going off. I can't make it stop."

When I attempt to push myself up, I notice I'm clutching the telephone receiver in my hand. *Oh no, my dad!*

I put the receiver up to my ear. "Dad?" I call into it, frantic.

But the ring tone is the only response that fills my ears.

"Are you okay, Mom?"

I look at Austin in horror. I must have passed out—fainted from the shock. I need to talk to my dad. I need to call him back. But, first, I must get that smoke alarm to stop blaring.

"Mom," Austin repeats with a scared expression.

"I'm...I'm fine." I push myself up from the floor and return the receiver to the holder.

I take his hand, and we trudge to the kitchen. The pot on the stove is bubbling over, smoke bellowing up.

I grab the potholder on the counter and remove the pot from the burner, and then turn the fan above the stove on high.

Austin, standing on his tiptoes, waves a dish rag in the air toward the fire alarm above him.

I pull a chair from the dining room table and climb onto it. I yank the fire alarm from the ceiling and remove the battery.

"You're not supposed to do that," Austin warns.

"I know. I just need to stop it from ringing right now. I'll put it back once the smoke has settled."

"My Spaghetti-Os are burned," he announces, looking into the pot on the counter.

I need to call my dad. I need to get Austin occupied for a minute so I can call him back. I need to figure out a way to get to him. I glance over at the clock on the wall. It's twelve thirty. I might have time to get over to him. I can maybe convince them that he's innocent. I do the math in my head. I have about five hours. I don't know how far I am from Connecticut, but maybe I have enough time. Then I remember the map I looked at in Marc's office yesterday. Connecticut seems like a world away from here.

"Mama? What's wrong?"

I look at Austin with a blank stare, deep in thought.

"I can just eat Spaghetti-Os out of the can," he says when I don't respond.

"Um...no. Sorry, sweetie. I just feel lightheaded. I think I might just be hungry too. How about if you go gather the eggs from the chickens outside and I'll reheat you some Spaghetti-Os."

"Okay," he agrees, satisfied with my response.

Once he heads to the backyard, I scurry over to the telephone and dial the number for the prison that's imprinted in my mind.

"Wargate Correctional Institution."

"Hi. I was just on the phone with my dad, Robert O'Reilly, and...we got cut off. He's getting...exec—" I force myself to say the word, but it hangs on the tip of my tongue, "executed...today and I need to talk to him."

"Ma'am, I'm sorry, you'll have to wait for him to call you back. I have no means of connecting you," the woman advises.

"No. You have to. I need to talk to him."

"Sorry, ma'am, I can't help you."

"But, please, I'm begging you. I'll do anything. I'll pay you. Just, please!"

Austin stands at the end of the hallway, hugging a basket of eggs to his chest. I raise my finger in the air, signaling him to wait a minute.

"Ma'am, as much as I'd love to entertain your offer since we don't get paid a whole lot around here, I'd get fired for taking your cold hard cash. So, I think it's best that we just end this call, and you do as I instructed you—wait for a call back."

"But he didn't kill my mom. Can I talk to someone? I need to tell them he's innocent," I beg.

"Right, they're all innocent here," she drawls, laughing.

She has the audacity to laugh?

"Let me talk to your supervi—"

The line goes silent.

"Sara."

I look at Marc.

"Honey, are you all right?"

I scan my surroundings and realize I'm sitting cross-legged on the overstuffed chair in the living room, my hands folded in my lap.

Austin sits on the couch, legs dangling, and Marc is hunkered down in front of my chair. Both are looking at me with intensity.

"It's okay, baby," Marc comforts me. "Austin told me what happened."

Austin told Marc what happened? He told him about my call? About my dad?

I burst into tears.

Marc leans over me, enveloping me in a hug. "I know that you didn't kiss Dean. I know you didn't cheat on me. Don't be upset, my love."

Wait a minute. *What?* Does he think I'm crying because of the incident at school? Oh no! *What time is it?*

I look around the room for a clock.

"What time is it?" I ask in a panic, swiping the tears from my face.

"Don't worry, Jacob is on the bus on his way home. And my mom is picking up the girls from school."

"No! What time is it?" I repeat.

"It's three thirty," he answers, looking at his watch.

How did I lose track of a few hours?

"Oh no, your lunch," I exclaim, looking at Austin.

"I ate." He doesn't look up from his lap.

I glance over to the kitchen and see an open can of Spaghetti-Os sitting on the dining room table, a spoon peeking out the top of the can. I sink further into the chair, feeling disheartened. I haven't been much of a mom today, when this kid needed me the most.

The front door flies open, and Jacob comes bounding through, throwing his backpack to the floor. The girls and Claudette follow behind.

"Memere said she's taking us to Tasty Treats for supper and ice cream," Abby announces.

"And then to go bowling," Emma adds. She runs over to me and throws her arms around me, plastering a wet kiss on my cheek.

"Yes. How about you guys get changed out of your school clothes and then Memere will take you out," Marc announces.

"Do I have to go?" Jacob whines.

"Yes, you're all going," Marc confirms.

Jacob's shoulders slump over, and he drags his feet upstairs. "I wanted to play Mario Brothers," I hear him mumble.

"How about you go get changed too," Marc states to Austin, who sits unmoved on the couch.

Without a word, he stands and does as Marc says.

Despite my pleas for the kids to stay, that Claudette doesn't need to take them anywhere, both she and Marc insist. And within twenty minutes, she and the kids have left.

Marc takes me by the hand and walks me to the bedroom and into the master bathroom.

"I've drawn you a bath. It'll help you to relax from your stressful day." He hands me a glass of wine. "And after, I figured we could go to Bernard's in St. Leonard for a Donair."

"You didn't have to do all this."

This is sweet of him. I just wish he didn't think that I'm upset because of the incident with Austin. And I can only imagine how Austin's feeling as well.

"Oh, my love, this is nothing." He kisses my forehead. "You've been through a lot this past week. Relax and take your time in the bath. I left you a book to read if you'd like."

Once he's gone from the room, I take a long swig of wine and refill the glass, and then remove my clothes and climb into the tub.

My tense body eases when I lower myself into the water. I close my eyes, and despite my efforts to push away any thoughts of the day, I can't help but wonder how my dad is doing right now. I'll be left in a world without parents, when just a week ago, not only did I think I still had both in my life, but that I was twenty-two and still living under their roof. Instead, now I'm the parent of my own kids. Talk about a change of events.

I grab the book resting on the side of the tub. I need a distraction. The title on the front of the book reads "Finding Savannah." I notice that a page is earmarked, likely where I last stopped reading. I unfold the page and begin to read, fighting away the thoughts of my dad.

After three full glasses of wine, I get out of the bath and take note that it's nearing five o'clock. Only an hour left. I can't imagine what my dad's thinking or feeling.

When I walk down the hallway, I notice the light in the office is on. Marc is sitting behind the desk, papers scattered about. He looks up at me with a warm smile. Putting his pen down, he stands and rounds the desk to me.

"Thank you," I blurt out before he can utter a word. "That was wonderful."

Despite what I know is going to occur to my dad within the hour, either the wine has relaxed me or I'm coming to terms with the fact that there isn't a single thing I can do to help at this point; time has run out for him. I need to redirect my attention to my family—my kids who are clearly affected by my erratic thoughts and actions the past week. My life is here, with them. And it appears to be a good life—a fulfilling one.

"You're welcome, my love," he replies. "Are you hungry?"

"Yes, actually, I'm starving."

"I'm famished. Let's blow this joint," he says, making me chuckle.

When we get to the immigration office at the Canadian border, Marc stops the car and lowers the window for the patrolman.

"Bonjour, Monsieur et Madame Theriault," the man in uniform says, addressing us.

"Bonjour," Marc responds.

"Où allez-vous aujourd'hui?"

"Nous allons simplement à Bernard's pour souper," Marc says.

"Ah. C'est bon. Enjoy," the gentleman replies, waving a hand, directing us.

We drive ahead, without another request or word said.

"Wait a minute. How'd you get through that easily?" I ask, surprised that I wasn't probed for identification or asked to get out of the car.

Marc laughs. He squeezes my leg playfully and then takes my hand in his. "It's that easy when they don't smell alcohol on your breath," he jokes. "I guess also it helps that I know him."

"Not fair. Simply not fair." I try to hold back a smile.

When we get to Bernard's, Marc places our order. He doesn't ask me what I'd like, but I don't take offense to it since it's clear he knows what I would want, like this is a natural occurrence for us.

"We'll take that to go," Marc directs the woman behind the counter.

"I figure we can take it to our spot," he says, turning to me.

I narrow my eyes.

"You don't remember where our spot is?"

I press my lips together and shake my head. I haven't a clue.

He cocks an eyebrow, nodding. "This is sure to be fun then."

"Hey, you guys," a gentleman addresses us in a familiar thick accent, shaking Marc's hand while we wait for our order.

"Hey. Looks like we had the same idea for supper," Marc states.

"Yeah, well, I needed to grab a quick bite. I haven't stopped all day."

"Your trusty sidekick not doing his job?" Marc jests, laughing.

"Well, he's not here today. He called me last night to tell me that he was taking a couple days off. When I arrived at the garage this morning, his dog was tied up on the porch. Her food bowl was overflowing and the water bowl full, and the poor dog was whining. I don't know where he went, but he never leaves that dog behind. He told me last week that his dad wasn't doing good, so I don't know if something happened to him or maybe Dean just needed a vacation. But, anyway, he left me with a lot of work to do by myself," the gentleman states, an expression of exhaustion and disappointment plastered on his face.

"I'm sorry to hear that," Marc tells him. "I hope everything's okay."

"I hope so too."

Marc grabs our order, and we exchange goodbyes with the gentleman.

By the sounds of it, Dean has up and gone. I can't say I'm surprised after my confrontation with him yesterday. Maybe he thought I'd rat him out, so he made a break for it. Or maybe I'm overreacting, he could have just taken a few days off, went on vacation somewhere to clear his head. But the timing sure is questionable.

When we return to the van, I glance at the clock on the console: 5:59 p.m.

A knot forms in my chest. I stare at the numbers as they illuminate, taunting my emotions, tugging at my heart. My dad had seventeen years in that prison to prepare himself for this very moment, but the me with the few returning memories has barely had a week.

The clock changes to 6:00 p.m.

Inside I feel like a two-year-old, having a temper tantrum, arms flailing, kicking and screaming and crying uncontrollably, but on the outside, I'm stone cold, unmoved, paralyzed.

I feel a hand touch my arm. I look to my side.

"You were so quiet, I thought you fell asleep," Marc says.

I offer him a tight-lipped smile.

I feel like a game of Jenga, about to dismantle, pieces of me ready to come crashing down and scatter about at any given moment.

"We're here," he announces, grabbing the take-out bag from the floor, between my feet.

I lean forward, looking through the windshield, and see a large white object. A massive structure of some sort, maybe even a building, I can't be sure. My initial thought is that it's a water tower like I've seen from the highway in Connecticut on more than one occasion, but this surely can't be that. Why would he have taken me to a water tower to eat dinner? Maybe this one's been transformed into something else? Or maybe there's a trail leading to something else next to here.

Marc exits the car, and I follow suit. He opens the side door to the van and removes a picnic basket and drapes a blanket on his arm. He takes my hand, and we walk over to the structure.

"Do you remember now?"

I glance up at the massive structure. It has the words *Van Buren Maine* imprinted on the front. A chuckle escapes my lips. The thought that this structure could be "our spot" seems comical.

"Is this a water tower?"

"Yes. You do remember?"

I shake my head. "No, sorry. I just know this to be a water tower, but I still don't know why we're here."

He wriggles his eyebrows at me, grinning.

We walk around the cylindrical object and approach a ladder attached to the side. "Ladies first," Marc directs, motioning to the ladder.

"Ha!" I snort. "You expect me to climb all the way up there?" I point a finger in the air.

He gives me a quick nod, a grin playing at the corners of his mouth. I take note of how his ice blue eyes sparkle.

I look away from him and scan the structure again. Without another protest, I grab hold of the side of the ladder, hoisting myself up.

About halfway up, I feel my stomach begin to sink. It's starting to get high. I look behind me, below, and see Marc a few steps down on the ladder, his eyes fixed on me. And then I realize that I'm wearing a short dress, and he likely has a view of everything underneath—everything he's seen multiple times, I'm sure, but it all feels so new to me.

When we reach the top, I crawl to the center of the structure and remain there until Marc joins me.

"It's a beautiful view," he declares.

Does he mean the view that he just had of what's under my dress, or the view that sits on display before us?

When I look out in front of me, I'm left marveling at the sight. This view, the one of the beautiful sun-filled sky above what feels like the entire world, is spectacular. It's unlike anything I ever remember seeing.

"How could I have forgotten this?"

"It's amazing, isn't it?"

"Incredible."

"When we first moved here, and Abby was just a baby, we'd often come here in the early morning hours to catch the sunrise. I can still picture her curled up in the carrier, resting on your chest," he says.

Marc lays out the blanket and I scoot onto it, sitting with my legs straight out in front of me, crossed at the ankles. He sits next to me, placing the picnic basket on the other side of him.

He hands me a Styrofoam take-out container, and I rest it on my lap. The smell of onions fills the air.

"What is this anyway?" I open the container.

"A Donair. One of the best things to ever hit your taste buds."

When I peel back the foil, I notice that it looks familiar. "Is it a gyro?"

He shrugs. "What's that?"

Examining it further, I'm certain it's a gyro. "This is a gyro."

I bring it up to my mouth, taking a bite. While it looks like a gyro, the sauce is a little different—a bit sweeter.

"Whoa! But these taste so much better than the gyro I remember," I murmur with a mouthful, my taste buds dancing.

"Isn't it the best?" he queries, scoffing his down.

He sets out another Styrofoam container between us and opens it. This one has a mountain of fries covered in gravy and cheese.

He sticks a fork into it and brings it up to my lips. "Open wide, my little chickadee," he sings.

I frown at him. This does not look appealing. But I part my lips reluctantly.

And when the taste fills my mouth, I let out a sigh.

Marc throws back his head, laughing.

He hands me a glass of wine and we both devour our dinner in record time.

"I'm sorry about today," I tell him after he's cleaned up the empty take-out containers and refilled our glasses.

"Don't be silly." He scoots closer to me. "You've been through a lot lately."

ISABELLE VAN BUREN

If he only knew just how much I've been dealing with.

"Is Austin okay?" I ask, feeling terrible that he thinks he's the reason I was distraught today.

"He's fine. He was just concerned about you. Don't worry, babe, we'll get you through this. You've started to remember things already, and every day will only be better than the last. And don't pay any mind to the rumors that scatter about this town. It's nothing more than small-town gossip. You and I have always been above that. We know what's true. We know that our love is stronger than all the nonsense talk. None of that matters to us. It's you and me. It's always been just you and me. I know that. And you do too. You're my everything."

He kisses my cheek and reaches a hand around my back.

Leaning into him, I rest my head on his shoulder.

"And you're my anywhere," I whisper, remembering my words from our wedding day. I reach up and press my lips to his neck, and he leans into my touch.

Wrapping my arms around his waist, we grow silent, content with each other's warmth.

"Do you remember the story behind why you call me your anywhere?" he asks.

"No. I just heard myself saying it during our vows on our wedding video."

"From the moment we met, it was like you felt lost in Portland. I could tell that you didn't care for it. You missed home. So, on the weekends I'd ask you where you wanted to go, just to get away for the day. Your answer was always 'Anywhere, but here.' But after a couple of weeks, your response changed to 'Anywhere with you.' And then one day I asked you, and you said, 'It doesn't matter where we go, as long as I'm with you, because you're my anywhere.' And calling me your anywhere just stuck. Every time you say it, even after all these years, it touches me in a way that no other words ever could."

I nuzzle into him, and he tightens his hold on me. "I might not remember the story of why I started to call you that, but…you feel so right."

I lift my head from his shoulder and look at him. "Is it all right that we're up here? I'm not sure people are supposed to climb water towers for sheer amusement, especially the town manager."

"Well, since I am the town manager, doesn't that make this water tower mine? So, I get to do whatever I want with it," he jokes. "I guess it helps that we aren't throwing rocks off it like the kids do," he adds. "Just last week a few kids were up here, throwing rocks, and one of them accidentally hit a windshield, shattering it. Those boys now have some community service to do."

"Yikes!"

The chill in the air runs through me, goose bumps covering my arms and legs.

"Maybe we should head back home. It's getting cooler out," Marc announces, noticing me shiver.

Propping himself up onto his knees, he removes his suit jacket and drapes it over my shoulders, rubbing his hands along my arms, warming me up.

He looks into my eyes and reaches up, tugging on my hair tie, my strawberry-blonde hair pooling in waves onto my shoulders. Desire fills his expression and it's clear that he tries to shake it away, reverting his gaze away from me.

Unable to help himself, he brushes my hair over my shoulder and leans in, kissing my neck.

Noticing that he's still in his work suit—a full three-piece suit, vest and all—it just now registers that he climbed a water tower in a tailored suit and tie.

I think it's safe to say that I've now fallen in love with this boy a bit more than yesterday.

Chapter Sixteen
— The Muddy Trails of Redemption —

I remove the thermometer from Austin's ear; it states 98.6 degrees.

"You don't have a temp, buddy."

"But I really don't feel good. Can I stay home with you just for today?" He pulls the covers up under his chin.

He claims to be sick, that his stomach hurts and he feels dizzy. Something tells me he's feeling fine, but he doesn't want to go to school today. Either he doesn't want to face the kid he punched yesterday, or I freaked him out with my episode involving my dad's call and he's needing some alone time with me. It's not like his mom has been normal lately.

"Are you sure you can't make it through the day at school?"

He shakes his head, giving me those puppy dog eyes.

I decide to keep him home. After yesterday, I don't feel much like being by myself, submerged in thoughts of my dad. I could use a distraction. I tell him to get dressed because we need to drive the girls to school, and we'll return so he can rest.

Once the bus has picked up Jacob, the rest of us hop in the van and we drop the girls off at school. On the way back home, Austin perks up, announcing that he's hungry, requesting some pancakes and confirming my suspicion that he feels perfectly fine.

"Are you sure you want to eat? Does your stomach feel better?"

"I think pancakes will help," he says.

I hide my smile.

When we arrive home, I ask him to gather the eggs from the chickens while I make pancakes. But by the time I'm done cooking, he still hasn't returned, so I go out to the backyard, calling his name. I notice another car in the driveway, but I don't see anyone, including Austin. And he doesn't respond to my calls. But I can hear something coming from inside the barn. When I approach the door, I hear talking, but still don't see where anyone is.

After taking a step inside, I stop to look around. I'd seen the barn sitting center of in the backyard, but I never thought to explore it. A wall is decorated with skillfully placed tools hung above a tool bench, two dirt bikes and three four-wheelers are lined up on one side, and a riding lawn mower and various other larger tools scatter about. Off to the far right, there's a gentleman standing next to a convertible, and Austin is sitting in the driver's seat, turning the steering wheel, acting like he's driving.

When I get closer and my eyes adjust to the darkness, my breath gets caught in my throat.

"I'm sorry, Mom. I'll get out," Austin searches for the door handle in a panic.

"Hi, Sara. I'm here to pick up the car to get it detailed before the parade this weekend," the gentleman says.

"Whose car is this?" I croak out.

"It's yours," Austin quickly states. "Well, it was Pepere's, but it's yours now. I know it's not my car. I know I'm not supposed to play with it. I'm sorry, Mom." He scrambles to get the door open.

The gentleman remains quiet, eyes fixed on me.

My feet are stuck in place. I desperately search my memory for anything that'll tell me how my dad's nineteen sixty-seven dark blue Pontiac GTO has ended up here.

"Pepere's?" I question, after registering what he said.

Austin exits the car, and the gentleman closes the door for him. Facing me, he bears a look that suggests he was just caught doing the ultimate crime.

"Yeah, it was his before he died," he finally speaks.

The realization that he's referring to Marc's dad hits me. But then, how would he have gotten it? Unless, of course, this isn't my dad's car. Maybe it's one like it, instead?

Willing my legs to work, I walk over to the passenger side and open the door. When I do, my eyes fixate on the custom foot mats that my dad had gotten made, embossed with the saying: *Work hard, play harder*. That was the motto my dad lived by.

This is, without a doubt, my dad's car. He was a car enthusiast and while I was a girly-girl, we always shared a love for cars. We'd sometimes go to car auctions and car shows together. It was our special time that we shared since my sister never enjoyed tagging along and Timmy was too young, only getting in the way. He won this car at an auction for thirty-nine hundred dollars.

But how did Marc's dad get his hands on it?

"Can you believe Jean bought this car for only two hundred dollars?" the gentleman chimes in.

"Yeah. That's…incredible."

"I'll be sure to get it detailed as quickly as possible. I have a few other cars ahead of this one, but it shouldn't be more than a couple of days, for sure by Sunday," he explains, seemingly unfazed.

When he starts it up and pulls it out of the barn, the familiar sound of the rebuilt engine fills my ears, and I'm back to feeling that sinking hole in the pit of my chest.

"Can we go for a ride on the four-wheeler?" Austin asks.

How am I supposed to move on, get over the fact that my dad—both of my parents, for that matter—are no longer around? No matter how many distractions I busy myself with, there are constant reminders of them and of the life I once had—or I thought I once had?

Austin tugs on my arm, gazing up at me through his long blonde eyelashes.

"Sure," I respond, absentmindedly. "Go eat your breakfast."

"Yes!" I watch him trot out of the barn and up the back stairs and into the house.

All my thoughts are jumbled between those that are reality and those that are mere fake thoughts that I weaved together while in a coma. Nonetheless, I did have a dad, a mom, a sister, and even a little brother that I remember and that I loved. And now, I'm left with a sister whose gone great lengths to mask our past, with good reason, I suppose, and a brother whom I've grown concerned about.

"Mama," Austin calls from the doorway, pulling me back to the present. "Dad is on the phone."

I scurry to the house, still feeling the heaviness in my chest.

"Hello?" I say into the receiver.

"Good morning, beautiful," Marc replies.

A smile grows on my face. "Hi."

"I heard that Austin didn't go to school. Is he sick?"

Wow, news travels fast around this town.

"He claimed not to feel well, but he's busy easting a stack of pancakes right now, so I think he's fine."

"Oh good. Maybe he just needed a day off. I can certainly relate."

I hear a woman in the background tell him that his ten o'clock meeting has arrived.

"Sorry. I hate to be so brief, but I'm running late for my meeting with the planning committee. But feel free to stop by the office later. I could use a beautiful distraction from my otherwise dull day."

Suddenly the weight in my chest is replaced with a flutter. And, while he can't see me, I feel my face flush.

"I have a couple cans of Moxie in the refrigerator that we can share," he adds with a hint of amusement.

"Well...in that case, I'll stop by for sure," I retort, returning his playful banter.

We exchange good-byes and I return to the kitchen to find Austin making good work of his tall stack of pancakes.

"What time can we go?" he asks, through a mouthful.

"Where? To see your dad?"

"No, four-wheeling."

My brow creases with confusion. "What are you talking about?"

"You said we could go for a ride. We can go have a picnic at the camp. Please, Mom," he drawls, bouncing up and down on the chair.

"Austin, I have no idea how to drive a four-wheeler, or the way to...camp?"

His big blue eyes widen. "Of course you do. It's easy. We went for a ride just before you had your accident." He raises his finger in the air. "Wait, did you forget? Daddy says that you don't remember some things because you lost your memories when you hit that moose. Sometimes, I forget to do my homework, but it's not because I had an accident. It's that I really did forget. And sometimes I just don't want to do it," he says, his voice low. "Plus, I can drive. I do it with you and Dad all the time. Did you lose your memories of me riding dirt bikes too?"

I can't help but smile at how he rambles on in his sweet, tiny voice.

"Fine, we can go. But I'll drive." I don't admit that I did, in fact, forget about him riding dirt bikes, or driving four-wheelers, or that he can down a tall stack of pancakes in under ten minutes flat. Boys and their appetites! They have so much energy that they need constant fuel. He reminds me of Timmy—the Timmy that I remember.

In his adorable authoritative tone, he tells me that he'll teach me how to drive, and that we need to pack a cooler for lunch, and I need to change into jeans and sneakers because it could be muddy. And immediately I'm left regretting my decision. But watching him bustle around, filling the cooler with lunch and drinks, I realize that his excitement is the kind of distraction that I need today. And he likely does, as well.

While I'm changing into a pair of jeans and a T-shirt, I hear a rumble coming from outside. I peer through the bedroom window and see that Austin has pulled the ATV out of the barn and he's waiting for me, extra helmet in hand. I doubt an eight-year-old boy should be driving on his own, but it doesn't appear to be his first time.

When I make my way outside, the fact that I haven't a clue where we're going or how to get there hits me. I really am just going along for the ride.

Austin hands me a helmet and scoots forward on the four-wheeler, making room for me to sit behind him.

"Do you know the way?"

He points in the direction of the overgrown grass at the back of the house. "The trail," he bellows over the loud roar of the ATV.

My stomach churns as the anxiety grows. I don't recall ever riding one of these, and the thought of it makes me want to run in the house and echo Austin's earlier claim, that I too am not feeling well. But, instead, I swing a leg over and straddle the seat behind him.

Austin motions for me to grab the handlebars, and placing his hands next to mine, he pushes a button with his thumb and the four-wheeler jerks forward, rolling us toward the tall grass. I help to steer us onto a gravel path, and he presses on the gas, sending the ATV barreling down the way. He's a pro at this; it's certainly not his first rodeo.

We ride for a while and come upon an open field. Austin slows and points off in the distance to a few large tractors, larger than the one that I had an encounter with last week.

"That's mon oncle Harold," he mumbles through his helmet while propping himself up from the seat.

"What are they doing?"

"I can see the tiller and seeder, so they must've already started planting the potatoes," he hollers. "Can we go see them?"

"No, Austin. Let them work, okay?"

He doesn't protest. He lowers himself back down onto the seat and sends the four-wheeler moving forward again.

Along the way, we pass old rundown barns, their rooftops caving in or walls hanging on by a nail, large fallen trees, and small shacks tucked away in the woods.

After a while, we happen upon a four-way intersection in the trail and Austin slows the ATV. "Can we go through the puddle? Please, Mom?" He looks back at me.

I gaze around his tiny frame and notice that the puddle he's referring to looks more like a river—a mucky, sludge-filled one.

I raise my feet from the floorboard, wincing. And Austin must take it as my cue that I'm all in because within a millisecond the ATV is charging forward. I let out a loud yelp, and squeezing my eyes shut, I clutch the handlebars tighter while we plow through the water.

Once we make it out of the grimy water and back onto safe ground, Austin jumps off the seat, raising both hands in the air and jumping up and down victoriously.

"That was awesome, Mom!" he exclaims with so much excitement his body trembles. Or maybe he's trembling because he's covered in globs of mud all the way up to his neck.

Feeling the cold wet water seep through my sneakers and pants, I look down in sheer disgust. Who knows what was lurking in that murky water—that very mud that's now clinging to my skin.

I'm not certain who starts laughing first, but suddenly, a chuckle rolls through us both, sending us into a fit of uncontrollable laughter. I never, in a million and one years, thought I'd find myself in the back roads in the middle of the woods, covered up to my knees in slime and mud. And now, with adrenaline coursing through me, I'm unpredictably finding myself enjoying it. I suppose it's impossible not to draw on Austin's sheer exhilaration.

"Come on. Let's get ourselves somewhere where we can dry off." My teeth chatter.

Austin hops back on the four-wheeler. He turns the key and presses the button on the handle to get it to start, but after multiple attempts, the ATV refuses to oblige.

"Are you forgetting a step?"

"No, Mom," he declares, annoyed. "Maybe it's out of gas."

Great. *How did I not check before we left the house?* It seems to be a natural occurrence with me lately.

Austin removes the gas cap from the tank between his legs. "There's gas," he announces.

"Try it again."

He does, but the four-wheeler doesn't even let out so much as a cough.

"Maybe going through the puddle wasn't a good idea," he admits, a defeated look on his face.

What now? I haven't a clue where we are or how far any main road is from here.

"We could walk to camp and call Dad," Austin says, answering my thoughts.

"Where's camp?"

"It's just over there," he directs, pointing right. He jumps down and I follow suit.

Once standing, I look in the direction he pointed and see an opening. There seems to be a camp about a couple of hundred yards in the distance. I'm not sure if we should leave the four-wheeler here unattended, but considering we can't move it, I'm not sure anyone else could either.

I unstrap the mud-stained cooler from the rack on the back of the ATV and Austin takes the lead down the trail.

When we arrive at the camp—our camp, I'm assuming—I notice that it sits along a lake. And as we walk onto the property, the water comes into full view. It's spectacular. I stop, taking in the scenery. While I shiver from the cool air hitting my wet clothes and skin, the sun shines down through the trees, fighting to warm me.

Austin bounces toward the camp and I follow him inside the log cabin. The interior is modest with only the bare necessities, but it's well-kept and has a way of feeling homey.

I rest the cooler on the table in the kitchen, and Austin appears from the hallway with a couple of towels in hand.

After we dry off as much as possible, I wrap a towel around him, and he walks to the telephone resting on the counter.

We call Marc, but the secretary tells us that he left for lunch about ten minutes ago, so we ask her to have him call us at the camp when he returns.

"I'm hungry. Can we eat lunch?" Austin pushes open the screen door.

"Didn't you just eat pancakes?"

"Yeah. But it's lunchtime and I'm hungry."

"Okay." I open the cooler to see what he's packed for us to eat.

"I want to eat outside," he announces, disappearing out the screen door.

I remove a loaf of bread and a jar of grape jelly. Clearly, he knew what he wanted for lunch. Rummaging through the cabinets for a plate, I find a jar of peanut butter and an unopened bag of BBQ Humpty Dumpty potato chips.

After fixing us both a sandwich, I grab the bag of chips and two bottles of red Gatorade that are tucked in the bottom of the cooler and go join him outside. He's busy skipping rocks by the water, but he comes running when he sees me.

As I'm laying our lunch on the picnic table, a truck pulls into the gravel drive. An older gentleman leans out of the driver's side window. "I saw you guys here and I thought you'd like some rhubarb that Margaret pulled from the garden this morning."

I walk over to the man, and he gives me a once-over. "Did you guys hop into the lake?" he asks, chuckling.

"No. Austin took us through what he calls a puddle on the four-wheeler."

He shakes his head, wincing.

"Mama," Austin calls out. "Hey, Mama."

I put up a finger to tell him to wait a minute.

"Um, Mom," he calls out louder.

Both the gentleman and I swing our heads in his direction. He sits on his knees at the picnic table, sandwich up to his lips, a bite taken out.

"Did you put peanut butter in my sandwich?" he murmurs, his mouth full.

The moment the last words reach his lips, a consciousness washes over me. He has a peanut allergy. I'd forgotten he was allergic to peanuts, but now I remember. And possibly a moment too late.

"Oh shit!" I exclaim. "Spit it out!" I sprint to him.

He spits the sandwich on the ground.

"I forgot. Oh, my God, Austin, I'm so sorry, I forgot."

"My pen," he croaks, through heavy, labored breaths.

Before I register what he's asking for, the older gentleman is rushing out of the cabin, an EpiPen raised in the air. "I got it," he announces, jogging toward us. I hadn't even noticed him get out of his truck, let alone run inside the camp.

He hands the EpiPen to me, and, in one swift motion, I remove the cap and stick the needle into Austin's thigh. I stare at him, willing him to catch his breath while I silently curse myself. *How could I have forgotten something as important as this?* Even if I've forgotten nearly everything about my life, as a mom, this is the one thing that I should have never let slip my mind.

I watch as his breathing, and my heart, slows.

"I'm so sorry," I manage to squawk out, tears forming.

"It's okay, Mom. I know it's just your memories that you lost. It's not your fault."

How can this kid, that practically stopped breathing only minutes ago, forgive this easily?

I drop down to my knees and throw my arms around him, enveloping him in a hug.

When I've just about squeezed the air he has left right out of him, I notice that the older gentleman has returned to his truck. Before he pulls away, I wave a hand in the air to get his attention.

"Thank you," I say, walking toward him.

"No bother. Glad I could help. Do you need a ride somewhere?"

"Well, the ATV is stuck down the trail a bit. It wouldn't start back up after we went through that water. We tried calling Marc, but he wasn't in the office."

"Is the bike far up the trail?" He throws a finger over his shoulder toward the woods.

"It's just a couple of hundred yards up that way."

"Something tells me you may have flooded the intake. If you want, I can call Conrad at the garage."

"You don't have to do that. I can call him."

"It might take him a bit to get here. I don't think Dean's around. Someone said he skipped town a couple of days ago, so Conrad might be a bit backed up with work on his own. It's worth a try, though," he explains. "And, if it'll be a while, I can drive you home."

"Are you sure?"

"Of course."

I look over to Austin, who shoves a fist-full of potato chips in his mouth. Thankfully, he looks to be feeling better.

He pulls his truck back into the driveway and I go inside. I find a local phone book next to the telephone and search for the number for Conrad's Garage.

After a gentleman—I'm guessing, Conrad—answers, I explain to him our situation and he tells me that he can be here within the hour.

Glancing at the clock, I realize that I've lost track of time and it's now nearly two. There's no way that I'll make it home and to town in time to pick the girls up from school. I scan the phone book for Claudette Theriault and dial the number. When Marc's mom answers, I tell her what has happened and without hesitation she offers to pick them up from school. I thank her profusely and hang up feeling blessed beyond measure.

When I return outside, I tell them that Conrad will be here in an hour.

ISABELLE VAN BUREN

"I need some Benadryl," Austin advises.

"I can drive you home and then return to wait for Conrad," the gentleman tells us.

While I feel that I can't let this man, who's done more than enough for us already, do that, I look to Austin and know that he's right; he needs Benadryl and it can't wait an hour.

The gentleman stands from the picnic table and starts walking toward his truck, and before I can think of protesting, he tells Austin to come along and that he'll let him turn the key in the ignition.

I quickly gather everything we brought, shoving it all back into the cooler, and lock the door to the camp before I join them. When I slide into the truck, Austin's sitting in the middle, absorbed in talk about dirt bikes and racing and farming, turkey hunting and fishing, and something about fighter planes and air shows. They both ramble on so fast I can barely keep up on our way down the road to the house.

When we pull into the driveway, I see Marc's car, as well as Claudette's.

"Since Marc is home, you don't need to return to wait for Conrad. Marc can do it," I tell the gentleman before exiting the truck.

"C'est bon."

"And thank you. Honestly, I appreciate all that you did for us today."

"Like I said earlier, no bother at all."

Austin hops out, and I take his hand and walk us toward the house.

"What's that man's name?" I ask, leaning close.

"That's Mister Lajoie. His camp is next to ours," he whispers back. But then he redirects his attention when we hear Jacob exit the barn on a dirt bike.

He releases my hand and runs toward him.

"Don't forget you need to take Benadryl," I call out to him, but he doesn't hear me over the noise of the bike.

When I enter the house, I find Claudette and Marc standing shoulder to shoulder in the living room, their attention focused on the television. As I place the stalks of rhubarb on the counter, I hear the sound coming from the TV: *"After seventeen years on death row, Robert O'Reilly may have finally caught the break he's been desperately needing."*

A photo of a much older version of my dad is displayed on the screen. The full head of brown hair that he once had is now thinning, his hairline receding, and sprinkles of greys are peppered throughout. And wrinkles surround his familiar green eyes that now look weary and gloomy.

My knees buckle from under me, and I drop straight to the floor.

Both Marc and Claudette rush to me. Marc lowers himself next to me and my limp body falls into his lap. My eyes remain glued to the television. I can't look away, I'm stunned.

"*With minutes before his execution yesterday, new credible evidence surfaced. Talk about a stroke of luck for the gentleman accused of killing his wife and two police officers back in nineteen seventy-six. It is said that a gentleman has come forth, admitting to his involvement in the crime.*"

A photo of my uncle Derry—my mom's older brother—flashes up on the screen.

"*Mr. Derry Sullivan of Stamford, Connecticut, is the only remaining son of the late Donald Sullivan, who was convicted sixteen years ago of a string of brutal murders and was said to be the prominent member of the Irish mafia back in the sixties and seventies. Donald Sullivan only served five months in prison before he died of cancer in March of nineteen seventy-eight.*"

Another photo flashes on screen; this one of Dean—my little brother, Timmy—and the reporter goes on to say, "*His involvement has yet to be confirmed, but it appears that this gentleman, a Dean Dumond of Van Buren, Maine, has also come forth with additional evidence to support Mr. O'Reilly's innocence. If the judge finds in Mr. O'Reilly's favor, he could walk free in as early as a few days. We'll bring you more details as the story continues to develop."*

An ear-curdling shriek escapes my lips and Marc rocks me in his arms.

"It's about time," I hear Claudette declare. "It's *about* time," she repeats.

When I look up at her, she gives me a slight nod and weak smile, a sign of recognition that she knows—that she's likely always known.

The front door flies open and Megan rushes in, stopping abruptly when she sees us. She raises both hands to her mouth, cupping it, muffling her cries.

Chapter Seventeen
— The Fog Has Lifted —

Megan's two kids enter the room, balancing a couple of pizza boxes in their arms.

"Whoa, is that Dean?" a small voice from behind us asks. "Is he a celebrity now?"

Before any of us can answer, the back door flies open, and both boys come bounding in.

"I need Benadryl, Mom," Austin advises, unaware.

"I'm hungry. They had that disgusting meatloaf for lunch. I only ate the mashed potatoes," Jacob proclaims, eyeing the pizza boxes in the middle of the table.

"Benadryl? Did Austin have a reaction today?" Marc asks.

"Yeah. We took the four-wheeler to the camp, and I mistakenly made him a peanut butter and jelly sandwich. There was a jar of peanut butter in the cabinet, so I grabbed it, forgetting he was allergic," I admit, feeling the guilt creep up inside again and anticipating him to chastise me.

"Brad used the camp last weekend. He must have left the jar there, not knowing. I'll have to tell him," he states, anger or disappointment absent from his tone.

"Let me get you some allergy medicine, Austin," Claudette states while I try to calm my spinning head. "The rest of you, come with me." She wraps an arm around Jacob's shoulders, directing him to follow her up the stairs.

"But I'm hungry," he protests.

Abby remains perched on the bottom stair, her eyes glued to the television screen.

"We'll get you something to eat, but right now Mom and Dad need a moment to talk."

Emma appears at the top of the stairs, swinging a Barbie doll by the hair. "Mama, can you braid my doll's hair?"

"Yes. Bring it here," I tell her without hesitation. Life doesn't stop because I've been keeping a deep dark secret all these years. These kids know nothing about any of it; they only know that they need their mom. And, while all their requests may feel small in comparison to my current situation, to them, these needs are grand and the most important in the moment. Kids are simple, adults are the complicated ones. I don't know when exactly that changes in one's life—when someone's needs and desires become often hard to bear. And then you throw the Irish mafia into the mix and your life takes on a whole new level of complexity.

"But—" Claudette tries to protest, but I cut her off.

"It's fine. They'll learn about it at some point anyway, it might as well be from us." I pick myself up from the floor. "Austin does need Benadryl though."

She nods and disappears down the hallway.

I motion for the rest of the kids to gather around the dining room table. Megan doesn't move from her spot in the entryway, so I go to her and wrap an arm around her shoulders, nudging her forward.

And then I proceed to tell them that they have a grandfather they've never met. "He was accused of killing your grandma many years ago, before any of you were born, and he's been living in a prison all this time. But now, it looks like the bad man who did kill your grandma has finally admitted to it."

"Can Grandpa come live with us?" Jacob chimes in, a mouth full of pizza.

I shrug. "I don't know. We still don't know if or when he'll get out of prison. They're working out those details right now and it could take some time."

"I thought your dad was dead?" Abby asks.

"I know," I admit, sorrow overwhelming me. "A lot happened in Auntie Megan and my life that is…hard to explain."

"Your aunt and your mama were protecting you— they were protecting all of us by not telling us," Marc interjects.

Both Megan and I swing our heads in sync in his direction, shocked.

"I knew and I should have said something to you. But when you came out of your coma and you had amnesia, I didn't know how much you had remembered and…I guess I didn't want to freak you out. You already had so much to deal with. And, if I'm being honest with myself, I was scared too. You told me the day before your accident that your dad was on death row and what had happened to your mom. You were headed to see him when you had your accident. I didn't know about Dean and his involvement though."

"Neither did I until a couple of days ago." I turn my attention to Megan. "Dean's our brother. He's Timmy," I tell her, her mouth dropping open before the last word slips off my tongue. I tell her about the investigator and the keychain and Dean's confession to me while the room remains silent, all seven sets of eyes fixed on me, Claudette having rejoined us.

"I'm sorry I didn't tell you guys. I was scared," I admit for the first time, not only to them, but to myself.

"I was too," Megan confesses.

"You both had good reasons," Claudette affirms. "I was scared too. Jean had told me about it before he died. I knew and didn't say anything either."

"So is Grandma alive too?" Emma asks, attempting to brush her doll's hair, not looking up.

"Is Dean our uncle?" Megan's daughter, Sierra, asks.

"No, Grandma isn't alive," I tell Emma, taking the mangled-hair Barbie and oversized brush from her.

"And, yes, Dean is your uncle," Megan says.

I realize that the kids don't understand the extent of what we've been talking about, especially Emma as young as she is, but I feel an incredible sense of relief now that they all know, and that there are no more secrets. Unless, of course, my memory has another secret yet to be revealed to me. I can only hope not.

"So, wait, if he's our uncle, then that means Josh was lying. You didn't kiss Dean the other night," Austin interjects, beaming. "I knew it!"

"Ew! Of course, Mama didn't kiss Dean. She only kisses us and Daddy," Emma says, her tiny face scrunched up in disgust.

Marc glances at me, winking, making me melt into the floor.

"You do know that the news about Dean will shake this town," Claudette states.

"I'm not worried," Marc replies. "We'll deal with that."

"It was on the news at Pat's Pizza when I stopped in to pick up supper on my way home from school. Everyone there was already stringing up predictions of his involvement," Megan tells us.

"Well, as of right now, no one knows that Robert is your dad. And unless the news stations figure it out, we'll have time to get things squared away before the town catches wind of it," Marc states calmly.

"I know I haven't talked to Dad in a really long time, but maybe we should try calling him?" Megan questions hesitantly.

I tell her that we can try but based on my unsuccessful attempts the past few days, we'll likely get nowhere. It's not like the guards are the most helpful, and now with the news swarming around, it's unlikely that they've changed their ways. "Unfortunately, we need to wait for him to call us or until things play out."

"Let's not talk about this with anyone until we find out more information. Okay, everyone?" Marc advises, looking at each of the kids intently. They all nod, but I think all the adults understand we're asking a difficult task of them. They are kids after all.

The doorbell rings and I shoot a look at Megan, my stomach sinking at the possibility of who could be on the other side of the door. *Reporters? Police? Someone from Mom's family?*

Claudette rushes to answer it. Within seconds, she returns with a gentleman in tow.

"I'm here to drop off some of the supplies for the cookout," he announces, looking around the room at the mass of people.

"Ah, yes, thanks. I'll show you where to put them," Marc tells him. "Will you be all right?" he whispers when he passes me.

"Yeah. I'm good."

He leans in and plants a soft kiss on my cheek, brushing his shoulder against mine, sending a bolt of lightning through me. And then he joins the gentleman and they both walk in the direction of the front door just as the doorbell rings a second time.

Marc opens it and Conrad's standing on the porch, a set of keys in his hand and Dean's collie by his side. "I have the ATV on the trailer on the back of my truck; I couldn't get it to start. I can either bring it down to the shop to have a look at or leave it here for you."

Marc looks in my direction, his brow creased.

I fill him in on Austin and my adventure and he laughs.

"The puddle was this big, Dad," Austin explains excitedly, arms spread wide at his sides.

"Well, that explains why you guys are covered in mud," he jokes.

The three men disappear outside, submerged in chatter about the new revelation they heard on the news about Conrad's trusty employee. And the kids scatter from the table, bellies full, minds overwhelmed, leaving Megan, Claudette, and me alone and wordless.

Later that evening, after a lot of coaxing to get the kids to do their homework and they've all fought over who's going to take a shower first, Emma asks if I can read a bedtime story "like we used to do."

"I think Mama might be too tired tonight. She's had a long day. I'll read you a book," Marc tells her, looking up from the stack of papers strewn across the dining room table. He's giving me the rundown on the Memorial Day festivities happening this weekend and the cookout that we're hosting here at the house tomorrow night.

"No. Of course, we can read a bedtime story," I interject.

"Yay!" she exclaims running up the stairs, announcing to the others that we're reading a bedtime book.

Marc looks at me. "Are you sure?"

When he returned this evening, he asked if I'd prefer to cancel the cookout, and he was surprised when I was instead excited and asked how I could help. With today's news that my dad will likely be exonerated and that I've finally come clean with my seventeen-year secret that's been weighing heavily on me, I feel like new air has filled my lungs, energizing me and clearing my head, allowing me to revert my attention on what matters most—my family.

"Of course."

Marc strings an arm around my waist, and we make our way to the bedroom, the little ones already claiming their spots on the king-size bed.

"I got a new book at the library today," Jacob announces, reaching out a book to me as I squeeze into a micro-sized spot on my side of the bed.

"*Astro's Epic Summer Adventure,*" I read the cover, and then open the book to chapter one where I begin to read about a cute alien who lives on the moon.

At the end of the chapter, I peek up from the story to find both Emma and Austin fast asleep, laying cozily between me and Marc.

Jacob looks up at me from the foot of the bed, barely able to keep his eyes open.

Abby gets up from her spot, yawning and mumbling that she's going to bed. Jacob follows behind, hugging his pillow.

I glance over to Marc, Emma curled up to his side, his arm encompassing her. He too can hardly keep his eyes open.

After laying the book on the nightstand, I lower my head on the pillow, turning to my side, facing him.

He reaches out a hand and I take it in mine, and he mouths "I love you." When he looks at me, the love in his eyes is real, sending heat from my toes to my nose.

While gazing at each other, the world melts around us as we fall into a deep, restful sleep.

The next morning, I awake refreshed, feeling like the dense fog has finally lifted. There's a lot to be said for a clean conscience and ten hours of sleep.

I nudge Emma and Austin awake, and it's back to life as usual.

Driving through town on my way to the girls' schools, we observe people putting up flags and decorations along Main Street, and there's a flurry of activity every corner we turn. Even the sign at the little motel downtown reads *No Vacancy*. It appears that this festival is shaping up to be quite an event.

When I drop Emma off at school, she kisses me goodbye and assures me that she won't tell Matthew that Dean's her uncle, adding, "because it's none of his business," making me smirk.

I swing by the restaurant for my morning coffee. Upon entering, I overhear talk about Dean, and while I can't understand everything they're saying, it's evident how shaken everyone is.

"Gertrude thinks maybe he's the one that started the fire at the old mill," a gentleman states. The others around him dismiss that claim, making up their own predictions instead.

The woman behind the counter—Madame Cecile—pays no mind to the whirl of gossip around her; she goes about filling up coffee cups and serving up breakfast, like it's just another day, making my heart warm even more for her.

After multiple exchanges of "Good morning" and Madame Cecile waving me off from paying for my coffee, I walk along the sidewalk to the post office, Starbucks in hand and hopeful that a new letter from my dad awaits me.

Sure enough, once the gentleman behind the counter hands me the new key, I discover an envelope in the box. Looking at the postmark, I see it was sent four days ago—two days before my dad's execution day and all the new developments. I contemplate not reading it; I'm not sure I want to know how he was feeling right before he was scheduled to die.

"Is your pig at home?" a woman calls out from her spot in line.

When I turn around, she's looking at me. I point a hand to my chest. "Me? My pig?"

"Yeah. I think it was Wilber I saw digging up Lawrence's lawn on my way here."

I shrug and she tells me it's the house with the horse stable on State Street, about five or so houses down from mine.

When I get to the stables, sure enough, the pink and black potbellied pig is doing donuts in the front yard, stopping every so often to raise his snout in the air to let out a squeal. A gentleman stands at the end of his driveway watching him, along with two majestic horses from their pen. The little pig gives off a show.

"He's cutting up a rug this morning," the gentleman proclaims, laughing when I exit the van.

"I can't believe he got out and made his way here."

"It's become a weekly occurrence. At least he's not digging up Annette's flowers this time," he says.

"How am I supposed to get him back home?"

The pig stops abruptly when he sees me and flops down, rolling onto his back like a dog.

"Wilber's the only pig I've seen do that," the gentleman declares, amused. "He won't let me get near him, but you should be able to scoop him right up and take him home in your van. I'm beginning to think he enjoys car rides more than his visits with the horses."

I should feel a repulsion at the thought of scooping up a pig in my arms but looking at Wilber with his little hoofs in the air, nose wriggling, eyes fixed on me, he makes me feel all warm and fuzzy.

Without a second thought, I walk toward him and drop myself to the ground, hoisting him in my arms and cradling him like a baby. He nudges his snout against my chest as if to say, *"Hey, sorry for running off. Please don't scold me,"* just like a little kid would do.

I slide open the door to the van and contemplate my next move. Eyeing Emma's booster seat, I lower him into it, and he sits back on his bum, his front two feet resting on the seat between his back legs. He lets me strap the seatbelt across him as I let out a chuckle, amused by my fifth child looking back at me.

After offering my apologies to the gentleman, I take my potbellied pet home.

When we arrive at the house there's a swarm of people in the side yard setting up large tents and tables. And after securing Wilber back in his pen and shoving the letter from my dad into my pocketbook, I make my way to them, asking if there's anything I can do to help. A woman—Doris, she introduced herself as—asks if I still have the flags and banners from last year's party, the ones that Marc told her were stored away in the attic.

I first tell her that I didn't even know we had an attic, making her laugh. And then I add that I'll try my best to find it and the decorations, but if I'm not back in twenty minutes, it's probably best to send someone looking for me since I'm not a fan of attics and cobwebs and spiders and whatever else lurks in dark places. She assures me that she'll come searching if she should hear my screams.

After I tug on the cord attached to the concealed pull-down attic ladder, I look up into the darkness and garner the courage to stride up the steps. At the top, I see that it's not as dark as I imagined it; the light from a vent on the wall at the far end seeps through, casting a glow across the floor. Eyeing a lightbulb above my head, I yank on the string, illuminating the room even more.

It doesn't take me long to spot the red, white, and blue flags and pennants stacked on the top of some boxes. But my attention is quickly drawn to an old black storage chest, a stack of cardboard boxes sitting atop. I know immediately that it's my trunk, the one I had as a teenager—the one that is lined with cedar and housed the oversized handmade quilt that my grandmother—my dad's mother who passed away when I was ten—had made me. She had sewn one for

Megan as well. One side was a dark blue wool fabric that had a scattering of white polka dots, and the other side was made up of scraps of various leftover pieces of material.

I remove the boxes and flip open the lid to be met with that very quilt that I insisted on using despite the fact the wool was so itchy. I'd pile it on top of me during the nights that I missed her most. She was a prominent part of my childhood since she lived next door and my dad and she were very close, especially after my grandpa died. Megan and I would often go over to visit after school, and we'd either play hide and seek in the house or accompany my grandma on her wooden porch swing. She left an overwhelming hole in my life when she passed away; one that I still feel as I stand here hugging the quilt to my chest while picturing her sweet face, glistening white hair, petite structure, and gentlest demeanor. I even smell her perfume. Every time I see Oreo cookies, I think of her since they were her favorite and she'd have just one for dessert after dinner.

I swipe at my eyes and gaze into the trunk. Lowering myself onto my knees, I remove a stack of envelopes all addressed to me at my P.O. Box, and all with the same return address: Connecticut Wargate Correctional Institution. There are well over fifty or so that line the bottom of the chest.

"Sara," a voice calls up to me, startling me and making me throw the envelopes back.

"Yeah..." I clear my throat. "I'm here. I found the decorations." I scramble to return the quilt back to its original spot.

"Thank goodness. I was getting worried that you may have come face to face with Freddy Krueger, or the world's largest tarantula spun you up in his web," Doris retorts.

"Well, you know, I wasn't scared until just this minute. Thanks," I jest, totally creeped out.

I grab the stack of banners and make my way to the ladder. As I approach, I hear the ring of a telephone, and thoughts of my dad fill my head. Maybe it's him calling to tell me he's okay? Or better yet, finally freed?

I cautiously climb down one step at a time, and in a hurry, hand the decorations to Doris. Running to the phone, I grab the receiver, but when I bring it to my ear all I hear is a dial tone. Who knows how long the phone was ringing, but apparently it was long enough for the caller to realize I was busy. If it was my dad, I can only hope he'll call back soon, knowing that I must have seen the news and want nothing more than to know what's going on and to hear his voice.

I busy myself around the house for the rest of the day, remaining within earshot of the telephone, until it's time to pick up the girls from school. But no call is received.

I make it back to the house just in time for the boys to be dropped off and a large RV to pull into the driveway.

All four kids bolt in the direction of the gentleman, exclaiming, "It's mon oncle Gerard!"

And when he hops out of the camper, they trample him in a group hug. A woman rounds the camper, and the kids wrap her in an embrace as well.

"Ma tante Rita!" Austin bellows.

"You guys sure have grown," she remarks.

"I'm in kindergarten," Emma offers.

"I can tell. You've gotten so tall."

The gentleman looks at Abby. "And you, there's no question as to why you're Miss Potato Blossom, my belle fille." He hands her a bag. "I meant to mail it to you, but I figured I'd deliver it in person instead."

Her eyes beam with excitement as she takes the gift.

He then proceeds to hand each of the other kids something, and they offer hugs as thanks before darting over to me.

"Look Mom, it's my favorite, a whoopie pie. It's bigger than my head!" Jacob exclaims. He's not joking, the thing looks more like a birthday cake than a whoopie pie.

"I thought of you when I saw it in Houlton. I remembered the whoopie pie eating contest we had the last time I was here. I'd love to see you try and finish this one," he jokes.

"Can I eat it, Mom?"

"You can have a piece, not the entire thing. How about you share it with your brother and sisters."

"Mon oncle got me a guitar pick," Austin exclaims.

"It has Elvis' autograph on it," the gentleman tells him.

"Wow! You brought it all the way from Nashville?" Austin exclaims. "I'm going to use it right now." He bounces toward the house.

The gentleman walks to me and hands me a bag of Starbucks coffee, and immediately I know I like this man. "I have three more bags for you in the RV," he tells me.

I reach up on my toes, hugging him.

A car pulls up behind us, Marc behind the wheel, his face cracked with a wide smile that reaches his eyes.

After they exchange hugs and hellos, we all gather in the yard that's been transformed from a field of weeds into an outstanding patriotic celebration, with even a DJ booth and a well-stocked bar, and a piñata hung for the kids. Claudette and Megan join us shortly after, and Marc reminds me that the gentleman is his uncle—the brother of Marc's dad—who lives in

Tennessee. And in a small corner of my mind, I remember that—I remember him.

While Claudette, Marc, and his uncle are engrossed in conversation about the new crop of potatoes being planted, Megan and I set out drinks and appetizers.

I catch Marc from the corner of my eye, his intense gaze on me. "You'll have to excuse me for a minute, but I haven't properly said hi to my wife," he announces, taking long strides in my direction.

Within the quick seconds it takes him to reach me, I drink him in. He wears a pair of black pinstriped slacks that hang just right on his hips, a white button-up shirt, the top button undone and the sleeves rolled up a bit, a satin pink necktie that drapes loosely from his neck, and a most mischievous grin on his face. Real men can *certainly* wear pink.

He gets within arm's length of me, and I can't wait a second longer. I grab hold of his tie and pull him to me. And with our mouths brushing and his body pressed against me, he tangles his hand in my hair on the nape of my neck, igniting my desire. It's not much longer before our lips part and I get lost in the sweet taste of him.

Well over a hundred people fill our yard—friends and family from all around. As I scan the yard, I see a lot of familiar faces; it's possible that the entire town is here. The growing group of kids is scattered about, playing various games and eating way too many sweets. And even Father Tom showed up, carrying a platter of Bismarck donuts, which Marc tells me is my favorite.

The rest of the evening is filled with food, drinks, laughter, and conversation—a lot of it surrounding the news about Dean, but at least there's no mention of him or my dad being linked to me and Megan, that piece remains undisclosed to everyone.

"Mama, what are drugs?" Emma asks, sitting at the table.

"Drugs are like smoking cigarettes, but a lot worse," Jacob answers before I can even register what's she's asking.

"Why do you ask?" I place a plate of food on the table in front of her and struggle with the right words to explain to a four-year-old what drugs are. And at the same time, I want to bottle up her innocence and shield her from the cruel, harsh world where she'll learn all about drugs and more in no time.

"I just heard Travis say that Uncle Dean must be on drugs," she responds. "I've seen him smoking cigarettes."

I dart my eyes around the row of tables, looking for anyone who may have heard her proclaim that Dean is her uncle. But everyone is engrossed in their dinner and small talk.

I lean into Emma's ear. "Remember, no one knows that Dean's your uncle, so let's not talk about it right now. All right?"

She shrugs and brings a forkful of potato salad to her mouth. "Okay," she murmurs, unfazed.

"And don't tell anyone that Uncle Dean was doing drugs. We don't know that." I feel a need to defend him, to protect him from the countless rumors. He is my little brother, after all.

After we eat, I pull Father Tom aside and tell him how I had seemingly already told Marc about my parents the day before my accident and fill him in on my new discovery about Dean. My close friendship with him quickly becomes obvious; he's not only attentive during our conversation, but he displays a sense of caring that suggests he's a true friend.

When the day bleeds into night and the air has cooled, a few of the men spark a campfire, and everyone drags chairs and blankets over, forming a circle. The kids gather sticks from the yard to toast marshmallows and make s'mores. And once they've had their fill of sugar, they run around the yard, chasing fireflies and capturing them in mason jars.

After pouring myself a hot cup of coffee, Marc pulls me onto his lap, and I bring my legs up and snuggle into him. He wraps us in a blanket while we enjoy the chatter of our friends and family, occasionally stealing glances and kisses.

It's well past midnight before everyone leaves and the kids are tucked in bed, finally coming down from their sugar high. And after the DJ and bartender pack up, I convince Claudette and Marc's aunt and uncle that they should head to sleep too, that Marc and I can clean up a bit and finish in the morning. The world suddenly grows quiet around, a stark change from earlier in the night.

Marc turns the radio on from the porch and then proceeds to diligently put out the campfire while I gather leftover food and drinks, bringing them inside the house.

And when we've both finished, I attempt to turn the radio off, but Marc stops me. "May I have this dance?" he asks in a distinguished tone.

I turn, facing him, and offer a curtsy in response. "It'd be my pleasure, sir."

When he wraps his arms around me and I lay my cheek against his, under the glow of the lights strung about, I confirm what my dad told me on the phone a week ago—that I'm right where I belong—in this extraordinary man's arms, for the rest of my life.

Chapter Eighteen
— A Lesson on Forgiveness —

I creak open the front door to the house and peek out. Marc turns his head to me, a tired look on his face. He stands on the front porch, sipping a cup of coffee, in a pair of track pants that hang from his hips, a worn T-shirt fitted across his shoulders, his hair tousled, and barefoot.

I take a couple of steps toward him and wrap my arms around him from behind, resting my head against his back. I run my hands up and down his chest, relishing the feel of him.

"Did you have a good night's sleep?" he asks.

"Mmm, I had a great night…sleep."

He reaches up his hand, threading his fingers through mine.

After the song ended last night, he took me by the hand to the bedroom, where we spent hours exploring each other, unrushed. While I was nervous—hesitant—at first, it wasn't long before I began to relax. He felt so familiar, so comforting—an old habit, rediscovered. And despite my body being foreign to me with its many imperfections from carrying four babies and, well, simply aging, he knew just how to put me at ease, kissing and caressing every inch of me. Neither one of us could keep our hands off each other, even hours later when we both felt completely spent and drifted off, tangled up together.

He hands me the mug of steaming hot coffee, and I gratefully take it, taking a step to his side and curling up under his arm. With only a couple of hours of sleep, I'll be needing more than one cup today.

The door squeaks open and a tiny Emma walks through in her Strawberry Shortcake nightgown. "Can we have donuts for breakfast?" she asks with way too much energy for six o'clock in the morning.

Marc and I look at each other, matching expressions of horror on our faces.

"I'm going to make you some green eggs and ham, Sam I Am," Marc jokes, scooping her up into his arms, earning a giggle from her.

"Can I set up my table next to Sheila," a woman—Pat, I learned, is her name—asks.

"Sure."

"Thanks. I think we'll attract more business if our tables are next to each other."

I'm helping—or more like leading—the set-up for the town's Saturday Marketplace. Claudette and Marc informed me that establishing this marketplace has been a pet project of mine. I've created it to bring more business to the town, while providing organic food and locally handmade clothes, decorations, and supplies to the citizens at reasonable prices. The past two years, people from neighboring towns, as well as folks from Canada, have frequented the market. It's become a popular attraction during the weekends between Memorial Day and Labor Day, even attracting more business to the shops and restaurants on Main Street.

There are tables lined between The Shipyard and a small diner tucked away next to the pool hall. During the week the space acts as a parking lot, but on Saturdays it's transformed into a marketplace.

I roam around while people set up their tables and tents, glancing at the various items for sale: Marty's Dairy Farm sells organic milk and cream and cheeses; Sheila's Handmade Quilts—the attention to detail is incredible; Pat's Handmade Dresses—it's evident that I've purchased many of them for Emma; Janice and Jerry's Florist, who have a wide selection of fresh flower arrangements and wreaths; Gladys' Fudge; Soucy's Woodworking and Primitive Wares—the craftsmanship is incredible; Nadine's Knitting, which includes everything from knitted wool socks to Christmas Tree decorations; Madore's Meat Pies—the very ones that I've salivated over since my first bite a week ago; Ouellette's Potatoes, which is Claudette's family's farm; Claudette's Canning, which is my mother-in-law who appears to be quite the experienced canner; Sierra's Handmade Soaps, which is Megan and her daughter, Sierra, who make soap out of goats milk and scented oils; Johanna and Carly's Sweets, twin girls about Abby's age sell cakes, cookies, and cupcakes; a few women from The Acadian Village sell books, postcards, and other Acadian heritage trinkets; Fern's Fertilizer and Hay; Marie's Maple Sugar—jars of syrup and maple sugar treats line her table; and Theriault's Garden and Eggs, that I'm told Abby, Jacob, and Avery—Megan's son—manage on their own. There's even a petting farm set up on the grass, where Wilber is currently enjoying the attention of the people around.

 The four kids, along with Megan's two children, picked fresh lettuce, spinach, radishes, peas, carrots, turnips, and gathered a few dozen eggs this morning.

They tell me that there would have been other fruits and vegetables as well, but with the late season frost we've been experiencing, they weren't quite ready yet.

And now the kids manage the table; it's their chore. The money that they make from the sales goes toward a family trip to Disney World. They've been saving up the past three years and have gathered enough money for the family to go on vacation this summer.

"I'm so happy to see you back." A woman rests a hand on my shoulder.

"Thank you."

"Mama, Madame Diane says that Emma and I won the coloring contest at Brooks!" Austin runs to me.

"Can we go get our prize?" Emma bounces up and down.

"We can go after the market is finished."

"You don't need to stay," Abby says.

"Yeah. We always do this ourselves. We know how to use the calculator for change," Jacob tells me.

"Are you sure?"

"Oh oui, they know what to do." Claudette appears out of nowhere.

So, once I'm certain everyone is set up and will no longer need me, I take Emma and Austin's hand and we cross the street. Entering the store, I look around for someone who can help us. But the only person there is currently busy behind the register, so I walk over and stand in line.

"Can I get a bottle of the Electric Youth by Debbie Gibson perfume?" a familiar voice asks. Without looking, I know it's the woman with the peacock hair that I sense has a thing for my husband.

I glance around the woman standing in line in front of me to see if I was correct. Today she wears a tight acid washed jean mini skirt, with a florescent pink crop top and matching high heel slip-on sandals. Her hair is fanned out with her bangs tightly curled down, and like the other day, it's clear that she has enough hairspray in it to cause a chemical warfare.

The young gentleman at the register can't seem to keep his eyes off her chest while she absentmindedly smacks her gum and hands him a stack of dollar bills, paying for her new perfume and tampons. She leaves without so much as a thank you.

When it is our turn, the kids ask about their prizes and the young gentleman fetches them from the office, bringing with him a Polaroid camera.

"Wow, Mom, it's a My Little Monster. I've always wanted one of those!" Austin exclaims.

"Is that a My Pet Sloth?" Emma squeals. "This is the best day ever!"

After the young gentleman takes a picture of each of them with their winnings, announcing that he'll be putting the pictures up by the door with the prior winners' photos, Emma and Austin thank him. Hugging their new stuffed toys, we make our way back outside.

"Can we have a root beer float?" Emma asks.

"Where?" I question, looking around.

"There." She points across the street to a business with a sign that reads "Harper's Pharmacy."

"At the pharmacy?"

"Please, Mama?"

I cave and tell them that they can. Crossing the street, I notice the sign on the building next to the pharmacy and it stirs up a memory, one that I don't believe I've made up while in a coma.

"Let's stop in at the music shop first."

Upon entering, a chime rings above the door. Scanning the room, I see a row of electric guitars line the walls behind the counter. In the glass showcase a variety of other instruments are laid out, next to it is a large selection of vinyl records with a sign that reads "On Sale $1 each," and off in the corner are a few drum sets.

"Bonjour, Madame Theriault—Sara," a gentleman says, greeting me.

"Hi…Eddy, is it?" He nods.

"Did I happen to order a drum set? Maybe a couple of weeks ago?" I pause, hesitant.

"Yes. I just got it in two days ago."

I recall ordering a drum set as a surprise for Jacob's birthday. I don't recall exactly when his birthday is, but I believe it's soon.

I breathe out a sigh of relief. "Okay, good."

"Did you want to bring it home today?"

"Actually, would you mind holding it for me until Tuesday?"

"Not a problem."

I thank him and tell Emma and Austin they need to keep this a secret until Jacob's birthday. Austin then proceeds to tell me that it's June fourth, in one week. I'm thankful I remembered; it would have been terrible to get to his birthday having forgotten this big surprise.

When we enter the pharmacy, the kids dart to the back beyond the shelves and to a countertop lined with steel swivel stools. They both hop onto one and start spinning around and around.

A gentleman appears. "Let me guess, you guys are here for…hmm…let me see." He taps a finger to his lips. "Pickle sundaes?"

"Ew, no," Emma says. Austin giggles.

"Oh, that's right, you like frozen liver popsicles!"

"No! Root beer floats." Emma's face splits open in a wide grin.

"Really? Oh, that's too bad, we're all out of root beer floats." The gentleman frowns, but looks at me, winking.

Emma's grin quickly turns upside down, pouting.

"But wait…how about you sing me a song and I'll see if I can find enough root beer just for you two."

Emma bounces on her stool. "Yay!" She starts singing Old MacDonald while the gentleman pours some A&W Root Beer into a couple of cups. And just as Emma finishes the last verse of the song, he tops them off with a scoop of vanilla ice cream.

They make quick work of their drinks while I eavesdrop on a couple of gentlemen at the other end of the counter, chatting it up about Dean. I can't make out everything they say since most of it's in French, but I catch enough to know that they're disappointed in him. One of them mentions that he can never forgive him for what he's done and for giving the town a bad name. "I gave him free room and board when he first moved here," he tells the other gentleman, hanging his head low.

"Oh!" Emma gasps, covering her mouth. "Mama, Austin just said the F-word."

"No, I didn't." Austin shoots her a look.

"He did, I heard him. He said 'shit'!"

I try to suppress a smile. I don't know if I should correct her or just leave it. Maybe I should tell the nuns that The Letter People haven't taught her much at school, after all.

"Oh my God, Emma, that's not even the F-word," Austin corrects her.

"That's okay. Nobody should be saying the F-word, and no one should be saying 'shit' either, right Austin?"

He wrinkles his lips and nods.

I feel a body press up against me from behind, and before I can look back, Marc whispers in my ear, "Have you seen my wife?" Earning him a smile while causing heat to manifest between my legs. I lean back into him, resting my head on his chest. He wraps both arms around my shoulders and kisses the top of my head.

"Daddy!" Emma exclaims.

"Look what we won." Austin reaches out the stuffed monster.

Marc left the house early this morning, after he prepared breakfast. A family in town lost their home in a fire a couple of weeks ago, so he went to help them get moved into a new place. It's apparent how much he cares about people and is always willing to lend a hand. I never used to love people very much, I was always guarded; I had my close group of friends, but that was the extent of it. He must have changed that in me. I suppose that's what love does—it changes people, while keeping them the same altogether, just a better form of themselves.

When we leave the pharmacy, Emma asks if we can stop in at a small gift shop. Upon entering, the scent of blueberries and candles fills the air. Looking around, I see greeting cards, candles, a collection of Smurf figurines and stuffed toys, and a large selection of stickers and trinkets. There's even a rack with some women's clogs, just like the ones I have on.

"They have my name!" Austin takes a small plastic license plate off a spinning rack. "Can I get it for my bike?"

"They don't have my name." Emma frowns.

"Don't feel sad, they don't have my name either," Marc tells her. "They have one with the wrong spelling, of course. But there's never anything with the correct spelling of my name." He looks at me, giving me an exaggerated pout.

I lean in and kiss the corner of his mouth. "I could buy a blank one and write your name on it. Then you can put it on your bike too," I joke.

"Daddy doesn't have a bike," Emma responds flatly.

"See, now you're even luckier than I am because you do have one," Marc says to her. She shrugs, still disappointed. "And you have a stuffed sloth," he adds. She gives her stuffed toy a squeeze and a smile fills her face.

After purchasing the plastic license plate and a blueberry scented candle that the woman behind the counter places into a red paper bag with a fabric ribbon attached, we return to Abby and Jacob. Most of the veggies have been sold, and only one dozen eggs remain. Impressive work for only a few hours.

When I round the table, my eyes are drawn to the ground. Dean's collie is curled up by Abby's feet, sleeping. "What is Dean's dog doing here?"

"Conrad came by earlier to buy some eggs and Penny wouldn't leave. She wanted to stay with us, so Conrad said he'd be by later for her."

"Can we keep her, Mom?" Jacob asks.

"No. I'm sure Conrad's going to keep her."

"No, he said that he's looking for a new home for her. We can take her, right?"

"I don't know, kids. We'll have to see." I look down at the dog and she continues to sleep, content. I've always wanted a dog for as long as I can remember. We never got one as kids because no one was ever home often enough to take care of it. My aunt in Portland had a collie and I recall how much I loved playing with him every time we went to her house.

Three o'clock rolls around and it's time for the kids to pack up for the day so we can head over to the four o'clock mass at church. I see Conrad crossing the street from his garage. "Looks like she's found a new friend," he says when he approaches. Penny the dog hasn't moved from Abby's side since she got here.

"Mom said we can get her," Jacob replies.

"I said *maybe* we can," I correct him.

"How about this, Jacob, if someone else wants her, I'll ask your mom before I give her to anyone else. If at the time your mom decides she wants to take her, then she's yours."

Jacob seems to be fine with that agreement. And I am as well. Maybe it's that I've always wanted one or that she belonged to my brother—either reason, I do want her.

Conrad has to nearly drag her away; she goes hesitantly with her head hanging low and tail between her legs.

After we pack up the remaining vegetables, we retrieve Wilbur, who dances on his hind legs in excitement when he sees me approach. And when we all pack into the van, Marc surprises me, laying a meat pie in my lap. I can barely contain my excitement, and it takes everything in me not to dig into it before we get home. Once we drop everything off at home and meet up with Marc's uncle Gerard and his mom, together, we slide into the church pew next to my sister and her kids.

A few moments later a woman approaches, bending down next to Marc, whispering something to him. I overhear him say, "She might. I can ask her."

He leans into my ear. "Nicolle was supposed to read today, but she's sick with the flu. Juliette wants to know if you'd be up to taking her place."

"Me?"

"Sure. You don't remember reading during mass before your accident?"

I shake my head, dumbfounded. "Um...I guess I could do it."

The woman hands me a book with a few pages marked and escorts me to the back of the church where Father Tom awaits. A moment later the organ begins to play, and we all form a line and walk in unison down the aisle. After we bow at the altar, I take a seat in the chair assigned for the lector. The service begins and I flip through the book to find what passage I am to read, when another passage catches my eye, making me pause.

While the service continues, I can't shake the passage out of my head. When it is my turn to take the pulpit, I turn to the page that's marked for me to read, and I begin: *"Jesus appears to the Disciples. On the evening of that day, the first day of the week, the doors being locked where the disciples were for fear of the Jews, Jesus came and stood among them and said to them, 'Peace be with you.'"* My eyes wander to the back of the church, seeking Dean—my brother—but his lone spot in the back pew is empty.

I clear my throat and lean into the microphone. "Excuse me a minute," I say to the large crowd all staring back at me, my voice cracking.

I cross the front of the altar and lean into Father Tom's ear. "Would it be okay if I read a different passage?"

He turns his head to me, looking at me expectantly. After a moment he nods, smiling in a way that tells me he recognizes there's a meaningful reason for my request.

I return to the pulpit, thinking of the many conversations I've overhead around town the past couple of days, and I flip the pages to Matthew 18:21–25: *"Then Peter came to Jesus and asked, 'Lord, how many times shall I forgive my brother or sister who sins against me? Up to seven times?' Jesus answered, 'I tell you, not seven times, but seventy-seven times. Therefore, the kingdom of heaven is like a king who wanted to settle accounts with his servants.' As he began the settlement, a man who owed him ten thousand bags of gold was brought to him. Since he was not able to pay, the master ordered that he and his wife and his children and all that he had be sold to repay the debt. At this, the servant fell on his knees before him. 'Be patient with me,' he begged, 'and I will pay back everything.' The servant's master took pity on him, canceled the debt and let him go. But when that* servant went out, he found one of his fellow servants who owed him a hundred silver coins. He grabbed him and began to choke him. 'Pay back what you owe me!' he demanded. His fellow servant fell to his knees and begged him, 'Be patient with me, and I will pay it back.' But he refused. Instead, he went off and had the man thrown into prison until he could pay the debt. When the other servants saw what had happened, they were outraged and went and told their master everything that had happened. Then the master called the servant in. 'You wicked servant,' he said, 'I canceled all that debt of yours because you begged me to. Shouldn't you have had mercy on your fellow servant just as I had on you?' In anger, his master handed him over to the jailers to be tortured, until he should pay back all he owed." I pause and look up from the book, scanning my eyes around the crowd. "This is how my heavenly Father will treat each of you unless you forgive your brother or sister from your heart."

    I close the book and return to my chair. I don't choose to elaborate; I let the townsfolk take what they will from what I read. But in this moment, I choose to forgive. I forgive my mom for making her career a priority above her family. I forgive my grandfather and other family members for not only putting my dad in prison, but for everything else that Megan, Timmy, and I had to experience because of our mom's death. I forgive my brother for lying to me and my sister all these years by getting caught up and brainwashed by lies told from my mom's family. And I also forgive myself. I may have already forgiven myself prior to the accident, that I'm not sure of. But if I hadn't, I am now. It's clear that I've harbored resentment toward my mother and her family, and even toward Megan for not speaking to my dad, but I'm ready to let it all go for my family's wellbeing and my own.

Another hymn is played before Father Tom takes to the pulpit. "It's Pentecost Sunday and we don't normally deviate from our usual sermon, but when something speaks to you and touches you in a way that it just did for Sara, I know that God would want us to continue to preach the powerful message of forgiveness. So, for today, I'm putting my planned sermon aside and will talk to you all about the importance of forgiving when it doesn't come easy."

He steps away from the pulpit and when he reaches the altar, he turns and walks down the two steps to stand directly in front of the crowd. "Sara read that Jesus told Peter he should forgive seventy-seven times. Some believe that he meant seventy-seven times as it's written, while others believe he meant seventy times seven times, or better put, four-hundred-ninety times. I personally don't think it matters. What Jesus meant was that we should forgive repeatedly, immediately, and regardless of whether the person asked for the forgiveness or not. How can we expect to be forgiven for our own sins by our Lord and Savior, if we, ourselves, do not forgive? I think it's safe to say that we have all been on the receiving end of forgiveness at some point in our lives. You see, forgiveness is letting go of the past, allowing for a fresh start. The key is, while you forgive, it doesn't mean you need to trust again. Those are not one and the same. Trust has to do with future behavior, but forgiveness is for what's already happened. God does not tell us to forgive and forget. He says you are to forgive them instantly."

He inhales deeply, glancing back at me in thought. He returns his attention to the people. "Dean needs our forgiveness and our prayers."

The service ends with Father Tom speaking about the festival. He tries lightening the mood by telling the kids he's planning to purchase ten rubber ducks so he can win the duck race on the St. John's River tomorrow and get the prize which is a new ten-speed bicycle. The kids all stir in their seats, eager to take him up on his challenge. And after everyone has left the church, Father Tom thanks me, telling me that it was exactly what everyone needed to hear.

Later, after Claudette serves dinner—blood sausages, or boodains as they call it, and mashed potatoes. The boodains is an acquired taste; I go from being reluctant to try to surprisingly enjoying it after only a few bites—Marc announces to the kids that we're going to the drive-in to see the new movie *The Sandlot*. And once we pay our entrance fee of five dollars, we drive through the gate and find a spot to park the van. Marc buys a large tub of popcorn, separating it out for the kids while they run around and throw a frisbee, waiting for the movie to begin. And then when the sun goes down and the large screen begins to show previews, everyone takes a seat, bundled up under a blanket, popcorn in hand.

The previews aren't even finished before Emma falls asleep curled up on my lap, hugging her stuffed sloth. Once the movie starts, I look into the back seat and see Austin nodding off. Abby and Jacob are still wide awake, engrossed in the movie. And when Marc hands me a hot cup of coffee, winking at me, I remark just how much he's doted on me all day—all week, really—and he leaves me completely enthralled.

Chapter Nineteen
— Down on Main —

"Where did you get all these clothes?"

"You."

I rummage through Megan's closet, searching for something to wear for today and tomorrow's festivities.

"Some of this stuff is great. Why would I have given it to you?"

"Because you got tired of it."

I raise a red-and-white maxi dress in front of me. Pressing it up against me, I examine myself in the mirror.

"Is it okay if I borrow this one? And that one too." I point to the blue sundress draped on her bed.

"You can take both. I haven't worn them."

"These are great. You should."

"They aren't my style. They're...too...revealing."

"Are you kidding? They aren't even revealing...anything."

"I'm happy in my tank tops and shorts, thank you. You do remember that you and I always had different tastes for clothing—and well, most everything else too."

I throw off my nightgown and slip into the maxi dress, twisting and turning in front of the mirror while folding down the top over my chest. I turn to her, running my hands down the front of the dress. "See. Nothing revealing."

She gives me a sideways glance. "It doesn't even have straps. And...you aren't wearing a bra."

"Yeah. And?"

"That's revealing!"

My mouth drops open. "You're making me sound like a slut."

"No. I didn't mean it like that."

"Okay...well..."

"Donna's a slut. You're just...you're just Sara." She struggles to get the words out.

"I'm not sure what you mean by that. *But*, what in the world is up with Donna with the peacock hair?"

Megan laughs. "She's an original around here, that's for sure."

"Does she have a thing for Marc?"

"Donna has a thing for every guy. She had a thing for Luc before you called her out on it."

"I did?"

"You don't remember?" She looks at me with an amusing grin.

I shake my head slowly. "No...I don't." But I suppose that could be the reason why she refused to look at me in Marc's office.

"And you don't remember—" She scrunches up her face. "And now that I know Dean's our brother, it makes recalling this so much worse."

"Oh my God, you have to tell me." I plop myself down on the bed next to her, folding my legs under me.

"Well, the story behind you calling her out isn't nearly as entertaining as what she and Tammy did with Dean."

"Wait...Tammy...the girl who works at the bar?"

"Yup."

"What happened?" I look at her expectantly.

"They were caught...having a threesome."

"Okay. Please tell me there's more to this story than just the fact that they had a threesome..." I lower my voice, "with our little brother."

"They were caught in the janitor's closet at the high school during a basketball game...by three fourteen-year-olds and the principal. And at the time both Donna and Tammy, who I forgot to mention are sisters, were married."

"Wait, Donna and Tammy are sisters?"

"You don't see the resemblance?"

"Now that you mention it, I guess. So, let me get this straight, Dean had a threesome with two married women who are sisters?"

"During a high school basketball game…and were caught by teenagers. Yup."

"Did their husbands find out?"

"Oh yeah, they did. They were the talk of the town for months after they were seen running through the hallways and out of the school buck-naked, clutching their clothes, trying to hide their privates. All three of them."

"Wow! Are they still married?"

"Tammy's husband 'forgave her.'" She waggles up her fingers in air quotes. "Donna's husband, who was a gynecologist in Caribou, kicked her to the curb and moved away. I guess he could have his pick of any woman he wanted in his profession."

"I know guys are infatuated with…woman parts." I wave my hands in front of me. "But what guy in their right mind would really want to stare…like literally stare…at cooches all day?"

"Every guy."

"But...you know what I mean, it's not like they're looking at porn."

"I guess to them, you've seen one cooch, you've seen 'em all?" She shrugs.

"Apparently he saw something different in Donna's cooch."

We both break out in a fit of laughter.

"Did I just hear you girls talking about cooches?" Marc leans up against the door frame to Megan's bedroom.

Megan's hands shoot up to her mouth, covering it. I laugh, falling back onto the bed.

"We're talking about Donna and Tammy," Megan informs him once her shock has worn off.

"Oh, that explains it."

I sit back up and look at Marc. His eyes change from an amused look to one of fascination.

"Nice dress," he remarks, looking intently at me.

"Nice suit, Mr. Theriault." I drag my eyes up the length of him. He wears a blue three-piece suit—mind you, not many thirty-something-year-olds could pull off such a suit. He's so distinguished at such a young age—and a red tie. Looking down at his feet, I laugh.

"What?" he questions.

"I just noticed you're wearing Chuck Taylor Converse sneakers with a three-piece suit."

"I always wear them. Are you just noticing my coveted Chucks?" he quips.

I slide off the bed and stride over to him, and forgetting that Megan is watching us, I press my lips to his, marveling at his ability to poke fun at himself and his childlike playfulness.

I don't recall ever being in love—ever knowing what true love feels like. The only relationships I remember having were all more along the lines of puppy love, lust, empty desire. As a young woman, I always prided myself on being a virgin, waiting for the right one. I never saw love as something that you played around with. Lust, of course, is easy; we long for and yearn to have that person with the perfect body who we fantasize making us scream in the bedroom— thanks to the many trashy magazines and movies that portray the opposite sex like they're meat on a stick— enough eye candy to satisfy even the biggest sweet tooth. We even envy people who are with those "perfect people," trying hard to find their imperfections to prove to ourselves that we are the more deserving ones. However, love, that's not easy to come by. But the feelings I get every time I look into Marc's eyes or when I hear his voice, I'm certain that's what love is.

The weekend festivities begin with a flurry of events. We start with the duck race, accompanying droves of people lined up along the river, watching thousands of tiny rubber ducks float by, all headed for the finish line. The kids' excitement is contagious; they all jump up and down, certain that their duck will win. And when the ducks get close to the finish line—the bridge that connects the United States and Canada—everyone watches attentively, waiting to see which duck will cross first.

The winning duck is pulled out of the water, and they announce that number three hundred twenty-six has won, and a hush grows across the crowd while everyone examines their tickets. It takes me a few solid minutes before I realize that three hundred twenty-six is one of my winning tickets. "I won! It's me! I'm the winner!" I call out, waving the ticket in the air.

While Abby and Jacob cheer along with me, a mix of looks are shot in my direction, but it's one in particular that catches my attention. A little boy, about Abby's age, remains quiet, tears streaming down his face. His mom's bent down, wiping his tears, consoling him. He looks like he's completely heartbroken.

The officials call two more winning numbers for the runner-up prizes that include a basketball and net, and an inflatable swimming pool, causing the crowd to stir once more.

"Mom?"

I look at Abby.

"Who are you planning to give the bike to?"

"I don't know. One of you kids can have it."

"Would you mind if we give it to someone else?"

"Who?" I ask her, intrigued.

"Connor." She points to the little boy that had caught my attention. "We all have bikes. And his family just lost everything in a house fire."

When we go claim our prize, Abby asks Connor to come with us, and I let her present him with his new bike. I don't think I've ever seen a child's face light up as much as his does. My heart swells, not only from his excitement, but from Abby's incredible selflessness.

I fish inside my purse and find the blank plastic license plate that I secretly purchased from the gift shop yesterday, with plans to write Marc's name on it and give it to him. Instead, I ask the girl at the table to use her marker, and I write *Connor* on it. And when I give it to him, he hugs me hard and thanks me repeatedly.

After he and his mom walk away, I hug Abby and tell her just how much she's not only made him happy, but me as well. Up until now I doubted my parenting skills, but she just confirmed that I must have been doing something right.

We walk up the hill, away from the river, to meet up with Marc, Emma, and Austin. The kids stand in line, waiting for their turn to ride a pony. I inform Marc of Abby's thoughtfulness, and he too is taken aback, filled with pride, enveloping her in a hug.

After the kids each get a ride on the pony, we leave, walking toward Main Street. Street vendors fill the path. We stop and get the kids each a balloon animal and have their faces painted, and then Marc asks if we'd like to eat lunch, telling us about the BBQ chicken that the firemen cook annually. As we cross Main Street, we can see the parking lot next to Conrad's Garage where there are four oversized custom-made grills, lined with small chickens, all slowly turning and roasting. The smell is incredible, and they look equally delicious.

While we wait for our lunch to be prepared, the faint sound of music can be heard. "Where is that coming from?" I ask Marc, looking around.

"There's a block party on Pine Street. A live band is playing." He points a finger toward the street behind the garage. "Do you want to go check it out?"

"Sure. That'd be fun."

"Hey Marc, I have the car ready for the parade tomorrow. It's all detailed. It looks good." I recognize the gentleman—he's the one that came by to pick up my dad's car a couple of days ago.

"Perfect. And you'll drive it over to the high school tomorrow for us?"

"Yup. I'll have it there well before the parade starts."

"Thanks!"

Once we get our food, we climb a steep embankment behind the garage and the music becomes clearer as we continue down the street. People sitting on chairs and blankets fill the front yards, and others are scattered about, chatting and even dancing.

When we approach where the band is set up, a woman sitting on her porch across the street invites us to join her. Two kids sell lemonade in her yard, so we buy a cup for each of us and then spread out on the porch.

We engage in small talk with the woman and her husband, while enjoying the band and our lunch.

"I hear that someone won my bike while I was busy giving a lesson on forgiveness during the nine and eleven o'clock masses this morning." Father Tom approaches, looking at the kids, giving them an exaggerated pout.

"But did you hear what Abby did?" I ask him. "She asked if we could give it to another kid who didn't have a bike."

The music to an ice cream truck is heard and all the kids jump up from their seats, begging and pleading for ice cream.

"For such a nice act of kindness, I'm going to buy you guys each an ice cream," Father Tom tells them.

"Of course, if Mom and Dad say it's okay."

"Please, Mom!" Jacob and Austin beg.

When I tell them they can, they all bolt toward the ice cream truck, Father Tom in tow.

The band begins to play a new song and suddenly it's like I'm experiencing déjà vu; not only is the song familiar, but so is this very moment. Maybe it is déjà vu or possibly a memory resurfacing from prior years' festivals, but when Father Tom returns asking me to dance with him, I picture us doing just that—dancing in the middle of the street. "We have to dance. This is our song." He extends a hand.

And so, we do. He twists and twirls me, and we dance toe-to-toe right there in the middle of the street. Other couples join in and it's the most fun I recall having in quite some time.

After the song ends, we return to Marc and the kids.

"Est-ce que vous faites le tir de la guerre?" A woman approaches.

"Oui," Marc responds to her.

"Il est sur le point de commencer en quinze minutes."

He tells me that he needs to head off to get ready for the tug of war across the river, so we thank the woman and her husband for their hospitality, say goodbye to Father Tom, and pack up the scraps left from lunch.

We make our way back down to the river where another large crowd has formed. A long rope extends from one side of the river to the other and a group of men is gathered at each end, most in their swimming trunks.

"Are you going to change?" I ask Marc, eyeing him in his three-piece suit.

"I don't think I have time. Plus, we never lose, so I don't think I'll be getting wet today."

"Don't be so sure, Marc. Did you see the size of some of their guys this year?" a gentleman interjects.

Glancing across the river, it's clear that there are quite a few men of grander size, but before Marc can respond, the announcer requests that all the men take their place. Marc gives me a peck on the cheek before taking his spot at the very front of the line, and within minutes the countdown is called. Just when the announcer says "Go," the men begin pulling in opposite directions, but it's not long before Marc and the rest of his crew are yanked headfirst into the water.

The crowd from Canada cheer and point, laughing, while Marc and his team trudge out of the water, drenched. The announcer offers Marc the microphone and he gives a concession speech, starting by congratulating them for their first win in eight years, and ending with, "You won't be so lucky next year!"

He marches toward us, hooking a finger in the knot of his tie, yanking it, and then removing his soaked jacket. Someone offers him a towel and he wraps it around his shoulders. He runs a hand through his wet hair.

When he gets close to us, he cocks an eyebrow at me, and then takes one quick step toward me. And before I can register what he's about to do, he wraps his arms around me. I let out a yelp, causing him to hug me tighter and swing me in the air, soaking me from head to toe right along with him.

The kids laugh hysterically, and before they know it, he's released me and chases after them too, eventually drenching each one of them as well.

Later that evening, once we've all changed into dry clothes, we meet up with Marc's aunt and uncle, as well as Megan and her kids, and we attend a dinner party at the local American Legion Hall. It's a catered affair, and a grand one at that. When we approach the buffet tables, I see that the incredible spread includes everything from garden and Watergate salad—a rare dish that I recognize from my childhood—to roast pork, fried rice, and Swedish meatballs. The servers keep up with the demand of the crowd while a gentleman keeps the line moving. I balance plates for Abby, Emma, and myself, while Marc helps Jacob and Austin.

"Donne moi ça." The gentleman limps around the table to us and grabs a plate from my hands. "Kelly-Sue, come help Sara here."

"You don't have to do that," I tell him.

He puts a large hand up. "She can help you." The woman takes the plate from him.

"Thank you," I say to them both.

"Lui donner d'autres Swedish meatball," he tells the other server, and she piles more meatballs onto my plate.

"We need to put some weight on you," he says to me in his thick French accent. "You look like you lost more weight."

"That she has, John," Marc responds. "She needs to keep eating your delicious food."

"You need to come over for supper more often," the gentleman says. "I'll be calling you when I make more pies." He rests a hand on my shoulder, giving it a light squeeze, and I offer him a genuine smile.

During dinner, the adults are absorbed in conversation while the kids finish quickly, running off to bounce around balloons and play tag with the other kids on the dance floor.

"It seems like you've done a good job with bringing new business to the town," Marc's uncle Gerard says to him.

"We're trying. It's been hard to keep the younger generation around, but hopefully if we keep creating jobs, they'll want to stick around instead of move once they graduate."

"Well, not even McDonald's could survive around here so you have your hands full."

"You know what, people say that our McDonald's was the first one to go bankrupt, but I'm not so sure that's true, there are other McDonald's restaurants that had to close their doors because of no business. A fast-food restaurant like that isn't going to survive around here. People would rather have home-cooked meals around the dinner table with their families. While the younger population has declined over the years, that's not the reason for them having to shut down. It's just the culture around here."

"You have a point," Marc's aunt agrees.

Marc rests a hand on my leg, rubbing my inner thigh, causing a throb to grow in my lower belly. He and his uncle continue to be absorbed in conversation.

The lights dim and the DJ starts to play music. A crowd gathers on the dance floor, and they begin dancing in rows, all in sync, swaying forward and backward, twisting, and clapping in time with the music.

"Let's go join them, Sara." Megan jumps from her chair.

"I can't dance to that."

"Are you kidding me? You usually lead every line dance there is."

I look at her intently, waiting for her to start laughing, but she doesn't. Is she serious?

"Come on. Let's go." She extends a hand for me to take.

When we join in on the dance floor, the familiarity of it hits me and I step right along with the rest of them. Megan looks at me, nodding.

We dance through two songs until a slow song begins to play.

When we approach the table, Marc stands. "Give me a minute, mon oncle, I need to dance with my wife. I'll be right back." He removes his suit jacket, draping it on the back of his chair and then takes my hand, leading me to the dance floor.

He wraps his arms around my waist, pulling me in, and when he runs a hand lightly up and down my back, I exhale, a desire to be closer to him building.

I lean back and unbutton his vest, and then curl my arms around him, taking in the warmth and comfort of him. He rests his cheek against mine and grazes my neck with his thumb, and when he whispers the lyrics to the song to me the rest of the room melts away. My body submits to his touch.

We dance through a second slow song and then Marc offers to get us drinks at the bar. Megan meets up with me when I walk to the table; she tells me she's tired and heading home. She offers to take my kids with her, saying they can all have a sleepover in her living room. All the kids are excited and don't protest when she tells them it's time to go. I walk them to the door, kissing them each good night, and then pay a visit to the ladies' room.

When I return to the table, everyone has their attention on the dance floor. It doesn't take me long to spot Donna—with the peacock hair—grinding on some guy in the middle of the dance floor. Marc wraps an arm around my waist. "This is what you call cheap entertainment around here."

"Good thing the kids are gone," I say, leaning into his ear over the noise in the background.

He tilts his head to the side. "Where'd they go?"

"Oh, you didn't see them before they left? Megan took them to have a sleepover at her house tonight."

A mischievous expression crosses his face. "So, are you telling me that we have the whole house to ourselves tonight?"

My lips curl into a grin and I nod.

"What the hell are we doing here then?" He places a hand on the small of my back, takes a big swig from his cup, and grabs his jacket as we sneak out the door before we're noticed.

We wake up on the living room floor at the crack of dawn the next morning. And after we delight in each other's company over a hearty breakfast, we share an enjoyable shower together. Within minutes of us exiting the shower, eight tiny feet come running through the front door, ready to take on the final day of festivities.

We gather at the cemetery for the traditional Memorial Day ceremony, paying tribute to those who fought for our freedom. People gather, heads bowed, arms filled with bouquets of flowers. The stillness of the graveyard allows for people to pay their respects and thank their loved ones. The only sound that can be heard are the many tiny flags waving in the wind. Shortly after speeches are said, songs are sung, and a band is played, the ceremony is finished off with a rifle salute. And then people return to their cars just as quietly as they came.

Before we leave, we visit Marc's father and brother's graves, and I notice the new floral spreads that the florist told me about. A single small flag adorns the large arrangement of red poppies, blue irises, and white gladioli.

"Thank you." Marc leans in and kisses me. "Both my dad and brother would be proud."

"Yes, they would," Megan adds.

While I stand here, I do feel proud, but I also can't decipher if my intentions are pure. Have I been placing flowers on their graves weekly more out of love or out of guilt? I know that I've carried around the heavy weight of guilt since they both died—were both killed—and while I like to believe I've been visiting them weekly and placing fresh flowers on their graves because I loved them and miss them, it's hard for me not to also believe I'm doing it because I'm guilt-ridden. Maybe along with forgiving myself, I need to stop carrying the burden of guilt. Maybe today's a good day to start. A fresh beginning on this day of remembrance.

After we watch a spectacular air show at the local Air Force Base—four forceful Thunderbirds whip and glide through the air, providing the crowd with a dynamic air demonstration—Marc's aunt and uncle join us, and we head to The Acadian Village for lunch. We feast on hot dogs, hamburgers, corn on the cob, and a variety of salads.

Just as we're finishing up, Marc looks at his watch. "The parade's going to start in about forty-five minutes.

Finish up your lunches, kids, we need to leave in about ten minutes so Abby can get changed into her pageant gown." He turns to me. "The car should be waiting for us there."

When we arrive at the high school, I quickly spot Claudette, and for the first time I realize that I hadn't seen her even once all day yesterday. She must have been just as busy with the festival as we were. When she sees us, she waves Abby over and leads her to the dressing room in the high school gym to get changed. The rest of the kids follow, all excited to see their grandmother.

Megan walks over to me. "I can take the kids with me to the center of town to find a spot to watch the parade if you'd like."

I feel a wet nose nuzzle against my hand. Penny, Dean's dog, stands by my side, wagging her tail, pushing her nose against me.

"Where did she come from?"

Megan's gaze drifts off to somewhere over my shoulder and her face pales. She places a shaky hand in mine.

"Megan?" I turn my head, following her line of sight. I see my dad's car driving up the parking lot. "Are you oka—" I can't finish getting the words out before my eyes set on the man behind the wheel—my dad comes into clear view, garbed in his Army dress uniform that I had forgotten about. A memory that had slipped my mind was the fact that my dad was in the Army before my sister and I were born. He came out of the military when we were only babies, he wanted to be around for us more, and that is when he decided to become a private investigator.

I feel my face whiten, mirroring Megan's own expression.

And when the car comes to a stop and my dad hesitantly opens the door and slides out, tears pool at the corners of my eyes.

"Dad?" My words come out a whisper. "Daddy!" I say louder.

I run to him, taking Megan with me, and jump into his arms. He hugs us both like he's been bottling it up for all of seventeen years.

When we finally pull away, a crowd has formed around us, and my immediate thoughts turn to what they're likely thinking and will possibly have to say about my father who they all saw on the news just days ago. But that all vanishes quickly when Marc, Claudette, and the kids break through the crowd and walk over to us.

"This is your grandpa," I manage, sniffling.

My dad kneels on the ground and all six kids envelop him in a group hug while he sobs like a child. Claudette comes to my side, wrapping an arm around me, drawing me into her. "Your dad is finally home." And when she speaks those five words, I know that she played a part in getting him here. This is the reason why she wasn't around yesterday. I know it. I feel it. This woman is incredible. She really is the backbone of this family—the family I'm so fortunate to be a part of.

Marc extends his hand to my dad, and my dad pulls him into an embrace. I overhear him thank Marc for keeping me safe and providing me with a good life.

Our reunion is cut short when we're told that the parade is starting, and we must take our places. Abby boards the pageant float, and she's simply stunning in her gown and crown. Claudette offers to take the rest of the kids to the center of town so that Megan can accompany us in the car, my dad the chauffeur.

And as we make our way through the crowds that line Main Street with Penny sitting in the back seat between us, instead of the predicted gossip and gawking, my dad receives a hero's welcome.

Later that evening, after we enjoy a spectacular fireworks show over the river, the kids bunk out in our living room with my dad. And while I change into my pajamas, he reads them a bedtime story with Megan sitting on the couch listening.

Exiting my bedroom and walking down the hallway, I overhear Emma ask him, "Do you miss Grandma?"

I pause, leaning against the wall, eavesdropping.

"Sure, I do. Every day. But, you know, it's okay because I get to talk to her whenever I want to. She always hears me. I don't need to pick up the phone to call her. I don't even need to speak out loud. I can just talk to her in my thoughts, and she hears me. You can do it too. You can talk to anyone in heaven, including God, without even speaking a word."

"Is Grandma in heaven?" Emma questions.

I feel Marc approach behind me, wrapping his arms around me, resting his chin on my shoulder. He kisses my cheek. "Come to bed soon."

I nod, leaning into his kiss. "I will."

"She sure is," my dad tells Emma.

"That's good, because Lori says it's hot in hell," Emma tells him, straight-faced. My dad suppresses a smile.

"Father Tom says that if you don't break any of the Ten Commandments, like not stealing, you're guaranteed to go to heaven," Sierra says.

"He's right," my dad tells her, pushing hair off her forehead.

"I stole a piece of gum from Jacob, but I can't return it," Austin admits, shrugging.

It's not long before all six kids, as well as my dad, are fast asleep, huddled up together on air mattresses and in sleeping bags. I tell Megan to take one of the beds in the kids' rooms, but she refuses to leave our dad's side, so she snuggles under a blanket on the couch.

When I finally get to my bedroom, I pause, taking in the sight of Marc laying on his side, hugging my pillow, fast asleep, and Penny curled up at the foot of the bed. I slide into bed, under the covers, and after turning off the bedside light, I lean over, kissing Marc on the forehead. While still asleep, he pulls me into him. I rest my forehead against his, the feel of his warm breath on my lips. He drapes an arm over me and strokes my hair.

And before I drift off to sleep, I take a moment to say a special prayer that Timmy will, too, find his way back home to us. And without speaking a word, I talk to my mom for the first time since waking up in the hospital bed.

Chapter Twenty
— The Road Less Traveled —

I reach for the blankets, the chill in the air nipping at my toes. I roll over, seeking the warmth of Marc's arms. When my body doesn't meet his, I slide myself to the center of the bed anticipating the feel of him, but instead I sense the edge of the bed.

Still tired, I squeak an eye open, glancing in the direction of the clock on the nightstand. My eyes shoot open. There is no alarm clock, only a bare white wall.

I blink my eyes open and shut a few times and shake my head. When I reopen them wide again, there's still only a white wall.

I clear my throat and sit bolt upright in the bed, an uneasy feeling settling in my chest.

ISABELLE VAN BUREN

In the dim light I can make out a thin figure sitting on the edge of a bed in front of me. When I narrow my eyes, I can make out that it's a girl and she's staring straight at me, eyes focused, unblinking.

I move my eyes left and then right, scanning the room. There are only two metal-frame twin beds, two small wooden nightstands, a large clock on the wall that reads eight thirty-two...a.m. or p.m.? I can't be sure. And there is a single square window on the wall to the right with a metal door beside it.

"Where am I?" I question, fixating on the girl. She doesn't respond. She remains unmoved.

The door flies open and in walks a woman dressed in solid green scrubs, rolling a metal cart. She flicks a switch on the wall causing the florescent lights on the ceiling to blink on, the sudden brightness making me jump.

She rolls her cart to the side of my bed. "Open," she demands.

"Where am I?"

"Open up," she repeats, raising a small paper cup in the air.

"Not before you tell me where I am."

"Fine, I'll play along again today. Open up first and then I'll tell you." She wears an expression of annoyance.

Against my better judgment, I open my mouth, and she drops four pills onto my tongue. She hands me a small cup of water.

I roll the pills under my tongue and take the cup from her, downing the water. Before I can return the cup to her, she rolls the cart to the other girl. With her back to me, I spit the pills into my hand, cupping it between my legs.

The girl across the room remains unmoved, eyes fixed on me while the woman repeats her demand.

Once the girl takes the pills and cup of water, the woman rolls her cart out the door.

With a trembling hand, I slide open the drawer to the nightstand. A lone black leather bible sits inside. I fish to the back of the drawer and when I open my hand to drop the pills, my finger brushes against something. I lean over the side of the bed and remove the bible, and peering into the drawer, I find a few days' worth of pills stashed in the far corner.

"Good morning, ladies." A woman rounds the corner into the room. I quickly release the pills from my grasp and slide the drawer closed, sitting up straight.

When I look up, I see the woman's wearing scrubs decorated in little puppies dressed in hospital gowns and she looks just like Claudette.

"Claudette?"

"Good morning, Amanda. Or is it Sara today?" When she speaks, she doesn't sound like Claudette—she doesn't have my mother-in-law's thick French accent.

She leans out of the doorway and pulls in a rolling hospital table, a green tray of food resting atop.

"Are we in New York or Maine today?" she asks. "Seeing as it's dreary out, how about we're at the beach today?"

She rolls the table to the side of my bed. "It's your favorite, bread pudding. And your Starbucks."

I peer into the tray of food; there's a Styrofoam cup with black coffee, a cup of chocolate pudding, a single bread roll, and a Styrofoam bowl and plastic spoon. "That's not bread pudding."

"Well, not until you mix it all in the bowl it isn't."

"Where am I?"

"The same place you were yesterday, and the day before, and the day before that for the last couple of weeks." She offers me a tight-lipped smile and then turns, heading for the door.

"Wait," I call out. "Where am I?" I repeat.

She reaches for another rolling table and pushes it to the other girl.

"Wargate, sweetie. Have you forgotten again today?"

"Wargate? The prison?"

She lets out a chuckle. "It sure feels like prison, doesn't it?"

I jump, instinctively covering my ears, when the girl's tray goes flying across the room, food littering the floor. The girl mumbles something indecipherable.

"You could have just told me you weren't hungry," the lady says to the girl. She walks to the side of the bed, and presses a red button on the wall, causing it to blink.

"Why am I here?"

The lady shuffles over to me. She pauses within a couple of feet from my bed, clasping her hands in front of her.

"Why am I here?" I repeat, my throat tightening.

Another woman strolls through the door, rolling a bucket and mop. The first woman pays her no mind, she remains focused on me.

"You were in a plane crash. You suffered a traumatic brain injury. You came to Wargate shortly after you came out of your coma. We're working on getting you better."

"I was in a plane crash…on my way to Bermuda?"

"Yes. I'm happy you're starting to remember. That's a great sign."

"With Tom and…Jayde?"

She nods, pleased.

"And where's Marc?"

"The boy from the airport?"

I nod.

"You talk about him every day, but I don't know where he is."

"Are Tom and Jayde here too?"

"No, sweetie."

"Is my mom alive?" I ask, expecting her to tell me she isn't.

"Yes, of course."

"So...my mom is alive? Is my dad in prison?"

She smiles. "Yes, your mom is alive. And your dad isn't in prison, sweetie."

"Can I have my cell phone? I want to call them. Please?" I plead with all I have left in me.

"You can't use your cell phone. But you can call them. You're allowed one ten-minute phone call a day. You can use the telephone in the common area."

When I don't respond, she turns on her heels.

"You know what not eating means, right?" she says to the other girl. "You're going to end up with that dreaded feeding tube again, Megan. It's in your best interest to just eat."

"Megan?"

She turns back to me. "Yeah, your roommate, Megan here, hates the tube, but when she throws her tray across the floor, we have no other choice."

The girl looks nothing like my sister, nothing like me. She's bone thin with beady brown eyes and stringy black hair.

The woman turns back around and walks to the doorway. "You have time to wash up before they arrive with the tube," she advises the girl. And then she disappears into the hallway.

Once the woman's out of sight, the girl mutters something.

"What did you say?" I ask her, recognizing what she said was in French.

"Mange la marde," she spats out in a thick accent, making me look away from her.

I gaze down at my lap to see that I'm wearing grey sweatpants with an elastic at each ankle and drawstring at the waist. Going down along the side of the right pant leg is the word *WARGATE* in bold letters. I trail my eyes up to my white T-shirt and notice it's inside out. Tugging at the collar, I glance down inside, certain it'll have an image of a large red cracked heart and the words *Achy Breaky Heart* scrolled across it, but instead it reads "WARGATE" in large black letters.

And when my eyes fixate on my chest and stomach, I see that it's void of any scars. Not a single stretchmark can be seen, no sign of any cellulite, my breasts as perky as a teenage girl's. My body is only a thin shell, unmarked, no story to be told.

My bottom lip quivers, fighting back a sob.

Lowering my legs to the side of the bed, I stand barefoot on the cold floor. I slip my feet into the pair of clogs resting on the floor in front of the nightstand. When I turn to the door, the girl on the other side of the room—Megan—begins rocking back and forth and recites something in a low tone. The only words I can make out are "red pillows."

Once I get to the doorway, I glance out into the common area. A few couches and chairs sit against the walls and a flat-screen television is hung from a partition in one corner, blaring country music videos. A boy sits alone on a chair, his focus drawn to the television. Diagonally to my room is a reception area, separated by a half wall and adorned with pots of large, bright tiger lilies. A woman sits behind a glass window, typing at a computer.

"I want my babies!" a woman cries out from an adjacent room. "Abby! Jacob! Emma! Austin! Ahhh! I want my babies!"

I raise my hands to my mouth, muffling my own cries at the sounds of those names being called out.

"My babies!" she continues until a nurse rushes into her room and closes the door behind her.

I bite down on my tongue and inhale, forcing the tears to stop. I take a step toward the common area and spot a telephone.

When I reach the phone, I slouch onto the couch and examine it. It's a video conferencing phone, with a large screen attached above the keypad. A sign posted on the wall above it reads:

<u>Telephone Rules</u>
You cannot use the telephone more than once a day.
Each call is for only 10 minutes to allow access to all patients.
Calls will cut out after the allotted time.
A prepaid calling card is needed.
If you do not have a calling card, you can only make collect calls.
To make a collect call, dial 9-1-800-COLLECT.
Don't abuse your privileges.

I don't know if I have a calling card, but I assume my parents will accept a collect call from me, so I pick up the receiver and put it to my ear. Then I proceed to dial 9-1-800-265-5328.

An automated recording answers, asking for the phone number I'd like to dial and then requesting my name. After a brief pause, the line rings.

"Don't tell my heart, my achy breaky heart. I just don't think he'd understand," the boy sings at the top of his lungs.

"Shut up!" I raise the receiver in the air, motioning to him that I'm on the phone.

He sits back in his chair, going silent, redirecting his attention to the television.

I hear my mom's voice answer and then the recording asks if she'd accept a collect call from me. After a beep the line goes silent.

"Mom?"

"Hi, Mandy. How are you doing today?"

"Mom. Where am I?"

"What do you mean?"

"Mom, I'm at some loony bin—mental hospital. I want to go home."

"Oh, Mandy. I don't have time to go over this with you again today. I'm on my way out. I'm running late for a meeting. Can we do this some other time?"

"But, Mom," I plead, my voice cracking.

"Really, Mandy. If you're feeling okay, I can't talk right now. George just pulled up. We need to rush off to a meeting with the planning committee for the new downtown offices."

"Mom, is everything okay at home?"

"Of course it is. What do you mean?"

"Is Dad there?"

"Yeah. I think he just got out of the shower."

"Can I talk to him?"

MY ANYWHERE

"Robert!" she hollers. "Mandy, I really must go. I'll talk to you tomorrow, okay?"

"Okay, Mom."

"Baby girl?" The screen on the telephone flashes, my dad coming into view.

I lose my breath. It's my dad. Just like I remember him.

"Daddy," I cry.

"Baby girl, what's the matter?"

"I don't know. I woke up and I don't know where I am. Daddy, help me."

"Oh, Mandy. Don't cry. You're where you belong right now. They're taking good care of you."

"I need to leave. I want to go."

"Go where, baby girl?"

"Anywhere, but here."

"I know. But you're making great progress. You won't be there much longer."

"Daddy, is everything okay?"

"What do you mean?" he asks.

"With you and Mom. And with Grandpa Don. Is everything okay?"

"Yeah," he responds hesitantly.

"Daddy, what aren't you telling me?"

He draws in a breath and bows his head. "It's Grandpa Don. He passed away last week. Your mom said she told you...and I know that it's a lot to deal with right now, but...well, I'm sorry."

"Where...was he?" I brace myself for the answer.

"He was still in the nursing home—at Riverview. The cancer had spread to his other organs."

"In the nursing home," I repeat. "Not prison."

"What, honey?"

I shake my head. "Nothing. And Timmy? How is Timmy?"

"He's taking it okay."

"No, I mean, how is he doing otherwise?"

"Oh. He's doing good. He just started baseball." He looks away from the camera. "Timmy, come say hi to your sister."

My brother's face comes into view. "Hey, Mandy."

"Timmy." I raise my hand, waving. "You're so young."

He laughs. "Yeah, well, I'm older than the last time you saw me. I turned fourteen four days ago."

"Happy Bir—" the line cuts off before I can finish. I lower the receiver back to the cradle and swipe the tears that stream down my cheeks.

When I turn in the seat, I see another boy has joined us. He wears a sticker on his shirt that reads "Hi, my Name is Dean." And around his neck hangs a chain with a large Celtic cross pendant.

I look away, the weight of the world crumbling down around me.

"Disney Land!" the other boy calls out. "Let's all go to Disney Land!"

"Quiet down, boys." A girl rounds the corner and plops herself on the couch facing them. She wears a white T-shirt knotted at her chest and she's rolled her sweatpants up to her thighs. But it's her hair that immediately catches my attention. It's long, black, and curly. And it's stretched as wide and as high as it'll go, fanned out like a peacock—like Donna's hair.

I stand and rush back to my room. When I enter, Megan turns, eyeing me. She hasn't moved from her spot on the bed since I left.

I walk over to the red button on the wall and press it. I need to get out of here. I don't belong here. I need to get home and back to my life.

A woman rushes inside the room and looks from me to Megan.

"I want to go home. Get me my things."

"Okay. I understand," she answers calmly. "But I think it's best that you stay. I can have Dr. Bouchard stop by during his rounds if you'd like to speak with him."

"No. I want to go home. I'm an adult. I should be able to go home. Either you let me sign myself out or I'll just leave."

"All right. Well, let me call Dr. Bouchard."

"I don't give a damn about Dr. Bouchard. I want to go home now!" I growl.

She raises her finger in the air. "Just wait here." She turns and exits the room, walking in the direction of the reception area.

Megan covers her ears and hums while rocking back and forth on the bed. And then once the woman is out of sight, she lowers her hands. "Keep you hostage," she growls, darting her eyes around the room. She lets out a loud, disturbing laugh.

I truly need to get out of here. I walk over to the doorway and peer toward the reception area. I don't see the nurse. The woman behind the counter speaks to a couple, the woman appears distraught, crying. A girl, about my age—twenty-two—sits on a chair in the waiting area, her legs drawn up to her chest, her fingers scratching at a scab at the corner of her lip, her eyes wide. A suitcase and handbag rest on the chair next to her.

Tapping my foot on the floor, impatient and aggravated, I start to plot my escape plan in my head. I'm not sure how far I'll get in a T-shirt and sweatpants that read "WARGATE," but I'm willing to try. I make eye contact with the fidgety girl and then briefly look down at the suitcase. I don't even know if the front doors are unlocked. I might not even make it further than the lobby. And what if they have some of my belongings like my cell phone? My thoughts are jumbled, sporadic, and panicked.

Taking a few steps across the hallway, I look over at the receptionist once more. She doesn't turn her head to me, she's absorbed in consoling the woman still.

I observe the suitcase again. And from the corner of my eye, I see that the girl's expression changes slightly from one of exasperation to possibly that of intrigue. She rolls her eyes to the side, as if motioning for me to grab the suitcase. I don't move my feet, but my eyes follow hers.

After another quick glance at the receptionist, I scan the room behind me, and don't see anyone except for the two boys, who are now fully engrossed in a detective show.

Squatting down behind the half wall, I drag my feet to the girl. Her gaze is fixed on me, and she nods quickly. I can't believe she's going to help me escape.

When I get close enough, she darts her eyes to her parents and back to me, and then quickly pushes the suitcase into my hands. She grabs the purse and throws it to me.

Without a second thought, I catch it and dash toward the front doors.

Not looking back, I push on the glass door, and it flies open, no alarms sounding to signal my escape. I run into the parking lot as fast as my feet will take me.

I crouch down between a utility van and a row of trees, catching my breath and slowing my pounding heart. Scanning my surroundings, nothing looks familiar. A row of large concrete buildings line the street and cars zoom by behind me. I haven't a clue what to do next; panic settles, a heavy weight pressing on my chest.

Lowering the suitcase to the ground, I realize that if I have any chance of getting home, I need to get out of this parking lot before someone notices I'm gone, and they come searching for me.

Inhaling deeply, I make a break for it in the direction of the nearest side street. I see the golden arches for McDonald's, and I run. Crossing the street, I notice that the restaurant is dark, parking lot empty, and as I get closer, it's clear that it's out of business, abandoned.

Taking a quick glance over my shoulder for signs of anyone chasing me, I see that I'm alone; not a single other person can be seen. I slow my pace to a jog and make my way to the back of the abandoned building.

I unzip the purse and then flip it over, causing a woman's wallet, an iPhone, cosmetic case, a hairbrush, a few pens, and a few dollar bills and a shitload of coins to litter the ground.

Grabbing the phone, I press the Home button and the screen awakens, a picture of a creepy clown as wallpaper in the background. Quickly, I press the Phone button, and the keypad appears covering the strange clown photo. I dial my dad's cellphone number and raise the phone to my ear. If anyone's going to help me, it'll be him.

The line rings and then his voicemail picks up. *Damn it!*

I end the call and quickly dial my sister, Becca's, number.

"Hello?"

"Becca?"

"Yeah. Mandy?"

"Yeah, it's me."

"Hey. How you doing?" she says in a hushed tone.

"Um, I'm okay, but—"

"I hate to cut you off, but I'm at my second interview right now for the teaching job in Portland. If I have to hang up quickly it's because they're calling me in," she whispers.

"Teaching job? Portland?" Damn it, she can't help me all the way from Portland, Maine.

"Yeah, you know the one that I told you about last week. I'm staying with Aunt Jan until the round of interviews are done. Mom's not happy of course. She thinks Portland isn't a big enough city. She told me that she expected more out of me, you know, in true Mom fashion."

"Are you going to teach...French?"

"Ha! Are you kidding? The only French I know is, 'Voulez-vous coucher avec moi ce soir,' that our little perv of a neighbor would always say." She laughs. "You sure sound like yourself today. Do they have you on some new meds?"

"I'm not taking them. I don't think I've been taking them for a few days now."

"Mandy!" she warns. "Oh, wait a minute, the secretary's coming my way, I have to go," she murmurs.

"Wait! Do you have Tom's number?"

"I don't, but I don't think you'll be able to talk to him since he's at Seminary."

"What?"

I hear her mumble something away from the phone.

"Listen, Mandy, I have to go in a second. But, yeah, Tom went off to Seminary right after the plane crash. He claimed that God called him, or something like that. But, anyway, I have to go. Call me tomorrow, okay?"

Before I can respond, the line goes dead.

Tom has always had a flair for the dramatics, but this is extreme, even for him.

I eye the suitcase. Sliding along the brick wall, I sit on the ground and drag the bag toward me. When I flip it open, a laugh escapes my lips. The only item inside is a hot pink string bikini. Apparently, the girl thought she was headed to a beach resort instead of the loony bin. This certainly isn't going to help me. I think I'd attract more attention in a string bikini than my Wargate sweatpants and T-shirt.

"Headed somewhere?" a voice calls out, making me dart my eyes up. A gentleman sitting behind the wheel of a yellow taxicab looks down at me.

I freeze, swallowing hard.

"You staying? Or coming?"

Is he serious? "Um." I shrug.

"If you're coming, hurry it up, I'm on the clock here."

I grin. He must be serious.

I gather the contents of the purse and shove them all back into the bag, flip the suitcase closed, and pick myself off the ground. I open the back door of the cab and slide in.

He taps on the steering wheel. "We can't go anywhere until you tell me where you're headed." He remains straight-faced.

"Where are we?"

"Bronx."

"Bronx?"

He looks at me in the rearview mirror. "Listen, lady, if you want to go somewhere, you better tell me quickly or I'll have to move on to the next customer."

"Stamford...Connecticut?"

"I need an address."

"I don't even know if I can pay you," I tell him, fishing through the purse for the wallet.

"Like I said, I need an address."

"78 Willow Street."

He nods and guides the cab out of the parking lot. He turns the music up—someone sings about last chances and having no regrets.

"Wait!" I scoot up on the edge of the seat, leaning into the small open window that separates us. "Can you take me to the nearest airport...shit, no. I can't do that, I don't have an ID on me."

"Where you wanting to go?"

"Maine," I say, feeling defeated.

"Greyhound."

He stops at a red light.

"Don't I need ID for that too?"

"I have connections," he says flatly. *Who is this guy?*

When the light turns green, he sends the car spinning, making a U-turn, causing me to fly back against the seat. He presses a button on his cell phone and it rings, the sound loud on speaker.

When a voice answers, he says, "Hey. I need one ticket to...where in Maine?" He turns his head to me.

"Um. Van Buren?"

"Van Buren," he repeats.

"The closest I can get you is to Portland," the voice through the speaker tells him.

"Portland good?" he asks me.

"Yeah. Sure."

"Okay. Portland," he tells the voice. "We'll be there in five."

When he hangs up, I can't help myself. "Who are you?" I ask him.

"A product of Wargate," he responds, not looking at me.

The rest of the ride is silent. When we arrive at the bus terminal, he opens my door and grabs the suitcase and leads me inside. Another gentleman hands him a paper and he simply nods at him before turning to me. He points down a hallway. "The bathrooms are down there. You have ten minutes to change before you board." He hands me the ticket and suitcase and starts to walk away.

"Thank you?" I call out, baffled.

He throws two fingers in the air over his shoulder and disappears through the doors. I can't help but think that lucky for me, Wargate must've done a serious number on him. Who'd help someone make an escape otherwise?

I scurry to the bathroom and look at myself in the mirror, frowning at the young face that stares back at me. I don't have a thing to change into; I certainly can't slip into the bikini. I drag the sweatpants down my legs and flip them inside out. It's the best I can do. At least now, the bold letters can't be seen.

When I exit the restroom, I walk toward the signs for the buses. I pass a Dunkin Donuts and then quickly turn back around remembering that I have a few dollars in the purse. I order a large latte and then hurry to find my bus. While standing in line, nerves bubble up inside. A map of the United States hangs on the wall next to me and I trace my finger up from New York all the way to the tip of Maine—Van Buren.

An announcement is made that it's time to board, and I hand my ticket to the attendant, not looking up. He scans it and directs me to walk on board.

Sliding down the aisle to the back row, I slump down into the seat and take long sips of coffee. Finally, when the bus pulls out and onto the road, I exhale, relieved. I lay my head against the back of the seat and stare out the window. This feels all too easy, impossible. Maybe I'm dreaming. Maybe I'm insane. Who knows? But I can't help but smile at the sheer thought that I've escaped so effortlessly and am now headed to Maine...to see someone who I dreamt about having a life with, but only knows me as the distracted girl who crashed into him at the airport. It's crazy—absurd—but invigorating.

A phone rings, and I realize the sound is coming from inside the purse. I fish it out and read the caller's name: Mom. Not my mom, but the bikini girl's mom. They must have finally found out that I took it—*someone* took it. A moment later the phone pings, alerting me a new text message has come through. When I check it, again I see it's from "Mom."

The message reads: *Whoever stole my daughter's phone, we know your location. We're tracking you with Find My Phone. You have 24 hours to return the phone and the rest of my daughter's belongings before we alert the police.*

Swallowing hard, I contemplate a reply. Instead, I choose not to respond.

I close out the text messages and tap on the Facebook icon. It pops up the login screen, displaying yet another creepy clown photo and the name Georgina Gladiola. I guess the bikini girl is Georgina and she has a weird fascination with clowns. The nuthouse might be just the right place for her.

After I tap *Log into Another Account*, I enter my email address and password. Scrolling through my newsfeed, I realize that I haven't missed much. Searching for Tom's page, I see that his last post was dated *May 20, 2015*, and it's a photo of the bible with a caption that reads: *Show God you love him. Share this picture if you believe in God, ignore it if you don't.*

I glance at today's date on the top menu of the phone: *June 12, 2015.* He shared that post twenty-three days ago, which was two days after our plane accident. *Tom, a priest?* I shake my head and grin, suppressing a laugh. But, who knows, maybe it is his calling. Who am I to judge? If someone had told me twenty-five days ago that I'd be headed on a bus to a small town on the edge of the universe, I'd have laughed in their faces. It's amazing what happens when you silence your life, if that makes any sense at all. I suppose it does to some people. New York is for the dreamers, those who search for the next big thing. And it's what I once thought I wanted, but now know it isn't what my heart desires. If Marc is anything like I dreamt up, he's where I long to be. I haven't a clue how I'm going to get to northern Maine once I reach Portland, but at least I can meet up with my sister and figure out my next move.

"Ma'am."

I open my eyes to a gentleman standing over me.

"We're here. We're in Portland."

I look around. No one's left on the bus but me. I must've fallen asleep.

"Thanks." I clear my throat. I grab the purse and suitcase and stand.

Upon exiting the bus, I spot a row of benches, so I walk over to the nearest one and sit, dialing my sister's number on the phone. It rings, but she doesn't answer; instead, her voicemail picks up.

I inhale deeply, taking in the cool air, and check the time. It's seven fifteen. I can't believe I slept the entire ride here.

Cabs line the street in front of the station, but otherwise the surroundings are surprisingly quiet. I sit a moment longer, absorbing the stillness.

I reach into the purse and take out the wallet. Opening it, I spot a driver's license and a few credit cards. And then reaching into the back pocket, I count out three hundred twenty-five dollars.

"I promise to find a way to repay you," I say into the silence.

After I walk to the first cab in line, I tell the driver to take me to 54 Mountain Avenue.

Fifteen minutes later, we pull up to my aunt's house, and after I pay the cabby, I knock on the front door. The noise of a dog barking responds on cue. But it's the only sound to be heard from within.

I ring the doorbell and wait. A minute later, the door opens, my sixteen-year-old cousin, Andy, looks at me annoyed. "Hey, Mandy," he says like I just saw him earlier today instead of over a year ago.

My aunt's collie nudges my hand. I pat his head.

"Hey, Andy! Is my sister here?"

"Nope."

"Do you know where she is?"

"She headed back home earlier today."

"She did?"

He doesn't respond, he just stares at me.

"Is your mom home?"

"Nope."

"Okay..."

"Kill 'em! Fuckin' shoot 'em!" he yells, making me jump back, dropping the suitcase.

He points to a headset wrapped around his head. "Sorry, I'm playing *Call of Duty*." He eyes me up and down. "Aren't you supposed to be in the funny farm or something?"

"Yeah. I got out. Long story...do you know when your mom's going to be back?"

"Four days."

I narrow my eyes. "Where is she?"

"She went with your sister to visit your parents until the weekend."

I frown.

"You wanna come in?"

"I guess." The blue Honda Civic in the driveway practically calls out to me. "Whose car is that?"

"Whoever's. It's just a spare."

"Really?"

He shrugs and nods.

"Do you think I could borrow it? I'll return it before your parents get back."

"Yeah. Whatever."

"And do you think I could maybe borrow some clothes from your mom?"

His brow creases. "Uh, okay."

After he lets me in, he disappears into the basement.

I rummage through my aunt's closet and find a white sundress. And then I stuff a couple of shirts and shorts into the suitcase and slip into a pair of my aunt's sandals. While a bit snug, they're better than the clogs.

In her bathroom cabinet, I find a brand-new toothbrush. I brush my teeth, pass a wet cloth on my face, and a brush through my hair.

Feeling refreshed, I return to the kitchen. I can hear Andy playing his video game in the basement, so I dig through the refrigerator, starved. Grabbing a couple of slices of cold pizza, I wash them down with a can of soda. And then I throw a couple of apples and granola bars into the purse and take a bottle of water from the fridge.

I grab the only keys hanging on the hook by the front door and walk over to the entryway of the basement. "Thank you, Andy!" I call down.

"Sure thing, Mandy," he calls back. "Don't let 'em get away, Jake. Shoot 'em in the head!" he bellows through the sound of shots being fired in the background. I take that as my cue to slip quietly out the door.

The sun has set, and the stars shine brightly. I slide behind the wheel of the car and turn the key in the ignition, country music blasts through the speakers. I lower the volume and turn up the heat. Realizing that I haven't a clue how to get to Van Buren, I press a few buttons, searching the navigation system, and it asks for my destination.

State: *Maine*

City: *Van Buren*

Street Number: …

Every city or town must have a Main Street, right?

I enter: *100*

Street Name: *Main Street*

The map appears, stating that my destination is 324 miles, 5 hours away. That means I'll arrive at three o'clock in the morning.

I contemplate waiting until morning. But against my better judgment, I throw the car into reverse and start on my journey. I'm not even five miles down the I95 before lights flash and sirens blare behind me. *Shit!* My first thought is that Georgina's family has hunted me down. Damn you, technology!

I pull the car to the side of the highway and start devising a believable lie as to why I have a stolen cell phone and other belongings when the cop taps on the glass.

Lowering the window, my hands shake. "I don't have my license on me," I blurt out.

"Excuse me, ma'am?"

"I...I...forgot my license at home," I stutter. "And this is my aunt's car."

He leans over, scanning the inside of the car. "I was just going to tell you that one of the taillights is out, but...do you have any form of identification on you?"

A burned taillight? I laugh and release my breath. "Uh, no."

The cop eyes me for a long moment before he speaks. "Where are you headed in such a hurry that you forgot to bring your license with you?"

"I'm just...headed to see a friend. I had my license but forgot my wallet on the counter." I quickly glance from the corner of my eye at the purse resting on the passenger seat. I look back up at the cop and, shifting my body over slightly to block the view of the bag, I offer him a tight-lipped smile.

"Make sure to never drive without your license again. And get that taillight fixed."

I nod. "Yeah. I will. Thank you."

Without another word, he returns to his car. I take a sip of water and watch as he pulls away. The phone pings, signaling another incoming text message.

I grab it and read a text message from "Mom" that simply says: *Portland, Maine.*

She's alerting me that she knows where I am.

I don't respond again. Instead, I throw the car in drive and head north along the very dark and quiet highway. Most of the way, there isn't another car to be seen, only endless trees on both sides of me, and the occasional exit sign. I turn up the music, bopping to the sound of a woman with a southern twang singing about working nine to five.

After about five hours or so, I see what looks to be a toll plaza a few hundred feet in front of me. But as I approach, a sign reads:

Welcome to Canada
Stop Ahead
For Customs – Immigration

Is Van Buren part of Canada, not Maine? I slow the car and frantically look around for somewhere to turn. I cannot go into Canada. I don't have a single form of identification on me. There's also no place for me to turn around. I release both hands from the steering wheel and shake them in the air, tension building, a lump forming in my throat.

The car slowly approaches the customs booth. Stopping, I lower my window and scan the area. I don't see a single person around, so I press the gas pedal. The car doesn't get five feet before lights overhead flash and a loud horn blasts, making me stomp on the brake. I clench my stomach, feeling like I'm going to pee my pants.

Glancing in the rearview mirror, I see a gentleman in uniform waving a hand in the air, signaling me to put the car in reverse.

I do so, and when I get to him, I stop the car.

"Bonsoir—"

"I'm just trying to get to Van Buren. I thought it was in Maine, not Canada. Um, maybe I can just turn around?" I say, cutting him off.

"À Van Buren?"

"Yes. Van Buren. That's in Maine?"

"Yes." He speaks in a thick French accent. "Uh, you have a driver's license to show me?"

"Um, well, you see, I forgot it home." I shrug and offer him a look that says "sorry."

"You forgot it," he repeats. "Ah, I see. Well, um, you are a resident of the United States? In Maine?"

"Yes, I'm from the US, but from Connecticut. My mom is the mayor of New York."

"Oh, yes? Your license plate is not from Maine, non?"

"Yes, it's my aunt's car."

"I see." He pauses. "Well, maybe you can give me your name and social security number so I can just run a check."

"Oh, yeah. Sure, that works. My name is Sara Ther— Uh, I mean..." I shake my head and look away. "I mean...my name is Amanda Marie O'Reilly."

He stares at me, eyes narrowed.

"I'd like you to pull over right there." He points off to the side and I immediately feel déjà vu all over again.

"It was just a mistake. You see, I had this dream, and it confused me. Can I just turn back around and head back to the United States?"

"Over there," he repeats, unamused, pointing for me to pull the car over.

I do as he directs, feeling completely defeated. When I place the car in the park, the low-gas light flashes in the console, and I see that the gas gage is on empty. Great, now I'm out of gas as well.

He disappears inside the office, so I turn the car off and slump back in the seat, tears pooling in my eyes. And it's the first time all day that I feel like I've made the wrong decision coming on this road trip to hunt down a boy who barely knows I exist. *What was I thinking? What am I going to do once I get there?* Try to convince him that he's my soul mate because I had a dream or whatever while hopped up on pills in an insane asylum?

A car approaches in the other lane—a taxicab. The driver looks my way as he passes. He reaches up and tips his riding cap at me, nodding. The cab slows at the booth, and the gentleman looks around, but the officer is nowhere to be seen. The car remains idle for a moment before I see the taillights flash red and the car reverses diagonally in my direction. He comes to a stop within feet of my car.

"Anyone here?" the driver calls out his window to me.

"Yeah. There was an officer a few minutes ago. I drove past the booth by mistake. I didn't even want to come into Canada, but there was no place to turn around. He had me pull over here since I don't have my license on me...and now I'm out of gas."

He leans forward, looking through his windshield. And then he glances back at me. "Where were you headed?"

"I wanted to get to Van Buren." I press my lips together.

"I can take you to get some gas if you want."

"Seriously?" I ask with a glimmer of hope. "Well, I can't go anywhere until he lets me go."

He scans the area once more and then throws a thumb over his shoulder. "Hop in."

I stare at him, wide-eyed.

"Come on. Hurry."

After I grab the purse and suitcase, I remove the keys from the ignition and swing open the car door. I take two long steps and slide into the backseat of the cab a second before he presses on the gas. When we cross the border, no lights flash, no sirens sound. Why does everyone else have good luck besides me?

"I can take you to the One Stop in Houlton," he says over his shoulder.

"Ha! I don't think I can return to get the car now that I've literally escaped from him. I'm basically screwed."

"Well, what are you doing here, then?"

"Take me to Van Buren," I tell him.

"Lady, don't you realize that Van Buren is over eighty miles from here?"

"I have money. I'll pay you."

He extends his neck, regarding me in the rearview mirror. "If you've got the money, honey, I've got the time."

I remove the three hundred dollars from the wallet and wave it in the air. He nods, redirecting his attention to the road. I turn in the seat, looking back at my aunt's car. "I'm in so much trouble," I whisper while the customs building disappears from sight.

"What's your name, miss?"

I take a moment before I respond. "Amanda. And yours?"

"Emile."

"Thank you, Emile."

He tips his hat and turns on his blinker, taking an exit. And after a few turns, we pass through a more congested area of gas stations and businesses. I relax into the seat and slip out the sandals, folding my legs under me.

A ping is heard and I run my hand to the bottom of the purse, removing the phone. Another text from "Mom." This one reads: *Houlton, Maine? Seriously? Of all the places in the world, you pick the boondocks of Maine?*

A grin creeps up, and I dig my teeth into my lips, forcing myself not to burst out in laughter.

I rest my head back and watch the sun rise while we wind through small towns. Suddenly we get up and over a hill and things begin to feel familiar. "Stop. Stop the car!"

Emile pulls the car over to the side of the road. "What's up?"

"There," I say, pointing off to the side. "That's where—" I trail off in thought. I open the car door and stand barefoot on the pavement, staring across the street where a large white farmhouse is supposed to be—Sara's house. But instead, it's an endless field of grass. Taking quick steps, I cross the street.

"You getting off here?"

I put a finger up, signaling him to wait while I saunter into the field, stopping right where I pictured the porch to be. Turning around, I see a white barn directly on the other side of the road and in the other direction is a sign that reads "Van Buren Welcomes You."

If the house isn't here, then maybe the rest of the town as I picture it, including Marc, isn't either. But I didn't come all this way to give up once I got here.

I jog back to the car and hop in. "Keep driving," I direct him.

He nods.

When we get to the end of the street, he stops. A street sign to our right reads "Main Street." We can either turn left, right, or go straight through yet another customs crossing. We certainly won't be going straight.

"Take a left," I tell Emile.

When we get to what appears the center of town, it doesn't look any different from any other small-town USA. Businesses line the street, a few cars parallel parked along the sidewalks. Where I recall a movie theater to be, instead is a restaurant. And where I remember the restaurant with the delicious bread pudding to be, is a store that sells cell phones. The mini mall is a second-hand clothing store. The music store, gift shop, and pool room are not there.

But what is there is the Town Hall. Not exactly as I recall from the dream, but it's there.

"We're here," I say.

Emile pulls the car over along the curb.

"Thank you." I extend the three hundred dollars to him.

He puts his hand up. "I think you need that more than I do. You sure you'll be okay? I can wait for you."

"No, I'm good." I inhale deeply. "I'm home."

"All right then. Have a good one."

"You too. And thank you. Are you sure you don't want—"

"You keep it, ma'am."

I sling the purse over my shoulder and grab the suitcase and exit the car. I start to cross the street before I realize that I'm still barefoot. I turn, but the cab is gone.

Turning back around, I cross the street. A gentleman stands at the door of the Town Hall, keys in hand. I walk up behind him while he turns the key in the lock.

"Hi. I was wondering if you could help me. I'm looking for someone. I think his dad is the town manager. His name is Marc."

The gentleman turns to me and when I look into his eyes, a sense of familiarity washes over me. He resembles Marc—they have the same piercing blue eyes.

"Marc, you say?"

"Yeah."

He pushes through the door and flicks on the light. We take a step inside, and he rests his briefcase on the chair by the door. He turns back to me and extends his hand. "I'm Charles. Charlie, to my friends. You can call me Charlie." He pauses, looking at me intently. "You're Mandy, right?"

I freeze in place, my hand extended in midair. I clear my throat. "Yeah...I'm Mandy. Amanda O'Reilly."

He nods.

"Wait here," he says before walking to the back of the reception area. He disappears up a set of stairs in the far corner of the room.

I rest the suitcase on the floor and fold my hands in front of me, fidgeting nervously with my dress while I try to make sense of how he would know my name.

The cell phone in my purse rings. My hands shaking, I fumble with the handbag, trying to open it. It slips from my grasp and falls to the floor, causing its contents to scatter.

I drop to my knees, and while reaching for the phone, I hear the front door open next to me.

Before I can move, a pair of black Chuck Taylor Converse sneakers come into view and my heart ceases to beat. I don't need to look up to know who it is, but I do.

When our eyes lock, his expression mirrors my own. And it feels like an eternity before he drops to his knees in front of me.

He leans forward.

And he kisses me.

About the Author

Isabelle is a small-town girl—born and raised in northern Maine—now living in the big city. As a writer of fiction, her stories are about love and life and include many plot twists and suspense.

She's always loved to write from a very young age, but it wasn't until Spring 2014 that she wrote her first novel, Deception. She enjoyed it so much that she decided to keep writing and sharing her stories with the world.

Facebook: www.facebook.com/isabellevanburen
Email: IsabelleVanBuren@gmail.com

Made in the USA
Middletown, DE
15 January 2025

68593955R00220